Until You
SAY I DO

An Until You Novel

Book Three

D.M. DAVIS

www.dmckdavis.com
Cover Design by Hang Le
Editing by Tamara Mataya
Proofreading by Mountains Wanted Publishing & Indie Author Services
Formatting by Champage Book Design

This is a work of fiction. Names, places, characters and incidents are the product of the author's imagination and are fictitious. Any resemblance to actual persons, living or dead, events or establishments is solely coincidental.

This story contains mature themes, strong language, and sexual situations. It is intended for adult readers.

Playlist

Welcome To The Jungle by Guns n' Roses

Never Be the Same by Camilla

One Woman One Man by Magic

Crazy Love by Aaron Neville

Have A Little Faith by Michael Franti & Spearhead

I Won't Give Up by Jason Mraz

You Are the Reason by Calum Scott

I Will Wait by Mumford and Sons

Still Yours by Jamie Lawson

Say You Won't Let Go by James Arthur

Perfect by Ed Sheeran

I Get to Love You by Ruelle

You Are the Reason - Duet Version by Calum Scott & Leona Lewis

To the readers who love Joseph and Samantha and wanted more.
This is their more. Their everything.
Their Forever. Always. I Do.

Until You
SAY I DO

Will you *Dance* in my *Darkness?*
Or *Relish* my *Light?*
Will you *Come* to me *Sweetly?*
Or *Take* me in the *Night?*

Will you *Add* to my Abundance?
Or *Grow* my *Shame?*
Will you be the *Fuel* to my *Fire?*
Or *Extinguish* my *Flame?*

D.M. Davis

One

WELCOME TO THE JUNGLE

AUGUST

Joseph

WHEN I WAS A KID, I BEGGED MY PARENTS TO take the training wheels off my bike so I could ride around like the big kids—like my older brothers. I was tired of feeling left behind, like the runt of the group, not so much in size but in ability. My dad was uncertain, sure I would hurt myself and damage my confidence.

"Let him try," Mom said.

"He's only four, Fiona. He's too young. He can't even tie his own shoes yet," Dad protested, ever my protector.

"Take 'em off, Hugh. He'll fall and come crying for you to put them back on." She was so sure.

With a sigh of resignation, and as I bounced on the balls of my feet in nervous anticipation, my dad removed my training wheels.

It took one good push with my left foot, while my right pressed down hard on the pedal, to get enough momentum to place both feet on the pedals. It was a millisecond, a mere beat of my heart, a gasp from my mom, and *yes!* from my dad, and I was off, tearing down the street.

1

My balance improved with every steady pump of my legs and the fierce support from my brothers as they ran beside me—not in front to lead me, or behind to push me—but *beside* me to guide and encourage.

That's been the story of my life, all twenty-three years of it. My need to prove myself before it was time, my family's ability to let me do it, and my brothers being by my side the entire time.

My proverbial training wheels as VP of Products and Technology for McIntyre Corporate Industries are off. Uncle Max is officially retired. I'm on my own. Only I'm not. My brothers are here, sitting in the chairs facing my desk, in my executive office at MCI's corporate headquarters in downtown Dallas. They're eyeing me expectantly, waiting for my next words, for my agreement, for *my* approval.

"Do you really think he's ready? That he's right for the job? Right for MCI?" I know the answer. I've always known the answer, but what happened a year and a half ago put a damper on my enthusiasm in bringing Samantha's brother, Jace, on board.

"He's changed, Joe. He's really trying. He had an impressive start at Solengers. They'd be fools to let him walk away, but I know he wants to be here as much as I want him here." Matt glances at Fin before his identical green eyes flash on me. "Jace won't accept our offer unless you okay the deal."

I pace to the wall of windows, not that I have to get up to see the view. I could have just turned my chair as two of my four walls are windows. But I need a break from their expectant stares. "You don't need my approval. Marketing is your baby." Matt doesn't need my approval, but he *wants* it.

He laughs. "Apparently I do."

A knock at the door brings a reprieve. "Mr. McIntyre." Lydia pokes her head in without waiting for my reply. Her face lights up when she sees me. "I…er." She looks between Matt and Fin as she enters the office.

I scowl at Matt, who's eyeballing her a little too appreciatively. When he sees me notice, he simply shrugs and looks away.

She throws her shoulders back, bringing her all-too perky breasts front and center. Her eyes lock on my crotch, and her tongue sweeps across her lower lip.

Christ, really? Have some self-respect. I internally sigh and roll my eyes. What to do about my new overly eager assistant, who spends entirely too much time staring at my dick and playing with her hair? Mary, my regular assistant, is on maternity leave, and I fear she may decide not to come back. I need her now more than ever. Lydia makes Mary look like a goddess among admins.

I clear my throat, and Lydia's eyes dart to mine without a hint of embarrassment, more like a dare. "Your two o'clock rescheduled to tomorrow."

I glance at my watch, noting the time, and wonder what Samantha's doing for lunch. Hands in my pockets, scowling, I clench and unclench my jaw, tempering my response. "You could have told me that between meetings."

She nods. "Yes, well…I thought you would want to know, given you'd requested it be set up for today."

True. I did. "Thank you for being thorough. I'm fine with tomorrow."

She smiles as if my thanks means more than it does. "I like to be hands-on and thorough." Her gaze darts to my crotch again, only this time she bites her lip.

Christ. She's trouble. "Thank you, Lydia." I usher her out of the office and all but slam the door.

I turn, letting out a punch of air.

"Brother, you have a problem," Fin states the obvious.

"I'm well aware." I return to my seat and run my hand through my hair as I call Michael.

"Boss," he answers before it even rings.

"Lydia. She needs to be gone today, before my wife sees her."

"She's not your wife yet." The humor in his voice is unmistakable.

I don't need the reminder. It was my brilliant idea to have the big wedding, talking Samantha out of the elopement she wanted. Or said she wanted, but deep down she really wants the full-blown affair: white dress, wedding cake, reception, first dance, and family. It's the *family* part that makes her think she doesn't need the fuss. Her family, not mine.

Four months. I have to make it four more months, then she's mine. Forever.

"Just…fix it."

"I'll talk to HR," Michael assures me before hanging up.

He's been a great addition to MCI's security team. Though he reports to Victor for all things security related, he's my man. My number one in security and getting things I don't necessarily have the time or tact for done. Not that Michael is full of tact. This is one thing he truly lacks, except when it comes to my wife. He and Samantha formed an unbreakable bond over the death of her father and his subsequent protection over her. After he and Samantha both shot her father's killer, he retired from the FBI, took some time off, and has since started working for MCI.

"What about Jace?" Fin brings me back to the topic at hand.

Jace. He's spent the best part of a year apologizing to me and Samantha in every way possible for bringing Tiff into my bed, and for all but abandoning his mom and sister when their father died. He's remorseful. I believe that. But has he truly changed? Am I the one to judge whether he's groveled enough to warrant a reprieve? Maybe. On the Tiff thing, yes. But on the family abandonment issue, no. That's all Samantha. It's her place to let him back in. She's trying, but trust doesn't come easy for her. Their relationship is vulnerable. I can sense her waiting for him to screw up, to prove she's justified in her doubt and mistrust.

I, on the other hand, still have no memory of Tiff and our drunken encounter. Rape. I was raped by Tiff. Samantha is outraged for me. I only remember my drinking-induced fantasy sex dream with Samantha. I can still see and feel her as if it were real. But it wasn't Samantha, it was Tiff. Samantha hates that I'm not more upset by it. I'm pissed at what Jace did and feel like something was taken from me that I did not offer or knowingly give. But because I still have a sweet memory of Samantha, I won't let it be tainted by dwelling on the Tiff aspect. I choose to focus on all that is Samantha Cavanagh. The fantasy of her, the reality of her, and the blessed day she becomes my wife.

Until Samantha is ready, though, I can't fully get on board the Jace bandwagon. I'm following her lead as Jace has caused enough damage to last her a lifetime. "Here's the thing." I steeple my hands, resting my elbows on the edge of my desk. "I think Jace has potential. The potential to be highly successful at MCI and bring our marketing to the next level with you, Matt. But, he also has the potential to break my wife's heart, irrevocably."

"She's not your wife," they both chime in. Fin smirks, and I can hear his silent *caveman* in my head.

I raise my hand dismissively. "Semantics." She is my wife—my life—in every way that matters. "I'm remaining on the fence. It's Jace's game to win or lose. I won't disagree with bringing him on board, but I'm not going to champion him, either." I meet Matt's gaze. "That's the best I can give you."

He nods and rises to leave. "Fair enough."

Fin stays behind and waits until the door closes behind Matt. He crosses his leg, playing with the seam of his slacks. "And Lydia?"

"You want her?"

"Fuck, no." He chuckles. "She's a lawsuit waiting to happen. HR needs to have a serious discussion with her, and then place her with a female boss."

"Or leave MCI."

He laughs again. "Yes, or leave." He stands and buttons his suit jacket. "That would make your life way too easy if all of your challenges simply up and left, brother."

"We're planning a wedding, I'm new to this VP gig, and my wife is getting ready to live apart from me for the next year while she finishes college in Austin. I could use fewer challenges."

"She's not your..." He stops mid-protest when he sees my scowl. "Fine. Fine. Call her your wife. You're already like an old married couple anyway."

"There's nothing old about us."

He laughs. "No, I suppose there's not, but you do have that couple thing about you. I don't think you'll survive a year apart from her."

I scrub my face. "Fuck. I can't ask her to stay. I can't ask her to give up her dream of graduating from the same college as her parents."

He shrugs. "She'd do it for you, you know."

"I know. That's why I can't ask."

"I hear ya. Regarding Lydia, I'll talk to Michael and Victor. We'll ensure she gets a job, somewhere outside of your organization and the view of your crotch."

I slump back in my chair in relief. He'll make it happen. "I owe you one."

He heads for the door. "I'll add it to the growing stack of IOUs." He looks back before opening the door. "Consider it done."

Samantha

"I'm sorry, ma'am, but you can't go in there without an appointment." The buxom blond darts around her desk to stop my progress to Joseph's office.

"I don't need an appointment." I try to walk around her, but she throws her arm out to stop me. I suppose I should have called first to let him know I was coming, but that would have ruined the whole idea of me surprising him.

I never had this kind of trouble with Mary. Sighing, I take a step back and don my friendliest smile. "I'm sorry. Let's start again." I stick out my hand. "You must be Joseph's new assistant. I'm Sam Cavanagh, Joseph's fiancée."

She wrinkles her nose, looking at my hand as if it's covered in something truly nasty. *Seriously?* I arch a brow, waiting expectantly.

She doesn't take my hand. Though, she does manage a stiff smile.

"Miss Cavanagh, while I can appreciate you *feel* you have the right to barge in on Mr. McIntyre without an appointment"—she grabs my arm and begins to turn me away from the executive offices—"you will have to make an appointment like everyone else."

Oh no, I don't think so. I slip out of her hold, pivoting around her. "Why don't we ask Mr. McIntyre how he feels about me barging in." The snottiness in my voice is undeniable. She's a piece of work. I hope she doesn't treat clients with the same condescending attitude. I barrel through Joseph's closed door, only stopping once I'm well inside and away from Miss Attitude.

"You can't—"

"Samantha?" Joseph stands, ignoring his assistant's protest. His eyes meet mine, and my insides clench at the sight of him in his black body-defining designer suit, looking ever the part of a corporate bigwig. It never gets old.

Oh my. My heartbeat goes into overdrive, and I strain to stop myself from fanning my face as heat creeps up my cheeks.

"Gentlemen, can you excuse us?" He escorts the men he was meeting with to the door, grabbing my hand as he passes, pulling me along.

After the men exit, he tucks me to his side and faces his assistant. "Lydia, cancel my afternoon." He releases me, and then he leans back through the door. "Oh, and Lydia, my wife takes precedence over all else. Don't try to stop her from entering my office again." He closes and locks the door without acknowledging her stammering reply.

"How'd you know?" My anger diminishes with his prompt admonishment of his assistant and claiming me as his priority.

He chuckles. "You walked in ready to decimate anyone standing in your way. I simply assumed you didn't arrive that way, but had a run-in with my new assistant." He steps closer. "Now, what brings you here?" He touches my cheek, studying my face. "You've got that look."

I lean into his touch. "What look?"

"That look that says you need me to show you how much I love you." He steps closer, his body pressing against mine.

I look away, feeling a bit foolish. "I know you love me," I softly reply.

His emerald eyes shine with understanding. His arms wrap around me as he nuzzles the side of my face, running his mouth along the curve of my ear.

He always knows.

I relax into him with a deep sigh. "I need you."

I squeal in delight as he sweeps me into his arms and heads to his adjoining bathroom. "I need you too, Sweetness."

Samantha

I think I could stay right here, in the arms of the man I love, for the rest of my life and be perfectly content. Forget sleep, food, school, or a career. This man is all I truly need. I burrow deeper into his chest. We haven't moved or spoken since he carried me from the bathroom to recover on the couch, wrapped in each other's embrace.

He traces circles up and down my back, lulling me further into the calm sanctuary of our post-sex haze. My eyes flutter closed, though I try to resist, to remain present and mostly conscious. His lips skim my forehead as a sound of pure satisfaction rumbles through his chest. A purr, nearly. I press in further to keep from laughing. He truly is such an animal at times, usually when he's extremely turned on or extremely relaxed. Both states he managed to hit in the mere thirty minutes since my arrival.

Heaven.

Home.

"Tell me. What got you out of sorts? Why'd you need the caveman?" His deep timbre makes my lady bits ache for him all over again.

"I came to surprise you with news, but the run-in with your assistant threw me off my game." I pull back enough to see his eyes. "I made a decision…that…well, I now realize maybe I shouldn't have made without you."

He kisses my nose. "Sweetness, I'm sure whatever decision you made, I'll be happy with, especially if it makes you happy."

I frown and sit up. "But you don't even know what it is. It's a really big decision. I shouldn't have made it without you."

His brow furrows. "Are you *wanting* me to be upset with you?"

"I…" Huh, do I? "No. I wanted it to be a surprise. You'd never ask it of me, but it's something I wanted to do. For us."

He sits up fully, his front to my side with his legs around me. "Now you've got me really curious."

I wait, wondering if he'll guess. Save me the drama of having to tell him.

He runs his finger down my nape and through my cleavage, which is fully exposed in his dress shirt I confiscated off the bathroom floor before he picked me up and settled us on the couch. "Tell me, Sweets. Don't make me play twenty questions." He cups my breast, running his thumb over my nipple.

I bite my lip to suppress a moan. "You're gonna have to stop that if you want me to talk."

"Hmm." He pulls me onto his lap as he leans back, his eyes caressing my exposed breasts, watching his fingers tease my hardening tips. "Maybe you could make it quick?"

Quick? Does he mean sex or my secret? "Oh!" His hips thrust, pushing his erection against my bare ass. I grab onto his shoulders as he swings my legs so I'm straddling his cock, pressing intimately against me.

He nibbles across my chest as he lowers his shirt from my shoulders. My hips sway, moving on their own, needing the friction. "Tell me, Samantha," he groans before his mouth consumes one lucky nipple, sucking it deeply.

"Joseph." I latch on to his hair. Jesus, I love it when he sucks my breasts as if he's starved for me. I reach between us, lifting up, and lower myself onto his hard shaft, groaning over every delicious inch.

"Fuck. You're so wet." He thrusts, burying himself deep, then holds my hips securely, ensuring I can't move. His eyes meet mine. "Tell me, before neither of us can speak with anything other than our bodies."

I arch back and contract around his cock, needing him to move, to take me, to make love to me.

His hand wraps around the back of my head, sinking into my hair, and he pins me with his gaze. He means business. My caveman has come out to play. I contract around him again. I love Joseph gentle, and I love him hard, but I think I love my protective caveman most of all. The one who needs to see me safe, happy, and, most of all, thoroughly fucked.

"I…I'm not going back to Austin." I close my eyes, afraid of his reaction. I'm met with silence, and when his hold on me softens, I open my eyes. My heart flips when I see such adoration in his eyes, though I also see a mix of concern. I cup his face. "I can't imagine a day, a night, without you. I tried to be brave. I did, I swear. I just can't leave this weekend and move back to Austin without you."

His hand drops from my neck and settles on my hip, mirroring his other hand's hold. His fingers knead at my flesh, making my hips jerk with want.

"More," he manages to rasp.

I'm not sure if he means my hips or more of my secret. So, I give him both. Leaning forward, placing my forehead against his and my hands braced on his shoulders, I start to move, slowly, with my words. "I transferred to SMU."

He cups my ass, helping me, guiding me as he begins to thrust into me. "Oh!" God. "I start in two weeks."

His lips find my breasts. "Tell me why, again." He bites my nipple and then sucks the sting away.

"Oh, yeesss." I wrap my arms around his head, pinning him to me. I move faster, urgently. "Because I know what it's like to live without you, and what it's like to live with you. And I don't ever want to be without you again."

"Fuck." He groans, encapsulating me, his arms and hands pressing me closer, controlling our thrusts, meeting our need to be one. "Look at me, baby." He tips my head, and our eyes lock. "You. Make. Me. So. Damn. Happy." He punctuates each word with a thrust. He sucks on my bottom lip and kisses me tenderly despite our urgency.

My body begins to tingle and reach for that pinnacle I've only ever known with him.

"Now, come for me, Sweetness. I'm gonna come so fucking hard for you."

His words send me spiraling. "I'm…"

"Ah, fuck. Yes, you are." He looks at me. "That's right, squeeze me, baby. Make me come."

"Yes. Yes. Yes." My vision blurs as I shatter around him, gripping and holding on as he continues to pump into me.

"So fucking hard!" he moans as he pulses and comes deep inside me. "Christ!"

I cry out again as he sucks on my nipple, driving me into a second orgasm.

"Fuck, yes. Just like that," he rasps before latching back on.

Once our bodies still, we collapse onto the couch, panting, him still buried inside me. "Never pulling out," he mumbles.

I sigh into his neck. "It might be hard to get any work done like this."

"I think *hard* is the relevant word in that sentence." He emphasizes his point by thrusting into me and growling. "Still hard for you, Sweetness."

Two

RELISH MY LIGHT

Joseph

THE AROMA OF DINNER ENTICES ME FROM MY HOME office. "Damn, woman, something smells incredible." I stride into the kitchen, grab her from behind, and bury my nose in her hair, taking a deep whiff. *Christ, she smells even better.* I latch on to her neck.

She giggles and squirms, pressing her ass into me. "Joseph," she moans as I tweak a nipple.

I'm hard. Instantly.

I had her three times at the office this afternoon. *Three* fucking times, and I'm rock hard again like a sex junkie on Viagra.

I groan and slip my hand between her thighs, cradling the gift that has been bestowed on me. The greatest gift I've ever received, besides that of her heart. Her moist heat permeates the thin fabric of her barely-there panties. "You're killing me, baby."

She squeezes her legs together, locking me in place. "I think you're the one trying to kill me, Caveman." Her hand caresses my arm. "You're the one who insisted I wear your shirt and only my panties after we showered."

12

On a sigh, I slowly disengage. "You're right. I'll try to behave, but you can't blame a man for admiring his woman."

Her sweet smile nearly has me throwing her over my shoulder and heading for the bedroom or couch. Shit. This counter right here would do just fine.

She cocks a hip, swinging her hair off her shoulder as she swivels to face me.

Stunning. Standing there in my shirt, hanging off her shoulder, and bare legs, looking like the siren she is. *My* siren.

"What's the deal with your new assistant?"

Visions of Samantha riding me on the couch in my office are derailed by the mention of my heinous ex-assistant. I swipe a hand across my mouth and down my neck as I think of the best way to approach this topic. Honesty. That's what we've promised each other. No more secrets that needle their way between us, filling in any gaps with doubt and darkness.

Honesty lets the light in, keeping the darkness at bay.

"Lydia is no longer my assistant. She's been reassigned."

Samantha's arched brow, smirk, and twinkling eyes have me grinning back at her. "What? Didn't she start recently?" She grabs the oven mitt, preparing to open the oven.

"Here, let me do that." I quickly maneuver around her to take over. We'll never eat if I see her ass peeking out from my dress shirt.

She giggles, knowing full well the effect she has on me.

I fill her in as discreetly as possible as we plate dinner and make our way to the dining room. She listens intently, not commenting, barely showing any reaction at all. It's making me a little nervous. My baby is usually so easy to read, but at the moment, she's playing it close to her chest. I'm worried this whole thing will upset her—allow old doubts to seep in.

"You...what? Had her replaced"—she snaps her fingers—"just like that?" She smiles, finding this humorous, surprisingly.

"Yeah, pretty much. I asked Michael to take care of it. Fin was in my office when I spoke to him about it. Fin followed up to ensure Lydia was moved to another department, far away from me."

Chuckling, she takes a bite, shaking her head, looking amused and disbelieving. "Poor girl. She thought she was gonna snag her a VP, and she ends up getting shipped off to Siberia."

"Marketing is not Siberia."

She laughs again. "It is if that's not where you want to be." She continues before I can protest. "I'm not questioning your tactics or motives. I'm thankful a shark like that won't be around you every day, causing you undue stress and putting ideas in my head." She slips onto my lap, wrapping her arms around my neck. Instinctively, I kiss her warm lips and pull her closer. "I forget sometimes how powerful you and your brothers are. You say *'jump'* and your employees ask *'how high?'* You each wear your power so effortlessly, it's easy to forget you run a multi-billion-dollar company."

Christ. She makes it sound like I leap tall buildings in a single bound. It's nowhere that glamorous nor fun, but I'll take her compliments any day. I live for her adoration, and right now the light shining in her eyes is nearly my undoing. I couldn't stand it if Lydia caused any further problems for Samantha. I'd endure heaven and hell for this woman. My. Woman.

"I'm glad you're not upset." I keep checking her eyes to be sure we're on the same page.

She pats my chest and returns to her chair. "I'm not that easily undone, Joseph; I can take a little flirting. But she was downright rude, and I worry who else was subjected to her wrath. I'm glad she's gone, but I do feel a tiny bit bad for her."

"That's because you have the heart of a saint."

She scoffs. "A saint would have forgiven her brother by now and worked harder to make amends with her mother." She glances out the penthouse windows into the lit-up downtown around us. "I'm no saint."

Her lightness of heart from a moment ago is gone. Her damn family and the heartache they bring her. I hate to even broach the next topic, but I can't keep it from her. Honesty—our motto—the string that ties our souls together, forever tethered, forever forged, forever one.

"Matt brought up the Jace thing again. He feels the time is right to bring him on. He believes Jace is ready."

Her focus returns to me. "What do you think?"

"I think I don't want to do anything that will bring you a single moment of unhappiness." *Shit, I should have talked to her before I gave Matt my answer.*

"Joseph." She cants a brow. "That's not realistic, and you know it. I saw the news report about Solengers. They're saying their latest product campaign could triple their profit margin by first quarter next year. That would be an impressive feat for a three-year plan, much less a target that's not even seven months away. If Jace had even one percent of impact on those numbers, you'd be silly to pass him up."

I pull her out of her chair and into the living room as I command the house computer to play *our song*. "Dance with me."

She slides into my embrace, the yin to my yang, fitting me with such precision it's hard to believe we are not one and the same.

"So, it wouldn't upset you?"

Her blue eyes meet my green ones with open vulnerability. "I would never ask you to make a business decision based on my personal preference." She lifts on her toes, leaning into my ear. I pull her tighter, supporting her. "Jace has caused both of us pain, and if you can look beyond it, then so can I." She kisses my cheek and gives me a squeeze before lowering to her normal stance. "I'm not saying it will be easy seeing him more often, or that we're best buds again. But I made a promise to him and myself: that I would stop purposely avoiding him. He can't make amends if I never give him the chance." She shrugs. "I guess this is life's way of telling me the time is now."

"Are you sure? Nothing's been confirmed. I told Matt I wouldn't stop him from hiring Jace, but that I still have my reservations."

"Are your reservations about his work ethics or his abilities?"

"No."

She smirks. "I didn't think so. You're a VP, Joseph. You have to lead with your head, not your heart."

"I prefer to believe there's a place for both. I will never let my head lead me where my heart is not willing to go. I nearly lost you by trying to use only logic. I won't let that happen again with you or MCI."

She nods and wipes away a tear. "That's why you're the man I love. You're not just one thing. You're so many wonderful things wrapped up in this amazing man I'm lucky enough to call mine."

My heart swells, and as our song starts again, I pull her close. "Enough talking, Sweets."

Our song and everything else is drowned out by my pounding pulse and her sweet gasps as I consume her mouth and ravish her body.

Mine.

Samantha

I climb into bed after having showered for the third time today. Thank god, I do so love our shower. It's the only competition Joseph will ever have to worry about.

"What's that smirk for?" Joseph asks over my shoulder.

My smile grows. "I was thinking how much I love our shower, which is a good thing considering your libido has me using it more and more."

He snuggles in close. "My libido?" He sounds incredulous as he wraps himself around me from behind. "I do believe your sex drive is as strong as mine."

I burrow back into him on a sigh. "You bring it out in me, my caveman. I can't resist your gentle heart and Neanderthal ways."

"Caveman is one thing. Neanderthal is quite another. I am a

well-educated man, with couth and manners, who happens to enjoy his wife's mind, body, and soul."

I chuckle at his mock indignation.

He squeezes my breast. "Did I mention rockin' body?"

"Yes, Caveman, you did."

His lips grace my shoulder, paying special attention to my scar. The scar is all that remains of the hole made when the bullet that killed my father exited my body. I shudder at the memory.

"Are you sure about this school thing?" He presses into me. "I don't want to live apart, but I'm willing to do it. I don't want you to regret giving up that dream."

I roll to my back and touch his cheek. "Life has a way of putting things in perspective. Things that used to seem so important-—like graduating from the same school my parents did—aren't really important at all. If my father were here, he'd tell me to do what makes me happy and not to fear the unknown."

Joseph kisses my palm and holds it over his heart. "And what makes you happy, Sweetness?"

Joseph is not a man short on confidence nor conviction, but sometimes—when it comes to me—he needs reassurance. Not so much in how I feel about him. He knows I love him. It's more about him giving me what I need. Loving me the way I need to be loved. I pull him to me and kiss him soundly before I answer. "You."

He smiles against my lips, his eyes searching mine. "That's it?" He seems shocked.

How can he ever doubt he gives me more than I need? "Yes, just you. Here. Not four hundred miles away from me. We could survive the year apart, but why? At what cost? And for what purpose? So that I can stick to some old goal I made for myself when I was a kid? We grow up and our goals should change with us, otherwise, we'd all be ballerinas, cowboys, and astronauts."

His laugh tickles my ear as he holds me close. "I love your mind, baby. I love how it works. I love how you meld your philosopher's soul with your intelligence." His lips graze across mine. "But, mostly, I love how you love me." He licks across the seam of my mouth before diving in with deep, penetrating precision, curling my toes and making me gasp for more.

Shifting, he settles over my naked body, nestling his hardness between my thighs. I open for him, always open to my Joseph and what he gives me—mind, body, and soul.

"Sweets." He pants, rubbing the tip of his cock against my clit. "But I also love that you're not leaving me." His voice cracks with emotion as he surges, filling me in one swift motion. "You chose to stay." He groans.

I contract around him, speechless, pulling him to me with each and every thrust. Telling him with my body how much I love him. Reassuring him that I'm here, and I'm not going anywhere.

"Fuck, yes. Squeeze me."

All sense of reason and words leave me as he takes me higher, rocking me into oblivion.

"You chose me," he chants with each thrust, with each gasp of air between kisses, with each glorious touch of his hands.

Ignited, I burst into flames, grounded only by his voice in my ear. "I'll always choose you, Sweetness."

Locked in my embrace, he grinds in deep and stills. "Always." He shudders with his release.

Joseph

"You alive?" She lies limp in my arms, so still and quiet I'm not even sure she's awake, but I'm pretty sure she's breathing.

"Mmm…barely," she murmurs and settles in further, rubbing her face in my neck, like she's scenting me.

I relax, knowing I haven't sexed her to death. I have to rein it in. She's not going anywhere.

This has been an emotional day. I didn't realize how anxious I was about her leaving for Austin until she told me she wasn't. Then all those pent-up feelings and anxiety over living apart from each other came crashing in and took over, making me need to claim her over and over again. Too much and yet, still not nearly enough. Never. Enough.

"I was gonna suggest something, but now I'm not sure it's such a good idea. We can't seem to stop having sex."

I laugh and relief floods my body. She can at least joke about it. And she said *we* can't stop having sex, so she doesn't think I'm mauling her.

"I'm just overwhelmed with relief that I won't have to live without you for the next nine months." I stretch and scratch my stubbly chin. Jeez, I need to shave. I probably gave her beard burn all over her body. She never complained, though. "Ignore the fact that I can't seem to keep my dick out of you. What was your suggestion?"

"You know you don't have to try to fit in a year's worth of sex."

I smile at that. "It seems my body hasn't caught up with my mind telling me you're not leaving."

She rests back on her pillow, allowing me to see her eyes. The blue eyes I love so much. "I was thinking that since you're out an assistant, and my internship is over for the summer…" She bites her lip.

I lean over and tug it free, giving it a quick suck. "That's mine."

She smirks and rolls her eyes. "You're like a two-year-old, think-ing everything is yours, or the birds in Nemo: *Mine. Mine. Mine*," she mimics.

Stifling a laugh, I take her mouth, keeping my kiss as chaste as pos-sible. "I don't think everything is mine, Sweets. Except when it comes to you, then yes: *Mine. Mine. Mine*," I parrot as I quickly kiss all my favor-ite parts of her.

Samantha squirms and giggles. "Forget my idea. We can't even have a conversation without your hands and mouth all over me."

Hands up in surrender, I flop back on my pillow. "Ok, no touching. Tell me."

She sighs as if she's frustrated with me, but I can see by the mischievous gleam in her eyes. "You need an assistant. I don't have anything to do for a few weeks, besides plan a wedding, get ready for school, and ensure my big strong man gets enough at home that he can keep his hands to himself in the office."

I scowl. "Keep my hands to myself? What does that mean?" Surely, she doesn't think I'd cheat on her.

"I mean I could be your assistant for a few weeks or until you find a suitable replacement. But none of this funny business in the office." She emphasizes with a nod of her chin and arms crossed over her luscious chest.

She's fucking adorable.

"You'd do that? Be my assistant?" I thought she was teasing, but she's serious about helping me out. I'm touched.

She softens. "Of course. You need help. I may not be fully qualified to be an assistant, but I'm sure I can manage to get you coffee, answer phones, and keep your schedule on track."

"You're more than qualified. You're *over*qualified. But I'd love to have your help. I could relax and find someone who really fits instead of taking the first person because I need someone."

"Good. You let Michael and Fin know. I'll contact Angela in the morning. I'm sure she can give me a few pointers. She manages to keep Fin on task, and I'm sure he's more difficult than you are."

"I wouldn't count on that. I'm the newbie, remember. I need a more hands-on approach than Fin does." I waggle my eyebrows.

This is gonna be fun.

Three

FUEL MY FIRE

Joseph

EARLY THE NEXT MORNING, MY FATHER KNOCKS on my office door, entering without waiting for my response. He doesn't need to, he's the CEO. He chuckles as he closes the door and sits facing my desk.

"Good morning, Dad. What's so funny?"

He shakes his head. "You're either crazy stupid or crazy brilliant, and honestly, I'm not sure which."

I follow his meaning as he motions to the door. "Brilliant." Having Samantha here with me day in and day out for as long as I can is pure genius. Too bad it wasn't my idea.

"I don't know how you talked her into it, but just remember to treat her with respect above and beyond how you would your normal assistant. Because you know each other so well, it will be easy to take advantage and let simple niceties slip. *'Please'* and *'thank you'* go a long way. Remember, you go home to her every night. Make it a good experience for you both—you're crazy brilliant. Make it miserable—you're batshit crazy stupid."

I laugh and bow to the master. "Noted. Thanks for the advice."

The intercom buzzes. I pick up the line instead of using the speakerphone. "Sweetness."

"I'm sorry to interrupt, but you have ten minutes until your nine o'clock meeting in the executive conference room."

"Is the team here?"

"They're setting up. Do you need something before the meeting, coffee or water?"

You are what I need. "I'll grab a water from the refrigerator in there. You'll be joining me, right?"

I'm met with silence.

"Samantha?"

"Is it expected that I join you as your PA?"

She's hesitant. This is her old team. She worked closely with them over the summer. This was her project, and she had to let it go to return to school. Now, I'm asking her to join me in a lesser capacity as my assistant.

"We don't have to tell them you're my PA—no one knows yet. Join me in an advisory capacity. One who knows the product backward and forward."

"Okay."

I hang up and look at my father. "I can see this could be challenging." I hadn't considered Samantha's role here in the past. Her tenured internship allowed her to work on highly sought-after projects. Appearing now as my PA could be considered a step down and be seen as preferential treatment, seeing as she's engaged to the VP of Product and Technology. It's a fine line we will have to maneuver, not only now, but in the future when she comes to work for MCI permanently.

Dad stands, buttoning his suit jacket, reminding me of how similar he and Fin are in their mannerisms. "I'm sure you're up for it." With a swift pat on the back, he follows me out.

Samantha

I settle in at the conference table, next to Joseph. He insisted. I'd rather disappear in the back in one of the chairs lining the walls. You know, for *observing*, and not so much *participating*.

Clasping my fidgeting hands, I force myself to breathe deeply and relax.

You know these people. You've worked with them for months. So what that you said goodbye to them last week, and—surprise—here you are sitting next to the VP of their department.

Ugh, these people are gonna hate me. Think I'm the teacher's pet.

And I thought I was doing a good thing by helping Joseph out.

Under the table, Joseph squeezes my leg and says, without looking at me, "It'll be fine. No worries." He squeezes again, leaving his hand in place. He turns and leans in as if to kiss me, then freezes, catching himself.

Shit. That was close.

He whispers in my ear. "It'll be fine. We'll find our way." His dimpled smile has me relaxing instantly.

I can do this. He's here, and he won't let anything bad happen. He's in charge. This is his meeting. I'm only here to observe...and probably take notes since I am his PA, after all. I focus on my laptop and begin taking notes as the presentation begins. There are no introductions; everyone here knows each other. I get a few quick glances, but for the most part, all eyes are on Joseph and Alex, who's the project manager.

Halfway through the demo of the mock-up application, it freezes up. As Alex works to reboot the system, I flip over to the server where the coding is stored. Thankfully, I still have access. I jump to the section I'm more than familiar with and spot what I'm looking for, unfortunately. I glance up at Todd, the head programmer on the project and not my favorite person. He's glaring at me with daggers in his eyes, daring me to say something.

Joseph leans over to look at my laptop. "What is it? Do you know what's wrong?"

"I'd rather not do this in front of all these people," I whisper and send a silent plea, hoping he can read my expression.

His eyes search mine. I know he wants to talk about it now. He wants it solved. With a small nod, he turns his attention to Alex. "Let's give it another minute. Then if it's not up, we'll reschedule."

That minute turns into five minutes with little-to-no progress. I'm embarrassed for them and frustrated at the same time. This could have been avoided.

Joseph stands. "Alex, let's reschedule. Fix the problem then contact me to see where I can squeeze you in." He doesn't wait for Alex's reply. Joseph looks at me expectantly.

I hop up, close my laptop, and head out the door with him hot on my trail. As we near his office, his hand presses to my lower back. "My office, please."

He closes the door and paces to me.

"I'm sorry," I blurt and fall into a chair at his conference table.

His brow furrows. "What do you have to be sorry for?"

"I knew there was a problem. I told them how to fix it, but I guess they decided against my recommendation."

He sits beside me. "Show me."

We spend the next half hour reviewing the code on the version Alex demoed, comparing it to the fixed version on my laptop, and then run the program from my code. The app works perfectly—as I knew it would.

"When did you discover the problem?"

"A few weeks ago. The app kept failing. I kinda went around Todd and took a look at the code myself."

He sits back, crossing his arms over his chest. "Did you report it?"

"Of course."

His pensive look has me concerned. I don't want to get anyone in trouble. "Who did you tell? And do you have a record of that communication?"

Oh god, they're all going to hate me for sure. I slump in my chair. "Yes."

"Show me."

"I'm starting to hate those two words," I grumble.

He kisses my cheek. "Don't. You didn't do anything wrong."

"Then why do I feel like I did?"

"Because you're about to show me how my employees dropped the ball and weren't smart enough—man enough—to take direction from someone younger and smarter than they are."

My head drops to his shoulder. "They're going to hate me."

"Shh. Stop. I'll handle it. I just need to have all the facts first."

I show him my email communication, my notes on the app, when I found the problem, and that I reported it immediately, starting with Todd, the lead programmer. Then followed up a few days later when I saw it still wasn't fixed. I followed up again asking if he could help me understand why he felt the outdated coding was better. I'd even appealed to his ego, saying he's more experienced, and perhaps there were details I didn't understand.

"Do you really think there are valid reasons for keeping the old coding?" Joseph asks after reading my last email to Todd.

"No, not really. But he's more experienced. I was trying to be open to the idea as well as not offend him outright. He dislikes me enough as it is."

He chuckles. "I think the mere fact you exist offends Todd. I saw the glare he was giving you in the conference room. He was not happy to see you when he walked in and even less so when the app crashed. I didn't really understand what his attitude was about. Honestly, I wanted to reach over and smack him for even looking at you with such disdain."

"Oh, god." My head falls forward.

"Hey. Don't do that." He tugs my arm. "Come 'ere." He pulls me into his lap.

"This is not proper boss/employee behavior," I chastise.

He pulls me closer. "No. This is boyfriend and girlfriend, husband

and wife behavior." His lips press to my forehead. "I'll fix it. I promise." He pulls my laptop in front of him. "Now, show me the rest."

Secure on his lap, I click the remaining emails. The final communication is to both Todd and Alex, where I again stress the importance of considering the new updated code statements. This will make the program run 50% faster, making it that much more efficient on system resources, increasing reliability, and reducing cost.

"Those assholes. I can't believe they completely ignored your insightful recommendations. Did they even respond to you?"

"Todd basically told me to mind my own business. Of course, not in writing. Alex never replied. I don't even know if he saw my emails."

He pats my butt. "Get up a sec."

I slip off his lap and take a quick glance at his calendar on my laptop. "You're going to be late to a meeting with Fin if you don't hurry."

Joseph punches a button on his desk phone. A second later it dials on speaker.

"Hi, Joe," Angela, Fin's PA answers.

"Can you reschedule my eleven o'clock with Fin? Something's come up."

"Sure. Oh…uh, hold a moment, please."

There's a click, and Fin's voice comes on the line. "It had better not be your dick that's *come up*."

"Fin, you're on speaker phone, and Samantha's in my office," Joseph says flatly.

"Shit. I'm sorry, Sam."

I stifle a laugh. "It's okay. Really."

"Fin, can you hold on a sec?"

"Sure."

Joseph puts him on hold and hands me a pin drive. "Can you call Michael and ask him to come up? Then copy your files to that drive."

"No problem."

He looks chagrined. "I hate to ask, but would you mind getting me some lunch? I'm starving."

I smile and walk around his desk. "Joseph, it's my job to get you lunch or whatever else you need during the workday."

He pulls me close, kissing me softly. "I'd like a blowjob later. Can you pencil that in?"

"I'll see what I can do, Mr. McIntyre." I pull away, grabbing my laptop. "Your next appointment is at two. Try not to be late. It's with your father and uncles."

"Yes, ma'am." He smirks. Before I reach the door, he calls me back. "I love you."

"I know, Caveman. I love you too." My smile doesn't nearly match the megawatt one blazing back at me.

Samantha

The MCI cafeteria is a familiar place. I've eaten here often with my co-workers and sometimes alone during the course of my two summer internships. This summer, though, was the first I never ate alone. If I wasn't dining with co-workers, then I was eating with Joseph. He would have preferred it that way every day, but he has a tight schedule, and lunch away from his desk isn't always possible. We'd eat in his office if we needed to, allowing us to spend time together. I feel at home there. It no longer feels like the huge powerful office of one of MCI's Vice Presidents. It feels like my fiancé's office.

As I wait in line, I shoot off a text to Margot. She's not happy about my decision to remain in Dallas instead of returning to the University of Texas with her. I don't blame her. I wish I could pay for her to join me at SMU, but she has a full ride to UT, and it doesn't make sense for her to blow that. Luckily, my financial situation is different. My dad set aside money for our college, and since I'll graduate after only two years instead of the normal four, I have the extra funds needed for Southern Methodist University, which is a private school.

Besides the fact that going to SMU allows me to remain with Joseph, it also affords me the convenience of being close to our wedding venue as the planning progresses. We're getting married at a church on campus. The Highland Park United Methodist Church is one of the prettiest churches I've ever seen. It has a small chapel as well, but now that I've given in to the whole "big wedding" ideal, I really want the large church with its wooden pews, stone floors, arched wooden cathedral ceiling, stained-glass windows, and a magnificent Dobson pipe-organ that encompasses the entire wall behind the altar.

We're getting married the Saturday before Christmas, not necessarily the best time for a wedding as everyone is already so busy with the Christmas and New Year's holidays. It was the best time for us, though, to be able to take a honeymoon immediately after the wedding since I'll have nearly a month-long break between the Fall and Spring semesters.

I order us lunch and wait. I never really felt out of place here at MCI until today. Now, I feel like I'm an interloper. I have to get over it. I love MCI and don't want this one project blip to color my feelings about working here, even as Joseph's temporary PA.

My phone chimes after I pay for and collect our to-go boxes. Grabbing a chair at an empty table, I respond to Margot's text. She leaves this weekend to return to Austin, and I'm hoping I get a chance to see her before she goes. Sadly, we didn't spend much time together over the summer, both of us busy with our summer jobs. We thought we'd have all year to catch up once school started, but that's all changed.

As our texts bounce back and forth, negotiating the best day to meet up, my ears prick up at the mention of Joseph's name somewhere behind me.

"He'll never marry her. She's just his plaything. Have you seen her?" one woman asks.

"No, but I hear she's quite pretty. But Joe's a hottie. There's no way

Until You SAY I DO

he'll tie himself down to one woman. Even if they do get married, he'll be getting some on the side. Guaranteed," another woman responds.

Are they talking about me? Us?

"I hear the pool's reached a thousand dollars," yet another woman chimes in.

A pool?

"I bet fifty they won't make it to Halloween."

"I said they'd make it through Thanksgiving and call off the wedding the first week in December."

Wow. I'm in shock. I stand to slip away. It's obvious they don't know who I am, or, if they do, they haven't seen me yet. I hate slinking away with my tail between my legs.

"I hear she got Lydia fired."

Shit. Now I'm getting blamed for that too? I can't. I can't walk out of here and not at least set *that* straight.

They never see me coming, too engrossed in their hateful gossiping. "That's simply not true. What happened to Lydia was her own doing. And for the record, she was transferred—not fired."

Four heads turn toward me.

"What—"

"Who are—"

"Shit. You're her."

"Yep, I'm *her*," I respond.

"Who her?"

"The fiancée."

"Shit."

"I recommend the next time you decide to talk smack about your bosses' boss's boss, you remember who signs your paychecks and works hard to ensure you still have a job to come to each day." I lean forward, looking each of them in the eyes. "But *if* I were a betting person, I wouldn't bet against Joseph and me. That's a sucker's bet, right there." I turn on my heel and strut away, leaving them wide-eyed with mouths-agape. I grab our lunches off the table on my way out.

29

I make it to the executive elevators before the implications of what I did hit me. Thankfully, a keycard is required for access, so I'm alone on the ride up. I hold on to the railing for support, feeling like I might pass out.

Hold it together.

What was I thinking?

Joseph

I'm fuming. Michael confirmed, through system logs, that Alex did in fact read Samantha's email and even sent a response to Todd. But there was no action taken to fix the code, at least none that I can see. I can read code, but I'm not nearly as proficient as Samantha. I trust her instincts. I trust her brainpower, her integrity, and her desire to see something succeed over her desire to be recognized for that success. She's not in it for the glory, at least not the individual glory. She's in it for the success of the company as a whole.

I've just gotten Alex on the phone when Samantha sets my lunch on my desk. She's pale and avoiding eye contact. I go on alert. She half-heartedly smiles and slips back out as quietly as she entered.

That won't do.

"Ten minutes, Alex. My office."

I call my Managing Director. "Ron, could you be in my office in ten?"

He sighs. "Yes. Is this about Project Nemesis or a new issue?"

I shake my head, disliking that project name. *Nemesis* sounds so combative, nefarious. "Yes. I've asked Alex and Michael to join us."

"Michael from Security? Is that necessary?"

"It is. I'll see you shortly." I hang up, not willing to address nor justify my decision to have my head of security join us. I have many reasons, none of which are Ron's business.

Opening my office door, I see Samantha isn't at her desk, and her lunch is in the trash. *What the fuck?*

I pull it out and examine the contents. Her chicken salad sandwich is untouched.

Samantha returns looking noticeably better, but still not her vibrant self. She glances at the container in my hands and down to her trashcan. "It must have fallen," she offers.

Really? If she knew it fell in the trash, why wouldn't she pull it out? *Samantha, why are you lying to me?*

"What's wrong, Sweets?"

"Nothing. It's been a trying day." She maneuvers around me. "You'd better eat." Her eyes hit my chest as she sits and starts clicking her mouse. "I've got some resumes to look through. And don't forget your two o'clock," she dismisses me.

"Michael, Ron, and Alex will be here momentarily. Please send them in."

She visibly swallows. "Of course." Her response is clipped.

My glare would tell her I don't believe a word she's said if she'd only look up and meet my eyes.

Dismissed? We'll see.

My meeting is wholly uneventful and not nearly the tongue thrashing I anticipated giving. Once everyone is seated at the conference table in my office, Alex jumps to apologize before I can even voice my findings. A preemptive strike to my planned attack.

"I was wrong not to give Sam's concerns the due diligence they deserved. I should not have taken Todd's word that the issue had been resolved. Obviously, by this morning's failed demonstration, the program has not been fixed as I was led to believe." Before I can respond, he continues. "It's not an excuse. I'm the project manager and should have confirmed for myself the app was working as designed."

Ron jumps in. "We appreciate your candor, Alex. I would like one of our other programmers to take a look at the code and make the required changes." He looks to me. "I know Sam could do this, but since she's returning to school, I'd rather have a permanent employee who will be around to support it going forward and understands the changes needed. Would you agree?"

"Yes." I do agree, but it chafes me that he doesn't consider Samantha a *permanent employee*. She'll probably be his boss someday soon—at least if I have my way about it. "However, Todd needs to move on. An honest mistake is one thing, but purposely letting a project fail out of pride or misplaced resentment is unacceptable. MCI is a business that thrives on new blood, new ideas with fresh perspectives. There's no room for ego in product and development. If we need a little housekeeping to ensure our team remembers that, so be it. I expect this to be fixed by tomorrow morning. And Ron, I want a plan by the end of the week to ensure this type of talent subterfuge doesn't happen again."

I glance at Michael, who gives a stiff nod, acknowledging the topic we discussed earlier. I'm concerned Todd may be a problem for Samantha if he stays, and even more so if he goes. There is a darkness in his eyes that makes me uncomfortable.

Four

COME TO ME SWEETLY

Samantha

HONESTY. THAT WAS THE TEXT I RECEIVED FROM Joseph before he left for his last meeting of the day.

I've avoided him most of the afternoon, uncertain how, or even if, I should address what occurred in the cafeteria. I allow my head to fall back, and flex and stretch my shoulders. I need to work out. The stress of the day has taken its toll on my old shoulder wound. It aches, every throbbing pulse reminding me how precious and fleeting life can be.

Honesty. I have to tell him.

I make it through the last of the PA resumes HR sent up. I pick a handful I think will make a good fit and block time on Joseph's calendar to review with him in the morning. I can set up interviews from there.

At five, I pack up and shoot Joseph a quick text.

Me: *I'm heading home. See you at the bar?*

We have a standing Wednesday night get-together. It's primarily the Six Pack: Fin, Matt, Joseph, Victor, Michael. Jace used to be a part of the pack, but he's keeping his distance. Then there's me, Sebastian, and sometimes Margot. The attendees always vary, depending on schedules and who's in Austin at school. But since summer, it's become regular for the whole lot of us to make it. The guys, besides Joseph, don't usually bring dates. It's not a *date* kind of atmosphere. It's a hang-out-shoot-the-shit-give-each-other-crap-I-know-you-better-than-most kind of atmosphere. And it's a blast.

My phone chimes.

Joseph: *Michael will drive you. I'll meet you there.*

My protective man.

Me: *I'll take a cab. Or walk. God gave me two good legs for a reason.*

Joseph: *Yes, he gave you 2 spectacular legs. Fuck, now I have visions of them wrapped around me.*

Good. Maybe that will sidetrack his thoughts of me walking.

Joseph: *Don't walk. Michael is on his way to the penthouse.*

Me: *Caveman!*

Joseph: *Always, when it comes to my girl.*

I reply with a heart emoji and give up on trying to assert my independence. Michael is going anyway, so it's not like I'm a hardship.

As I push the button for the elevator, it dings and the doors open.

Michael. Standing there with a shit-eating grin. "Princess."

"Do I even want to know how you knew I was still here instead of on my way home?"

"No." His smile warms as I join him. "I'm sorry you had such a shitty first day as Joe's assistant."

"Thanks. It was one for the record books, I think."

He tilts his head. "What else happened?"

I hedge, not sure whether to temper my feelings about what happened today with Michael, or wait and unload it all on Joseph.

"Hey." He touches my arm. "You know you can tell me anything. I've always got your back."

I nod and blink away impending tears. I wish it didn't upset me so. "Did you know there's a betting pool on whether Joseph and I will get married?"

He scowls. "Who the fuck would make that wager? They obviously don't know you two very well."

"Maybe."

He sighs like a gale-force wind. "Please tell me you're not letting this get to you. It's crap."

"The pool's up to a thousand dollars."

"Maybe I'll bet against all those schmucks, then when you marry, I'll be a grand richer."

The doors open on the crossover bridge floor. I move to exit, but Michael grips my arm. "Wait." He steps out, placing his hand on the elevator door to keep it from closing and scans the area. Satisfied, he motions me forward.

We fall into step, Michael to my side with his hand on my back. "You know protocol," he softly admonishes.

"Why are you in protective mode?"

"Precaution."

We pass through the open double doors leading to the crossover bridge to MCI's Omega Tower. He stops me again to determine if it's safe to proceed; only then do we move on.

The hairs on the back of my neck prick. Visions of my father's killer flash before me. I take a cleansing breath and push them aside. I've spent too much time dealing with my self-doubt and fear to let it get the best of me now. "Precaution against what?"

"Todd, that asshole programmer, was fired today."

I stop in my tracks, halfway across the glass-enclosed bridge. "What?" I'm shocked, and yet I probably shouldn't be, given what he did and the menacing way he glared at me. Joseph wouldn't have taken any chances, not with MCI, and not with my safety.

Michael wraps his hand around my arm, looking around. It makes me nervous, so I start looking around—like *I* know what I'm looking for.

"Princess, you're making my job harder if you stay here in broad daylight in a glassed-in enclosure. We need to move."

"Precaution, huh?"

He smiles down at me as we walk to the elevators that will take us to the penthouse level. "Like I said, whoever bets against you and Joe getting married is an idiot. That man is not taking any chances with your life, and there is absolutely no way in hell he would ever break up with you."

"You would never assume I'd break up with him?"

He looks stumped like I just said something in a foreign language he doesn't understand. "No, of course you would never break up with him either."

"But that's not what you said."

"It's what I meant."

"You think, like those people betting against us, if anyone was going to get dumped, it would be me." Of course he does. Why wouldn't he? Everyone thinks that—even me.

I rush into the apartment, knowing good and well Michael will follow. Grabbing a water in the kitchen, I head to our bedroom, hollering over my shoulder, "Can you tell Joseph I'll see him later? I'm not going tonight." I slam the door behind me and lock it, knowing if Michael wanted to come after me, a locked door would not stand in his way.

"Dammit, Sam. Don't do this." He hits the door. "Please, I'm sorry. I didn't mean it the way it came out. You know I'm no good at this touchy-feely crap."

I stop. It's not his fault. I open the door. The big lug is nearly pouting. "Michael, it's been a really…difficult day. I'd like to punch the hell out of something, take a bath, and go to bed."

"Punch me," he eagerly offers.

He'd let me too—that is something Michael understands—how to punch, how to work out your frustrations on a punching bag or a willing sparring partner. "I appreciate the offer, but I'd really like to be alone."

"Please, Sam," he softly pleads.

I slip my arms around his waist and give him a hug that he quickly returns. He's been a great friend over the last nearly two years that I've known him. He's Fin and Victor's best friend, and Joe's good friend.

He's essentially adopted me as his little sister, but one you treat well and take care of—not one you call names and dismiss. "Michael, I'm really not feeling up to it, and it's not really what you said. It's a culmination of all of it. I need time to unwind, clear my head, and distance myself from the emotions of it."

He tries to talk me into watching TV with him, or keeping each other company while we read our separate books. He's a book lover like me. He offers to spar with me, to pick up dinner, to even talk if I need to. But I finally convince him to go. I'm safe in the penthouse. There are no threats here, except for the negative voice in my head, threatening to undo all the progress I've made with believing I'm good enough for Joseph—that I'm enough for a man like him.

Joseph

The penthouse is quiet when I enter. Dropping my laptop bag and jacket at the entry, I make my way to our bedroom and quietly slip off my clothes, moving closer to the bathroom. The sound of water sloshing and the smell of vanilla tantalize my senses before I even see my girl luxuriating in a bubble bath. She slowly rotates her neck and stretches her shoulders on a deep sigh. The stress of today has taken its toll. As much as I want to absorb this moment of seemingly blissful relaxation, I know she's like a duck under the water—paddling and paddling to stay buoyant. She's not nearly as relaxed as the ambience suggests.

"Sweetness." I slip off my shirt as I enter.

"Joseph." The weight of my name, full of emotion, confirms I made the right choice to come home—to her.

"Is your shoulder giving you trouble?" It's rosier than her other one, telling me she's been rubbing it, trying to alleviate her discomfort.

"A little." She sits forward, her fingertips rimming the edge of the tub.

"Mind if I join you?"

She shakes her head but remains silent.

My boxer briefs, the last piece of clothing, hit the floor. I step in behind her. The water is nearly as hot and seductive as she is. I pull her close, wrapping around her like a barrier between her and the outside world.

She buries her head in my neck, whispering my name in sweet veneration.

"I'm here." My lips press to her cheek, her temple, anywhere I can reach without disturbing our embrace. "I'll always be here."

A tremor sends goosebumps rippling across her body with a small whimper. I turn her sideways on my lap, and her chest presses against mine. I hold her tightly, whispering to her as she slowly lets go and starts to cry. "You are the air in my lungs, the beat of my heart, the genius in my every thought."

She moans as if my words wound her, but I can't stop. She has to know.

"You are the moon to my night. The sun to my day. The fuel to my fire. There is no me without you." I kiss her bad shoulder, wishing my kiss—my love—could heal her shoulder and everywhere else she hurts. "Don't you know that by now? There's no one who can hold a candle to you. The world is a blur to me with my focus fully on you."

My hands find her shoulder and slowly go to work to loosen the strained muscles tightened with stress. She melts into me, holding me with more than her arms, every inch of us bonding to the other more deeply than the physical, more powerfully than the mind, more abundantly than the emotions. In this moment, we are untethered, yet bound only by our love—eternal.

As her tears wane and the water cools, I help her out of the bath, wrap a towel around myself, and tenderly begin to dry her off.

Her fingers snake in my hair as I kneel to run the towel down her legs. "How do you always know?"

Her trembling voice has me looking up into her water-cast eyes. "Know what?" I place a soft kiss on her stomach before standing.

"The right thing to say." She drops her hands to my shoulders, watching me intently as I continue to run the towel over every lovely inch of her.

I cup her cheek, my thumb grazing her bottom lip. "I tell you what's in my heart." Discarding the towels, I carry her to bed, lying down with her in my arms. "I don't want you to doubt the depth of my love. There is no time limit, no expiration date, no cause for termination. It is a permanent—beyond *'death do us part'*—soul-binding kind of love, Samantha."

She nods, her eyes welling up again. "It's the same for me." She kisses me sweetly. "It's always been forever for me," she breathes across my lips.

"Shh, no more tears." I press my mouth to hers, wanting to draw out her passion to still her emotions.

Once we're panting, and there's no sign of tears, I speak again. "Why didn't you tell me about what happened at lunch?"

"I wasn't sure how to proceed." Her head rests in the crook of my arm, and her eyes search mine. "I don't want to get anyone else in trouble. And it's entirely possible I'm blowing the whole thing out of proportion."

"If it upsets you, I *want* to know about it. No matter how small or inconsequential you may think it is. I don't want to hear from Michael how upset you are. He's a mess, by the way. He wanted me to apologize again for his careless remark." I smile, thinking of him storming in the bar, upset. It wasn't funny then, but the idea of my girl getting him so worked up was a sight to behold. The stoic Michael, brought to heel by my girl's hurt feelings.

"I told him it's okay. I know he didn't mean to hurt me with what he said. I'll talk to him tomorrow."

"You might want to call him tonight. I left him drinking at the bar with the gang."

"Lord. That man. He can't stop beating himself up," she mumbles as she reaches for the phone by the bed. She hits his number and puts it on speaker.

The phone only rings once before he answers. "Princess."

"Michael, what are you doing? I told you I wasn't upset with you, yet you send Joseph home to apologize for you like a pussy. What's up with that?"

He groans. "Why do you always cuss at me, Sam? And I'm no pussy. I was worried. You know I'd never mean to hurt you."

God, he's groveling. She's got him so wrapped around her finger, I think she could say *"jump"* and he'd ask *"how high, Princess?"* I'm not jealous. Michael's a stand-up guy and would never hit on another guy's woman. Plus, I'm pretty sure he sees Samantha more like a sister.

"I know, you big lug. And you know my insecurities around Joseph. You hit a sore spot that was already irritated. Okay?"

"Yeah, okay." He clears his throat. "We good?"

"We're good. Except I could use a good workout." She winks at me.

"Your shoulder?" he asks.

"Yeah."

"I'll be there at seven in the morning. Eat breakfast, drink lots of water, and be prepared to bring it. 'Cause you know this Weeble's not going down," he teases.

"It doesn't mean I won't try."

"I'm counting on it. G'night, Princess."

"Goodnight, Michael."

He hangs up, and she looks at me. "Satisfied?"

"Satisfied? Me?" I take the phone and set it back on its base. Rolling her to her back, I settle between her legs. "There are lots of things I love about you, but the fact that you don't let Victor, Fin, Matt, and especially Michael, intimidate you—turns me the fuck on." I flex my pelvis, rubbing my cock against her moist heat. "But as you can feel, no, I'm not satisfied."

"What do you need, Joseph?" The light in her eyes shimmers with mirth.

I run my nose along the column of her neck, breathing in her sweet scent. "I need to make love to you, Sweets." The hitch in her breath has me hardening further. "I also need you to promise that you'll come to me next time when you need support and validation of what you're feeling."

Her hand slides up my back and into my hair. "I'm sorry. I really was planning on talking to you, but I didn't want to do it at the office, especially after the day you were having with Project Nemesis. But you're right. I should have come to you sooner, or waited. I shouldn't have talked to Michael, at least not until discussing it with you first." She kisses my shoulder, her legs wrapping around mine. "Forgive me?"

"Forgiven. Always."

My adoring words from before are replaced by my desire to show her how much I love her and my need to connect with her—I let my body do the rest of the talking.

Our Yin and Yang.

Fire and ice.

Dark and light.

Feed and devour.

Mine.

Hers.

One.

Joseph

The next morning, I find myself staring out my office window, contemplating the resumes Samantha left me to peruse before we meet later this morning. When I left the penthouse, she was seriously working hard to take down Michael. If I didn't have such a busy day, I would have hung around to see how it played out.

My office phone buzzes. It's Fin's admin. "Good morning, Angela."

"Good morning, Joe. Fin would like you to come to his office."

Why didn't he call me himself or text? "Sure. Now?"

"Yes, please."

"I'll be right there."

"Thank you."

I freshen my coffee on my way to his office at the end of the hall. Angela smiles and motions me to go on in.

Fin's on his cell phone when I enter. He glances up with a grimace and turns his back to me. "It was great to see you." His voice is low, hoping I won't hear, I'm sure. He's quiet, listening to the other person talk. "Me too. I'm sorry I won't get to see you again before you leave. But…I'd like to…check in…see how you are from time to time." He laughs. "Yes, I'd like that." He clears his throat. "Joe just walked in." Silence. "I don't think that's wise… No rush. Take your time… Yes… Soon… Goodbye." His last words seem hopeful.

When he turns, I don't miss the wistful look in his eyes. I'm more than intrigued, but I need to move this along. "So, your phone's not broken, then?"

"No." He looks confused as he sets his cell on his desk and takes a seat.

I sit across from him. "Why the summons from Angela? A text would have sufficed."

"Sorry. My phone rang as I was getting ready to text you. I quickly asked Angela in my stead."

Sounds reasonable. "What's up?"

"I heard about the bet going around MCI. Is Sam okay?"

All these guys protective of my girl warms my heart. "She is now." I'd already filled him in on the project issue and firing yesterday, even though it's my department. We always share challenges, especially firings, across business units to keep us informed, consistent on best practices, and to stay on top of trends.

He nods. "I'm glad. Let me know if I can help."

"Is that it?" I stand.

"No." He glances to his open door and back to me. "Who's the blonde?" he asks matter-of-factly.

With a scowl, I sit back down. "What blonde? Where?"

"At the bar. Last night. There was a blonde all over you before Michael pulled you away." He's full of censure.

"Brother, are you accusing me of something?" Agitation courses through me as I stand, leaning forward, matching his glare.

He slowly rises and walks around his desk, leaning his hip against the side and sliding his hands in his pockets. "Do I need to?"

"No!" I step back, thinking about last night. "There was a group of British tourists. A few of the women got a little tipsy. They asked for selfies with me. You know..." I stand up straight and pose like a GQ cover model with smoldering sexuality. "Pics with the good-looking American to show their friends back home."

He laughs. "Fuck. Don't ever do that shit-ass pose again. You look like an asshole."

I punch his arm. "You're just envious 'cause I'm better looking than you."

"Whatever." He pushes away from the desk. "I'll walk you back to your office." I join him as he strides past Angela's desk. He's pensive. "It looked like more than that."

I stop, forcing him to turn and come back to me. "Fin, they were drunk. Maybe a little too touchy-feely. The whole thing lasted like two minutes. It was a blip in my crazy day yesterday. Was one of them a blonde? Yeah, maybe. I really couldn't tell you what any of them looked like. It was so inconsequential, I barely remembered it happened." He nods. "The wager about Samantha and me, please tell me you're not buying into that crap about me not being able to be faithful."

He steps closer, placing his hand on my shoulder. "I don't." His eyes reflect the truth in his words. "It looked bad, though. The blonde was hanging on you, and you had your arm around her waist. I didn't see any selfie action, or much attention from the other girls. I might have missed it, but if Samantha had walked in at that moment, it would not have been good. You're a friendly guy, Joe. You're no longer the college kid who's everyone's best bud. You're a Vice President of one of the largest companies in the US. You have an important, prestigious job. There will be women who will seek you out because of it. You need to be prepared to respond to it quickly, efficiently, without drawing undue attention."

"Shit. You're right." I should have stepped away. The minute their hands touched me, I should have removed myself from the situation. I shake my head and look to my PA's desk, not fifty feet away, where Samantha will be sitting shortly. "I wasn't thinking. I was trying to be nice, accommodating. It seemed harmless, but I can see from an outsider's perspective it was anything but."

We move toward my office. "I'm glad you understand. Next time you'll be prepared." He stops at my door after I enter. "And make no mistake, Joe. There *will* be a next time. Lydia and the chick from last night are only the tip of the iceberg. Some will be innocent, others calculating. And the fact that you're taken, and not interested, will only make you more of a challenge."

"You're a ray of sunshine today."

"Do that pose you did earlier—you'll scare them off." On a chuckle, he heads back to his office, leaving me with visions of women chasing me down the street trying to get selfies.

"Fuck," I mutter, shaking it off, and get back to work.

Five

ADD TO MY ABUNDANCE

Samantha

THE FIRST WEEK AS JOSEPH'S PA IS BEHIND ME. I managed a little wedding planning with Joseph's mom, Fiona. We finalized everything for the rehearsal dinner, wedding ceremony, and only a few things remain in flux for the reception. Joseph is handling the honeymoon. It's coming together more quickly than I thought and more easily than anticipated, but I know that's because of Fiona and Jackie, our wedding planner.

As for my replacement as PA, thank God, we narrowed down the prospects, interviewed potentials, and…WOOHOO…he picked one. I tried not to give my opinion when it came down to the final two. Joseph is the one who has to live with the decision, not me. I had influence over the applicants, but I didn't want the burden of the final choice. Thankfully, though, he picked the one I wanted. The one I would want as *my* assistant should I ever need one.

I knock on Joseph's open door before I enter.

"Baby, you don't have to knock. I told my last assistant my wife has precedence above all else. Do I need to reiterate that fact with you too?" The edges of his mouth twitch, trying to suppress a smile.

"Yes, Mr. McIntyre, I believe I do need a refresher on the impor-tance of your *wife* in the hierarchy of your priorities." I close the door behind me, locking it.

He raises his brow at the sound of the click. He slowly rises from his desk. "Is there a reason we need privacy for this discussion, Miss Cavanagh?"

"I thought it best, given the nature of the topic."

He stops directly in front of me, as close as he can get without touching, his hands buried in his pockets. "I see. And what topic are we discussing, exactly?" His green eyes gleam with possibilities.

"You requested an item be added to your schedule last week, and given that I begin training my replacement tomorrow, I believe today is the last day I have full control over what items appear on your cal-endar." I trail my finger along his abdomen above his belt. His muscles contract, and his breath hitches.

"It appears we have two items on the agenda then? The priority of my wife—"

"Yes." I love that one. I can never hear that enough.

"—and the other item, Miss Cavanagh?" His eyebrow arches. "You'll have to remind me." He presses closer, his erection fully present now.

"Perhaps you'd like to sit in your desk chair? This is your office, af-ter all. You should have the seat of authority for this agenda item."

He grabs my hand and pulls me behind him as he moves to his chair. "I believe that position of authority applies to both agenda items. Please remember that. I am the utmost authority when it comes to my wife and the importance she holds in my life."

"Joseph." I break our role-playing personas. Even playing, my cave-man holds me in such reverence.

He turns and cups my cheek tenderly, leaning forward and whis-pering against my lips, "You are my world, Sweetness." His eyes search mine, and with a slight nod, he waits for my confirmation.

I nod and swallow around the knot in my throat. "Sit," I whisper, having trouble slipping back into my role. I really just want to sink into his lap and let him love me.

He does as I ask, and also what I want, by pulling me down with him. "How long do we have, baby?" His voice is strained with need.

"Not long enough." I kiss his cheek and take a moment to relish the feel of being in his arms. On a sigh, I stand.

He reluctantly releases me, his hands grabbing onto the arms of his chair.

I clear my throat and square my shoulders. "Mr. McIntyre, we don't have time for more than this."

"Perhaps something could be rescheduled." He's serious.

My man. He knows me so well, better than I know myself. I will my love to show in my smile—he lightens me. I kneel before him. "Oh, no, Mr. McIntyre, that won't be necessary. It won't take me that long to bring my agenda item to conclusion." I smirk, thinking I'm so clever.

"Miss Cavanagh, I hope it will be a very happy ending." He shakes his head in amusement. He's as silly as me sometimes.

I rise, trailing my hands up his thighs, butterflies fluttering in my stomach. I want to make this good for him. Memorable. "I hope so too."

His fingertips trail along my jaw, and he tenderly lifts my chin. Green eyes overflowing with love stare back at me. "Always," he whispers, sensing my uncertainty. His warm lips press to mine. "You don't have to do this. It's okay."

I don't want him to think that. "I want to." My hands find his belt and get to work freeing his erection from its confinement while my eyes stay on his. "I'm nervous. Ignore me."

He chuckles. "Miss Cavanagh, rule number one of *my wife takes priority*, is I never ignore her." His breath catches as I stroke his freed cock.

"I never ignore her needs..." He groans as I lick his length. "...her wants and desires." He struggles to speak as I wrap my lips around its head and suck.

"Christ," he exclaims as I take him deep.

His hands white-knuckle the arm rests as his head falls back. "Fuck. Yes," he chants as I increase my tempo. His words give way to moans and sighs of pleasure.

Watching him fall apart, giving himself to me so completely, turns me on and makes me want to please him all the more. I stroke him in time with my mouth. His hips flex and still, fighting his desire to thrust. He's letting me give him this pleasure instead of taking it from me—from my mouth.

"Fuck, baby, I'm gonna…ah!" He groans as his body jerks, and he comes. "Yes, Sweets…fuck."

Languid and satisfied, he collapses in his chair. I sit back on my heels, out of breath and throbbing with need. A dimpled smile spreads across his face. "Miss Cavanagh, you surprise me. You're timid one moment and a succubus the next."

"Are you complaining, Mr. McIntyre?" I wipe my lips and under my eyes, fearing I look as undone as I feel.

"Hell no." He finishes tucking himself in his pants and pulls me into his lap. "I'm the luckiest man alive." His hand trails up my thigh.

I swat at him. "We don't have time."

"Nah uh, this is not a one-sided deal here. I come. *You* come." I struggle, but he stills me with a single look. "My wife takes priority." His lips graze my neck. "Now spread those sweet thighs and let me in."

I shudder and suck in a breath as anticipation tingles through my body. I comply as he situates me so that I'm sitting on his lap, my back to his front, my head on his shoulder, and my legs dangling over his—spread wide—my skirt up to my hips. "That's better." His lips trail up my neck as his hand slips inside my panties. "Fuck, Sweetness. Always so wet for me."

I moan.

"Shh. I know. We're in no rush remember? You're my priority." His finger enters me, and I instinctively thrust to take him deeper. "My creed." Another finger slips inside and begins to move in and out. "My heaven."

I can't stay still or stop my sighs of pleasure. His words as much as his body are going to make me come.

The hand around my waist slides up my body, slipping inside my blouse and bra, and squeezes my breast, tantalizing my nipple. Shamelessly, I roll my hips, riding his fingers, and push my breast into his hand.

His warm breath skates my ear. "You're making me hard, Sweets, watching you make love to my hand." He bites my ear lobe and squeezes my nipple, sending pleasure straight to my clit. I cry out, and he does it again. "As soon as you come, I'm burying my cock deep inside you and we're gonna do this again. I want to watch you writhe in my arms as you ride my cock."

"Oh, god."

His palm presses on my clit as his fingers increase their tempo. "I need you to come for me, baby." He squeezes and pulls on my nipple, sending me over the edge with explosive force. His arms hold me as I shake and tremble. "My girl." He kisses the side of my face and down my neck. "My beautiful girl."

I'm spent. Somehow, Joseph maneuvers us to the couch, slips his pants and underwear to his feet, and his cock inside me in one quick motion.

I shake and clench around him with aftershocks of my orgasm.

"Christ, you feel good." He was serious—he wants me in the same position—my back to his front.

He sets the pace, grinding his hips, his finger on my clit, a hand on my breast, and our mouths captured in a deliciously slow kiss as if we have all the time in the world—but we don't. I sever our kiss and glance at the clock. "Joseph, you've got to pick up the pace. You have ten minutes."

"That's plenty of time, baby."

No. No it's not. "Harder." I brace my bare feet on the edge of the couch—*Bare? When did he remove my shoes? And hell, where're my panties?*—and my back against his chest, lifting my lower half, giving him room to move. "Harder."

His growl tells me he's not happy, but as he pounds into me, the growl that follows tells me how very much he likes the idea. "Fuck." He pants.

Each thrust hits that magical place inside, and I cry out, biting my lip to stifle my outburst. He places one hand under my thigh, helping me meet each thrust in counter motion. His other hand snakes around to rub my clit.

The smell of sex, the sound of our bodies joining, our combined groans of pleasure, and the feel of him pounding into me sends my mind whirling and my orgasm climbing. "Joseph," I call out, my legs shaking with fatigue.

"Go, baby. I'm right there with you," he rasps in my ear, increasing the pressure on my clit. "Take it."

And I do, in a cataclysmic explosion that makes me lose all control of time or space. All I feel is Joseph's arms around me, protecting me, soothing me as I violently contract around him, taking him with me, hearing him moan his release in the recesses of my mind.

Minutes, hours, millennia pass. I come back hearing Joseph on the phone. "Charles, I need to reschedule."

I try to lift off the couch, but it's of no use. I'm like a cracked egg on a hot Texas sidewalk in August—fried. What the hell was I thinking?

"I'll get you rescheduled… I appreciate it… Thanks." He hangs up.

I hear the padding of bare feet and manage to look up. Joseph comes into view in his boxer briefs, nothing else.

"Where are your clothes?"

He grabs a bottled water from his minifridge. "I was burning up. I had to strip before I passed out." He kneels next to me. "Here, baby, drink." He helps me sit up and slides in next to me, pulling me against him as I guzzle half the bottle. He finishes the rest.

"What the hell happened?"

His chest rumbles with a chuckle. "I wore you the fuck out—correction—we wore each other out."

"Oh, god. We can't keep doing this in your office."

He sighs. "Sadly, you're right."

"Shit. Your meetings," I panic.

His hold on me tightens. "Cancelled."

"All of them?"

"Yep."

I relax into him. "We really can't keep doing this."

"Nope." He kisses my brow. "But I wouldn't trade this for anything."

An hour later, the sun is setting, and we're still lying on his couch. The last part of his afternoon is a bust, but it's been nice stealing these precious hours alone, the two of us, before his new assistant starts tomorrow, and I start school next week.

"I'll miss this." I turn to face him. "It was nice having this last week and a half with you, even though we were working. It felt like we were a team."

His hand caresses my hair. "It was nice. We work well together." He presses his lips to my forehead. "We're still a team."

"You know what I mean."

He smiles. "I do. It gave us an idea of what it'll be like once you graduate. You by my side—*not* as my assistant," he clarifies adamantly. "We'll be an unstoppable team."

"I think I like the sound of that."

I'm graced with his sexy dimpled smile. "Really? Because I'm serious. I want you by my side, not working four floors away from me, where I only get to witness your brain at work during staff meetings. I want you. By. My. Side."

I lift up and kiss him softly. "I got it, Caveman. You want me by your side."

"You're okay with that?"

"Joseph, you know I love watching you work too, and I'd be honored to work for you in whatever capacity you feel I'll most benefit MCI. And if that's by your side or in the mail room—I'm all in."

"Christ, I love you, Samantha." His lips crash over mine. "So…so fucking much."

"I'm glad it's mutual. I'd hate to be in this alone."

"Don't even jest." He frowns.

I laugh and touch his cheek. "I'm not kidding. I'd be lost without you. I'm the luckiest woman in the world. You love me mind, body, and soul. And I'm honored to be the recipient of such love."

"Sweetness." His voice cracks.

With a quick kiss and a moment of staring into the green eyes I love so much, I pat his chest and sit up. "Now, take me home and feed me. I'm starving."

"Miss Cavanagh, you're awfully bossy on your last day as my PA."

"You'd better get used to it. I have a feeling Teddy is gonna whip your ass into shape," I tease as I start to get dressed.

"Hey, I think my ass is in fine shape."

I swat it as he walks by. "Yes, Mr. McIntyre, that is a mighty fine ass."

Hand in hand, we make our way home. Luckily, it's only two private elevator rides and a crossover bridge away. Why did I ever think I wouldn't want to live so close to work? This is a dream. I need to apologize to Joseph for being such a baby about it when I first came to stay with Fin.

"Have you talked to Margot since she's returned to Austin?" Joseph brings me back to the present.

"Oh, shit! I forgot to tell you. I saw her. Here. Leaving MCI twice last week. I can't believe I forgot to tell you."

"When?"

"Thursday morning—the day after happy hour and my meltdown." I blanch at the memory. "I was late that morning because I worked out with Michael." I stop on the crossover bridge and point down to the curb, past the main entrance of Alpha tower, the tower we just left. "She was there, getting in the car with Victor."

"Victor?" He's surprised.

"I thought maybe I was imagining things, that it was someone who looked like her, until I saw her again on Friday afternoon. She was walking to her car. I know it was her because it was loaded down for her drive back to Austin."

"Shit."

"What?"

"Fin."

"Fin?"

"Yes, Fin." He pulls me along as we continue home. "I knew it!"

"You knew she was here?"

"No, Sweetness. I knew he had a thing for her. He has since he met her nearly two years ago."

"Really?"

He looks at me sideways. "Don't say anything. Let them tell us. Maybe it's merely a hookup."

"Maybe it's love. Oh my god!"—I tug on his arm—"She could be my sister-in-law."

"Don't get all worked up. It could be nothing."

"Or it could be something." My smile nearly cracks my face.

He pulls me into the elevator that goes directly to our penthouse floor. "You're so cute." He kisses my nose. "You want everyone to find a love like ours, don't you?"

I throw my arms around his neck. "I do. I really, really do."

His arms wrap around me, pulling me close. "So fucking cute," he breathes across my lips.

Joseph

I'm wrapping up a conference call when Samantha knocks on my door, slipping inside and closing it behind her. I want to chastise her for knocking, but I'm struck dumb by the goddess in front of me in a black fitted skirt that flares at the bottom and has a ruffle that cascades down the right side. If she's wearing a shirt, I don't even notice as I can't get past the come-hither sway of her hips and the sight of her gorgeous legs in black pumps with a little strap around the ankle.

Fuck me. My dick gets hard.

"It's a damn good thing Teddy's here. If you wore that skirt yesterday, we would have lost more than the afternoon fucking in my office."

She giggles as she rounds my desk. "We wouldn't have been able to do what we did yesterday in this skirt." Her skin pinkens at the memory.

I stand and press her to me, my hand gripping her ass as I trail a finger down her cheek. "Believe me, I would have found a way." Her eyes flicker with want—want that I cannot satisfy—at least not now. On a sigh I step away, returning to my chair. "Sadly, that will have to wait."

She bends, holding on to the arms of my chair, and presses her lips to mine, softly, tenderly, pulling away all too quickly.

"Fuck it." I grab the back of her neck and pull her back to me, consuming her delectable mouth, urging her into my lap. But she resists, pushing away and stumbling back. I grab her hand to steady her.

"Shit," she sighs.

"Yeah," I groan.

She motions to the door. "Uh, I really came in to tell you that Teddy is here. I…uh." She runs her hands down her skirt, her blue eyes searching mine. "Shit, Joseph, you've scrambled my brain."

I throw my head back in a laugh. "I know the feeling. At least you don't have a raging hard-on."

She shakes her head. "No, but I may have to run home to change my panties."

With a growl, I stand, hovering over her. "You're killing me, Sweetness."

Her hand presses to my chest. "I'm sorry. Think of baseball and puppy dogs or whatever you men think about that is totally not sexy."

My girl is cracking me up. "See, the problem with that is, I think of baseball—I think of you in a baseball jersey, little shorts, and a baseball cap on your head. You're cute as fuck, and I just want to sink into you."

Her breath catches, and she whispers my name.

I fall back into my chair. "Now, puppies. That should be a safe topic, but then I see you on the ground, laughing and playing with this little fur ball that's jumping around and licking your face." I sigh and rearrange my junk to make room in my pants. "You're cute as fuck—aaand I just want to sink into you."

Her soft giggle has me smiling. "I love you, baby, but you've got to get out of my office, and don't tell me about changing your panties while I'm working."

She's still laughing as she heads to the door. "Oh!" She snaps her fingers. "-I remembered. Do you want to meet with Teddy before I start training him?"

"Yes, but not with you." I point at her, motioning her out of my office. "Go change your panties or whatever you need to do. I don't want to see your sexy ass before lunch." My firm voice softens as I remember. "We *are* still having lunch together today, right?"

A mischievous smirk overtakes her face. "Meet me at home." On that, she exits my office, closing the door as she goes.

Great, I'll never get rid of this hard-on, thinking about what she has planned. I adjust my pants and command my body to heel.

Teddy knocks on my door a few minutes later. "Good morning, Mr. McIntyre. Sam said you wanted to see me?"

"Good morning, Teddy. Yes, please come in." He closes the door behind him, which pleases me that I didn't have to ask.

Once he's seated, I get right to the point. "I know Samantha will show you the ins and outs of the job and how I like things to work, but she won't tell you these things."

He nods slowly and opens his tablet to take notes.

"It's important to me that you and I work as a team. What happens in this office, stays in this office. No gossiping about what you hear, see, or presume. Respect, trust, loyalty, and diligence are key in your role as my assistant. I will, in turn, grant you the same. This team,"—I gesture between us—"this partnership, if you will, can only succeed if we both hold up our end of the bargain." I pause, letting his fingers catch up to my rambling. Once he looks up, I continue. "This is a family business—*my* family's business. We are vested heart and soul in this company, our employees, and the success of both. However, because we are related, the normal family dynamics do seep their way in occasionally, and you will be privy to things you might not otherwise know. Discretion, Teddy, is very important to me."

"Of course. Absolutely," he responds while still typing.

"Good. Any questions so far?"

"No, sir."

"When it's only us, you can call me Joe, if you like."

"Thanks, I'd like that." He smiles and his shoulders visibly relax.

Am I making him nervous?

"Now, for the main reason I asked you in here alone." I glance at the door, envisioning Samantha on the other side, or maybe she did run home for that change of panties. *Damn! Now, I'm getting hard again. Shake it off, man.* I stretch my neck and stand, pacing to the window. "Samantha is my life. She is my number one priority. If she calls, you put her through. If she shows up, you let her in. There is no reason, ever, to keep her away from me or my office. If she asks you for something, you do it." I face him, meeting his gaze. "She. Is. My. Priority. Understand?"

His eyes are wide with surprise. "Wow."

I chuckle. "Don't get me wrong, this job, my family are important too. But none more so than my wife."

His brow furrows. "I thought you weren't married…yet."

I wave him off. "Semantics."

He laughs. "Okay. I get it. I'm on board."

I think he'll work out just fine. "Excellent."

Samantha

I ring Joseph's office line. "Sweetness." The warmth in his voice spreads all over my body, and my skin ripples with goosebumps.

"Hey, Caveman," I whisper, my heart reacting to the mere sound of my lovename on his lips.

"Don't start," he gently growls.

I shiver and shake my head. "I'm not. Honest. I hate to interrupt your meeting with Teddy, but your nine o'clock is here."

"Thanks. When Teddy comes out, you can send them in."

"Great. Thank you."

"Always." His animal magnetism comes through the phone line and wraps around me, heating me to my core.

I hang up on a sigh. *My man.* I can't laze around in the visions he sparks. I've work to do. Movement in my peripheral reminds me I'm not alone. I walk over to the gentlemen waiting. "Mr. McIntyre will be with you in a moment. Can I get you something to drink while you wait?"

The tall, lanky one jumps to his feet, awkwardly sticking his hand out. "H…Hi. I'm Gregory…from…from robotics."

I take his proffered hand, my brain lighting up. "Robotics. Wow. It's great to meet you. I'd love to come down and see your lab sometime. That is, if it's not an inconvenience. I wouldn't want to stop the progress of genius."

"Really? You're welcome anytime." The other guy in the ill-fitting suit and friendly smile offers his hand. "I'm Jackson."

It's funny they think they have to introduce themselves, like I don't know who they are. When it comes to next gen robotics, these guys are *it.* They're famous—at least in the tech industry. Their combined brain power could probably light up both MCI towers alone. I stop fangirling long enough to shake his hand.

"You're Sam Cavanagh, right?"

"Yes." I'm shocked. "How'd you know?" The thought that they know me from the rumor mill/betting pool has me wanting to slink away.

"Samantha." Joseph's voice shivers up my spine. He's walking toward us with Teddy in tow. Joseph shakes Gregory and Jackson's hands with a warm greeting. "I'm sorry to keep you guys waiting." His eyes lock on mine as he places his hand on my lower back. "I see you met our robotics team." His smirk tells me he knows how much I loved meeting them.

Gregory speaks up. "I was about to tell Miss Cavanagh—"

"Sam, please," I insist.

"—uh, yes…Sam…" He looks between Joseph and me, finally settling on me. "We know who you are because you wrote an integral piece of code last summer that breached the gap in the robotics program, allowing it to become fully integrated into 1025D."

I'm both delighted and confused. "1025D?"

Jackson jumps in. "That's the name of a confidential project we can't really talk about." He smiles in apology.

"Huh, and what happened to 1025A, B, and C?" I tease, knowing they can't tell me.

Jackson and Gregory exchange a knowing look. "That's confidential," they chime.

"Anyway, we'd be honored to have you visit our lab anytime." Jackson looks to Joseph. "Pending your approval, of course."

"Approved." Joseph advises without hesitation. "Email Samantha the NDA beforehand." His hand slips around my waist and squeezes lightly. "Gentlemen, please have a seat in my office. I'll be right there."

The robotics twin gods say their goodbyes and head off to Joseph's office.

"Teddy, would you mind heading down to Starbucks and getting us two iced coffees? Get anything you want, as well. Oh, and one of their cinnamon crumble muffins." He flashes me a smile. It's my favorite. I guess I'm in for a treat. "Charge it to our MCI account. Call Samantha if you have any trouble."

"Sounds good. I'll be back." Teddy dashes to the elevators.

"You cleared the floor rather effectively, Mr. McIntyre. Any particular reason?" I tease.

He pulls me into his arms, his forehead resting on mine. "To tell you I love you." He kisses my head and smiles. "And to tell you I love hearing my robotics guys fawn all over your brain."

I can feel the flush creeping up my neck. "Please. Those guys make me look like a kindergartner."

He shakes his head. "Still. They were impressed with you. You have to come see me after you visit their lab. I don't want to miss the all-cylinders-firing-lightshow look you'll be bursting with."

I giggle. "That's quite a look. Deal."

"I gotta go. Love you, Sweets."

"Love you, Caveman."

He moans and kisses me quickly before pulling away. "Have Teddy bring in my drink when he returns. Enjoy your muffin." He backs away.

"Do you want me to save you some? And why don't you want me to bring you your drink?" I frown.

He rakes my body as if I'm standing before him gloriously naked. "Baby, if you come into my office looking like that, sashaying like you do, neither I nor the robotics twins will be of any use. And no, I plan to eat my favorite muffin later." He winks and leaves me throbbing in his wake.

Shit. Now I really need that change of panties.

NEVER BE THE SAME

Samantha

I HAD A NIGHTMARE LAST NIGHT. I HAVEN'T dreamt about my father and Rodrick, his killer, in a long time. I'm not even sure when the last time was. A heavy weight lingers like a cloak of darkness. As if my injured shoulder is truly bearing its weight, the ache is more prevalent today. A constant reminder of my waking with a scream ringing in my ears and Joseph wrapped around me like the safe vessel he is. My constant, my barometer, my guiding light showing me the way home—to him.

When he proposed six months ago, I was shocked and yet surprised he'd waited so long. I knew he wanted to ask sooner, but he gave me the time I needed to grow into our love and come to truly trust him as *the man* in my life who would never leave me. Who would never abandon me for something better. Who didn't think there were greener pastures than the one he's cultivating with me. *I'm* his greener pasture, and he's my horticulturalist. *I'm* the one he wants. The one he desires. The one he looks at with love and reverence. As remarkable as it still seems to me, I'm the *one*.

And he is, most definitely, the one for me. But he always was. From that breathtaking moment when we first met to every moment that followed, he is my other half, my protector, my champion, my caveman.

He tugs on my hair as he passes the dining room table where I'm supposed to be studying. School started a week ago. "What's got you lost in thought?"

I meet his gaze over my shoulder. "You."

His dimpled smile says he's pleased. "Oh, yeah? What about me?" He pivots and joins me at the table.

I blush at the memory. "Your proposal."

He lights up like the beacon he is, proud and confident. "You liked that, huh?" He scoots closer, leaning in, his arm over my chair, his fingers running along my nape. "What was it you liked best? Jumping from the waterfall hand in hand? Sailing the Caribbean at sunset? The moonlit dinner on the beach? Or making love in our oceanfront cabana?"

My dreamy mood lingers as the memories come flying back. "Those were all amazing. Each and every one." I lean into him, take a deep breath, and allow the tantalizing smell of him and the memories of our trip to swirl around me like a warm ocean breeze. "It was a great vacation." I squeeze his thigh under the table. "You've set a high standard, Caveman. Do you think you can top that for our honeymoon?"

"Abso-fucking-lutely."

I laugh and stand, holding out my hand. "Come." He takes it without question and follows me to the couch. We sit side by side, me tucked under his arm, looking out over the brilliantly lit-up downtown skyline. "All of that was amazing. But none of those are my favorite moment."

His hand runs up and down my arm. "No? What was?"

"Do you remember at the airport when that guy bumped into me, scattering my purse and all its contents across the floor?"

"Yeah," he says with confusion.

"You grabbed me, ensuring I was steady on my feet before kneeling down, handing me my purse, and then you carefully picked up and handed me each expelled item, giving me time to place them back in my purse where they belong—instead of simply scooping it all up in your big hands and dumping it in my purse like a trash bag."

"Okaaaay."

"Then each and every day you carefully, dutifully, covered my body with sunscreen to ensure I didn't burn. You kept a water bottle by my side and fresh fruit within arm's reach to ensure I didn't get dehydrated or hungry."

"Rubbing your body with suntan lotion was purely selfish on my part." He winks when I look up at him.

"And then there was that fateful day we tried street food, against your better judgment." I shudder at the memory. "I was so sick. Luckily, you weren't, but you didn't write me off to go play in the sun and sand. You stayed by my side. Held my hair when I threw up. Carried me back and forth from bed to bathroom when I was too weak to do it myself. Bathed me. Tried every trick in the books to keep me hydrated. Held me through my fever and clammy night sweats. You gave me everything I could ever need without even having to ask."

"Who would leave you to be sick on your own?"

I chuckle. "I can think of more than a few I'm quite sure would've been out snorkeling or jet skiing—any place other than stuck in a hotel room with their sick girlfriend."

"Fiancée," he corrects.

"I wasn't your fiancée yet."

"You've been my fiancée since I slipped that promise ring on your finger." He kisses my head and squeezes me. "You just didn't know it."

I laugh and adjust to face him. "My sweet Caveman, you've had it all figured out from the beginning, haven't you?" He nods with certainty. "You've been waiting for me to catch up?"

The back of his hand sweeps the side of my face, anchoring at my nape where his thumb continues to caress my jaw. "And I would wait for an eternity, Sweetness."

I lean into his touch, believing he would. "And that brings me to my favorite moment of our trip." His eyes light up as if he can't wait to hear it. As if he doesn't already know, but I'm not sure he knows *why* it's my favorite moment. "You could have proposed in any of the amazing places we visited: the sunset sail, the romantic dinner on the beach, the water-fall before we jumped."

I smile at the memory of him diving under the water, after we jumped, to find me. I hadn't come up right away. I'd gone deep, pulled out of Joseph's grasp by the impact of our plunge. I wasn't hurt as he feared, I was simply enjoying the peaceful moment—the elation of jumping and then the feeling of weightlessness as I slowly rose to the surface—that is, until Joseph grabbed me by the waist and hauled me up, as fast as he could, with a look of pure panic on his face when we broke the surface.

"But you didn't do it in any of those places. Instead you took me to the highest peak, on the highest island, where we met the dawn and ushered in a new day by you getting down on bended knee, pledging your love for me and endless days of sunrises and sunsets—together. Where you said it didn't matter where in the world we lived, where we worked, where we traveled, whether we had kids or not, whether we were rich or not. All that mattered to you was that I was in your world—for I *was* your world. Your. World." My voice cracks. I'm still amazed.

He tenderly wipes away my tears as they fall. His lips kiss along their trail. "You are my world. I breathe for you. My heart beats for you. My every thought, every emotion, every action, are with *you* in mind."

I nod, wiping at my tears as my chin quivers. "But I didn't truly believe it until that moment. I knew I would love you forever, Joseph. I knew it to the core of my being, with every fiber of my body—I knew you were *it* for me." I hold his open palm against my cheek, cradling it with my hand. "You told me over and over again how you felt. But it was something about that moment, the stillness of the morning, the purity of the new dawn breaking, the earnest sincerity of your words, and the light shining from your eyes. It finally clicked—you love me, truly, deeply, eternally—just like I love you. It wasn't one-sided. I didn't imagine it, or embellish it. Your love is true, honest, and pure. And that was the moment I knew I was *it* for you."

"Yes, Sweetness." He pulls me into his lap. His lips find mine before raining kisses all over my face and neck, burying his head in my shoulder. "Why didn't you tell me? I would like to have known, to experience that epiphany with you."

I shrug. "I needed to live with that revelation a bit, let it take root and grow." I pull away, finding his face streaked with tears. "Oh, Joseph. I'm sorry. I think mostly I'm ashamed it took me this long to get where you are." It's my turn to wipe and kiss away his tears. "We were always on the same page, on the same journey, except my self-doubt kept me from seeing you right there—next to me—at the same point in time that I was. We were always in sync. I was too blind to see it."

"But now you see me?" His soul, his heart is wide-open for me.

"I see you, Joseph. I see the love reflected in your eyes is the same as mine. We are one hundred percent in this together."

He smiles mischievously. "One hundred and fifty percent, Sweets."

I press my forehead to his. "Yes, one hundred and fifty percent to infinity."

"Infinity," he breathes.

"Infinity." My love.

Joseph

The days that follow come and go quickly, with a natural rhythm I haven't found before. I'm lighter: an unrecognized weight has been lifted by the knowledge that Samantha knows I'm not going anywhere. It's more than that, though. It's that there is an equality now. A balance has been reached where she knows she's the one for me, just as I've always known she was it for me. I'm sorry it took her six months to tell me, but I believe that for her, it took that long for the knowing to work its way to the surface, fully vested and indestructible.

Teddy, with his cock-sure way about him, has been a godsend. He's working out better than I could have hoped. Samantha comes in a few days a week after class to touch base, answer his questions, and fine-tune any processes he doesn't fully understand or believes could work better.

I step out of my office when I hear her laugh. She's early. I still as I spot her leaning on Teddy's desk, her face lit up with amusement, her shoulders shaking with laughter.

Teddy spots me and stiffens. "Sir."

"Relax. I never said you can't have a little fun," I respond to Teddy. With a nod and a smile, I move to my girl. "You're early."

She slides to my side as my arm wraps around her waist. "A little. My last class ended early. My professor had to be somewhere, and his TA didn't show up." She shrugs. "Lucky for me."

I kiss her temple. "No, lucky for me." Her smile widens, and I feel it in my cock.

"Actually, it's lucky for me. I need your help on that spreadsheet I mentioned. I'm hoping you'll have time to look at it." Teddy brings us back to reality.

Samantha gives me a quick wink before turning her attention to him. "Of course. Does he have a few minutes before I get started?"

"Don't talk about me like I'm not here," I grumble.

"Hush. Let Teddy do his job, which is to handle you and keep you on track. I don't want to mess that up."

I shake my head and walk to my office, knowing I have seventeen minutes before I need to leave for my next meeting.

"He has seventeen minutes," Teddy confirms.

"Great. I'll be right back." She enters my office and closes the door.

I'm leaning on my desk, my arms crossed. "You could have asked *me* how much time I had."

Her smile softens as she sashays toward me in black jeans, boots, and a sweater. My girl loves her black. "Don't pout. You only have a few minutes." She throws her arms around my neck, forcing me to uncross my arms. "Wouldn't you rather spend that time kissing me hello?"

I grip her waist, brushing her lips with mine. "For the record, I don't need anyone 'handling' me, except for you."

"Duly noted." Her eyes crinkle with mirth.

Enough teasing. I need these few precious moments with my girl. I kiss her slowly and tenderly, savoring her taste, the feel of her in my arms, and her sweet sighs.

With a heavy sigh of my own, I pull back, resting my forehead against hers. "Tell me you'll go home after helping Teddy and get all your homework done. I'm going to need a bit of your time when I'm there."

She smiles. "Only a bit?"

"Okay, hours. I'm going to need hours of your time." I slip my hand between her jean-clad thighs. "Fuck, I can feel your heat." She grips me tighter as my hand slides back and forth. "I'm going to need hours loving you, Sweets."

Her head falls against my chest. Her breathing increases, and I have visions of her nipples hardening in anticipation of my touch.

"Ah, fuck, baby, I can't wait."

"Wha…" her response is lost in the sound of me undoing her jeans.

I slip my hand inside, cursing the tight fit of her sexy-as-fuck jeans, but manage to slip two fingers inside her.

"Oh god," she moans.

"Look at me." I grip the back of her neck. Her face rises to meet mine with eyes shining with need. "There's my girl." I pump my fingers in and out, my palm rubbing her clit. "Do you hear that?" I breathe against her lips and then move to her ear. "Your wet pussy pulling my fingers back in."

She moans, her breath licking at my ear.

"You make me so hard, baby. I want to sink into you and feel you squeeze my cock like that, sucking me back in over and over again."

"Joseph." She trembles and tightens her hold on me.

"I want to feel you come all over my fingers." I pump faster, my breath quickening, my heart pounding. If she touches my cock, I'll come like a teenager in my pants. "When I get home, I'm going to take you against the wall, bent over the couch, on the kitchen counter, on the floor, pressed against the penthouse windows. Wherever I find you, that's where I'm taking you, Sweets." She shudders and clenches. "I want to give this to you, but you make me so fucking hot, I want to tear your clothes off and fuck you right here."

"Yes!" rips from her lips as she comes undone.

I wrap my arm around her, holding her up. "My girl, how I love to see you fall apart for me."

My desk phone intercom beeps. "You have ten more minutes. Your father's meeting is running late." Teddy's voice sends a reprieve.

Thank fuck, we have more time.

Before I can respond or stop Samantha, she's on her knees, unleashing my cock. "Baby." I try to tell her that's not necessary. I need the ten minutes to calm the fuck down.

"You're so hard." She looks up at me, all eyes and innocence, her cheeks flushed from her orgasm.

And fuck if I don't want her mouth on me more than my next breath. "Make it hard and fast, Sweetness." I touch her cheek. "I won't last long." With a sweet smile that belies the act she is getting ready to perform, she licks the cum off the tip. "Ah, fuck." When her mouth consumes me, I lean against my desk, gripping its edges, and let my head fall back. "Fuck, yes, like that."

She takes me deep, so fucking deep. Her hand pumps my shaft as her tongue flicks over the underside before she sucks me back in, over and over.

I look down, my hips thrusting, her head bobbing, her hand pumping. It's all too much, and yet it's not nearly enough. "Stop."

I lift her off the floor and swivel, pressing her to the wall, her back to me. "Hands on the wall." I push her jeans and panties to her ankles. I spread my legs and bend my knees, position my cock. "Hold on."

"Yes." She gasps as I fill her up.

Her wet heat swallows me, squeezing me like I knew she would, like she does every time. "Fuck, Samantha, my love. This is gonna be fast and hard. Are you okay with that?"

A tremor runs through her body. "God, yes."

Thank fuck.

I grip her hips and thrust. The feral groan that escapes my mouth is sure to be heard down the hall, but at this moment, I can't give a fuck. My girl calls my name, and I do it again and again, pounding into her, relishing the sound of our bodies joining. Mating. Doing what we were meant to do, becoming one. The perfect design of yin and yang. My cock to her pussy.

Pounding.

Pounding.

Pounding.

She tightens and grips, squeezing and milking me as she comes, sending me over the edge with her.

I groan as I pump into her, leaving my mark, my soul, the very essence of who I am. All for her.

With a quick kiss, I leave Samantha recovering on my couch, locking the door behind me. I send Teddy on an errand to give her more time. I catch up to Fin and Matt on my way, which is no great feat considering we work in the same wing.

"Did I hear you're flying to Austin tonight?" Matt asks Fin as we wait outside of Dad's office.

I perk up at that notion. "Austin?"

"And where did you hear that?" Fin deflects. He glances at me and does a double take, his eyes squinting, giving me a once-over.

Shit. Can he tell I just had sex? I fight the urge to squirm under his scrutiny.

"From Monica," Matt affirms.

Fin frowns but looks away. I silently sigh in relief. *Have to stop having sex in the office.*

"And who did Monica hear that from?" Fin glances at his phone before looking at Matt.

"From Angela." Matt smirks at me with a wink. He's messing with Fin, like I would if I had heard that news first.

"Hmm. I would think our PAs have more important things to do than gossip about my travel plans."

"So you're not denying it?" Matt pushes.

"No."

"Would your visit have anything to do with a slight brunette who's been spotted visiting MCI before returning to Austin a few weeks ago?" I can't resist pushing him a little. Though, I can't push him too hard, or he might call me on my shit I'm quite sure he's aware of—or suspects.

Fin's eyes widen momentarily before he regains his composure. "I'm not sure who you're referring to." He scowls at me again for good measure as censure for conspiring with Matt.

Deny. Deny. Deny. He's not ready to talk about it. That's obvious. With a shrug and a quick glance to Matt, I change the subject, focusing on the topic at hand—second quarter earnings and third quarter projections. This is in Fin's wheelhouse and a much safer topic by the way he jumps right in and visibly relaxes into the discussion.

We're an hour into our two-hour earnings meeting when I get a text from Samantha.

Samantha: *Can you let me know when you're out of your meeting?*

Me: *Anything wrong? I can step out.*

Three dots bounce on the screen, disappear, start again, then disappear again. Either she's distracted or she's contemplating her answer, which means it's *something*. Finally, she responds.

Samantha: *No, don't do that.*

She didn't say there wasn't anything wrong—which means there is.

Me: *Where are you?*

Samantha: *Finish your meeting. I'll be home when you get there. It's not urgent.*

I can barely concentrate the rest of the meeting. Fin keeps eyeing me, which brings me back to the here and now. The moment the meeting is over, I head to my office, picking up my laptop and a few reports before advising Teddy I'll finish up at home.

"Goodnight, Joe. Enjoy your evening." His smile is bigger than it should be, making me think he knows what happened earlier in my office. Well, he'll have to get used to it. I'm sure it won't be the last time, despite my best intentions.

Samantha is coming out of the bathroom, wrapping a towel around her body, head down, when I enter the bedroom. Her wet hair is clipped up high. Drops of water cascade down her shower-warmed skin. She's beautiful, all undone, not a stitch of makeup, only her angelic face, tender curves, as beautiful on the outside as she is on the inside. My Sweets.

She stops cold when she sees me, eyes and lips puffy. She's been crying.

"What's wrong?" My instincts were right, I should have come home the moment she told me not to. Dammit!

Her eyes dart to my dresser. "That came today. Addressed to me." Her voice shakes with emotion, ripping at my heart.

I step closer, pulling her to my side as I reach for the piece of paper sitting on top of the dresser.

He's mine. You'll never make him happy.
Leave now and I'll play nice.
Stay and you'll wish you'd taken my advice.

Sincerely,
The ONE Joseph really loves

What the fuck? Anger rages through me. "Where did you get this?"
She pulls back, reacting to my anger, her eyes big, scanning my face,

trying to read my thoughts. "It was in the mail. Teddy handed it to me before I left."

"Did he see it?" That came out way too accusatory. Fuck!

"No!" She steps back, extricating herself from my grasp. "I didn't read it until I came home." Her head tilts, piercing me with her glare. "I texted you right after."

"Fuck." My head falls forward, and I grab the back of my neck. "I'm sorry." I look up to see tears staining her cheeks. I rush to her, wrapping her in my arms. Thankfully she doesn't resist. "Christ, you know it's bullshit, right?" Her whole body sags against me. "I'm sorry. I'm not angry at you. I'm angry at the situation." I cup her head to my chest and kiss her wet hair. "I'm not angry with you," I whisper, my lips still pressed to her hair.

She simply nods and squeezes me tightly.

"It's probably some jackass trying to win that stupid bet. Trying to get you to break up with me by a certain date so he or she can win," I offer the first solution that pops into my brain.

"Maybe it's Lydia," Samantha pipes in.

Christ. "Maybe it is." I lift her chin. Her eyes lock on mine. "It's not true. Tell me you at least know that much."

She nods. "I don't believe you'd cheat on me."

I sigh in relief. I knew she knew that, but I had to be certain. "Why the tears then?"

Eyes cast down, her shoulders rise and fall. "It makes me question if I'm enough."

The sorrow in her voice squeezes my chest. "Samantha."

She pulls out of my embrace. "I know." She sighs, starting to pull clothes out of drawers. "It's old news. It's *my* old news." Clothes gathered in her arms, she looks at me pleadingly, sad. "It feels like the world is conspiring against me, against *us*, continually ripping off the scab of my insecurities as soon as I start to heal and feel confident."

After the events of the past few weeks, I'm not surprised. First it was Lydia, then the bet against us, and the overheard discussion about me never being satisfied by only one woman, and then Michael's poorly worded comment making her feel like she was the one who would be dumped- if it happened—not me.

I open my arms. "Come here, baby."

She doesn't hesitate. She drops her clothes and walks right into me, wrapping herself around me as I do the same. "We'll figure out who sent it." I kiss her swollen, soft lips. "I don't want you to give it another thought." My lips brush hers again. "I need you to listen to me, focus on my words—the *only* words that matter."

Her lips curl in a seductive smile. Her eyes shine with love as she waits patiently.

I walk her backwards. "You own me. Heart and soul. Mind and body. Everything I have, everything I am, everything I will be—is yours. There is no *me* without *you*. No other women even exist for me. They are monotone shades of gray compared to your shining, all consuming incandescence."

Her smile falters when the back of her legs hit the bed, startling her.

Slowly, I release her towel, letting it fall to the floor. "I will love you to the end of time, Samantha." My arm around her back, I gently lower her to the bed. "Every inch of you inside and out is my heaven, my sanctuary."

"Joseph," she gasps, bowing off the bed when I draw a taut nipple into my mouth and suck deeply.

I repeat my ministrations on her other succulent peak as I work to remove my tie. Her nimble fingers work to free my shirt from my pants. In moments, it's discarded, and I settle myself over her, bare chest to bare chest, my hard cock straining against my slacks, pressed between her legs. "My world, my life, is yours."

With racing breath, her lips find mine, her tongue pressing for admittance. I gladly let her in, taking all she has to give and returning it with equal vigor.

"Mine," she growls, coming up for air.

"Fuck, yes," I agree with relief to see the sadness gone, replaced with desire and possessiveness, making my steel-hard dick throb with the need to claim her as mine, too. I want to claim her, love every silky inch of her with my mouth, but my need to mark her with my cock wins out.

"Finally," she exclaims when I'm naked and pressing into her.

"My greedy girl." I sink in to the hilt, reveling in her gasps of pleasure, and still. Our gazes lock, her panting breath wafting over my face. "This, Samantha, is my favorite place. I love you in all things, in all ways. But here—buried deep inside you—is where I find my solace, my home, my respite. When we make love, I'm not a McIntyre, an heir to a Fortune 500 company. I'm not a VP. I'm not a son, a brother, a friend. All I am at this moment is a man, *your* man, making love to *his* woman, trying to express with my body the depth of my love and devotion."

"Joseph." She trembles below me, squeezing me tightly with her legs, her arms, and her pussy as tears stream down the sides of her remarkable face. "You make me feel like I could fly." Her chin trembles, and tears continue to fall into her wet hair. "Like I'm somebody special."

My heart bursts. "Christ, Samantha, you *are* somebody special. You're *my* somebody special." I grind my hips, pressing into her slowly and deeply.

She cries out, already so close. My words, my love, taking her faster than my body can alone.

"Fly for me, Sweets. I'll be here to catch you when you land."

Seven

DANCE IN MY DARKNESS

SEPTEMBER

Samantha

'M UNRAVELING. JOSEPH HAD TO LEAVE TOWN FOR four days for a tech conference in Las Vegas of all places. Sin City. Before he left, it had been three weeks since that fateful letter arrived. We'd moved beyond it, quickly falling into our normal stride, the letter all but forgotten. Michael is looking into it, but other than that, I haven't heard any further news. Joseph didn't want to leave, not because of the letter, necessarily, but because neither of us wanted to be apart for four days. In the big scheme of things, it seems silly. It's only days, not weeks.

In Austin, I had Joseph and Margot to hang out with. Jace was there, but we only saw each other occasionally. Being back in Dallas, going to school at SMU, has been an adjustment without Margot. And now that Joseph is gone, I'm feeling lonely, but it's good for me to remember what it's like to hang out by myself. I used to do it all the time. Four days is no big deal. Plus, I have Michael if I need anything, and

I could always call Sebastian, though he's been picking up extra shifts and hasn't had much time to hang out lately.

The day after Joseph left, I received a package. There's no return sender, but I assumed it was an early wedding present. A few have been trickling in now and again. Inside the box was Joseph's blue tie. The one he bought to match my eyes. It was such a sweet, thoughtful gesture, and then there it sat in a box.

I pushed it aside and found a note.

This is as tame a package you will receive.
Leave now and I won't be forced to take this any further.
He's mine. Leave.

Sincerely,
The ONE Joseph thinks about when he's fucking you
P.S. Loving Vegas!

I gripped the kitchen counter, my stomach churning. I tried not to give its words life, meaning in my head, but it was hard to ignore.

How do I know it's Joseph's tie? I rushed to our closet to see if his was still there.

I didn't find it in our closet.

Like his father and brothers, all of Joseph's ties are handmade silk with his initials stitched into the back. I turned over the tie in the box, praying I didn't find what I was looking for, but right there in perfect calligraphy stitched letters was JPM. Joseph Patrick McIntyre. How did she get Joseph's tie? When was the last time I saw him wear it?

P.S. Loving Vegas.

He's not cheating on me. She's not there. She wants to put doubt in my head. Play with me. She's succeeding!

All those thoughts swirled in my head, and when he called that night, I feigned a headache so he wouldn't know something was wrong. I can handle this. I trust him. It can wait. If he knew another package came, he'd screw up his trip to fly home to make it right, to ensure I know it's not true. My heart *knows* it's not true, but it's his tie—his tie for *me*. How did *she* get it? Whoever the hell *she* is.

True or not, someone is fucking with us. And this someone is capable of getting hold of such a personal item and knows Joseph is in Las Vegas. This is not good.

For the next few days, I go to school and back. Bury myself in my studies and help Teddy when he needs it, but with Joseph out of town, he doesn't seem to need much help. When I talk to Joseph, I make it short and sweet, trying not to give anything away, keeping the conversation on him and what new technology caught his eye. It's not hard for either of us to get lost in tech talk.

"Are you sure you're okay, Samantha? You seem a little distant." His low voice makes the ache in my heart that much worse.

"Yeah, I'm just busy with school and tired. I haven't slept well with you not here." All of that's true. I don't tell him that the thoughts racing around in my head are contributing to my lack of sleep.

"I miss you."

"I miss you too." Madly. Deeply. Truly. Heart-wrenchingly miss him.

"I can't wait to see you tomorrow. I'm going to devour you as soon as I see you."

"I can't wait." I squeeze my eyes shut, tapping my forehead, trying not to think about the letter. *Signed, the one Joseph thinks about when he's fucking you.*

No! He's not interested in anyone besides me. I won't let her get under my skin.

"Oh, I have that thing with my mom tomorrow. So, I'll see you when I get home." I'd completely forgotten about it. Jace and I are supposed to join my mom for a family counseling session. I'm dreading it nearly as much as showing Joseph the package.

"That's right. Do you want me to meet you there? I could cut out of the afternoon session and catch an earlier flight so I can go with you."

"No. Don't miss the end of the conference. I'll see you when I get home."

"Are you sure?"

"Positive." No, I'm not sure at all. But it's the right thing to do, to say.

"Okay. I love you, Sweets."

"I love you, Caveman."

"Bye, baby."

"Goodbye, Joseph."

The silence that hangs in the air after I hang up is stifling and eats away at my confidence to remain silent. I can't tell anybody about this. I promised Joseph I would come to him first, but I can't tell him now and mess up his trip. It can wait. I'll survive.

I combat the loneliness with working out. After I change, I head to our ensuite gym. I could go to the Omega Tower Gym two floors down, but I don't need fancy equipment. I only need the treadmill and blaringly loud music to beat the thoughts out of my head and exhaust my body so I can sleep.

Tomorrow.

He'll be home tomorrow.

Joseph

My intuition is screaming at me. *There's something wrong.* But I choose to listen to what Samantha is telling me. She's not being distant. She's tired and missing me. I can relate. I haven't slept well since I've been gone either. I miss *her*, but I also miss her sexy body pressed against me all night long, reminding me what my dick was made for. I head home tomorrow, and I can't wait.

It's the last full day of the conference. Tomorrow morning, we have meetings scheduled with a few tech companies that have promising products I'd like to acquire. These are not the products we saw during the dazzling expo. These are the little-known hush-hush products that are not quite off the ground and might be a few years away from the marketplace. Now is the time to secure and foster them to fruition. Whether that means partnering with them or full acquisition remains to be seen.

I meet Charles and the rest of my team for a strategy planning breakfast before we tackle today's full agenda.

Securing my seat at the head of the table, I address the team. "I won't be in the main session today, so I'll rely on you to be my eyes and ears." I get a few questioning looks, but I go on to explain. "I'll be attending a break-out session with other leaders in the technology industry, brainstorming what we can do to reduce our carbon footprint by minimizing the fallout when our new tech becomes legacy."

"Everything is about becoming green," Jackson mirrors my thoughts.

"Exactly. We need to leave the world a better place than how we found it, which includes not leaving our new inventions to be shipped off to other countries to be burned, scrapped, and piled into already overflowing landfills when they become outdated," I recap.

That leads into ten minutes of them giving me their ideas, which ends up giving me some great feedback to take to the session. Once these guys get going and their free thinking is set loose, it's hard to wrangle them back in. Their neuropathways ignite as ideas are tossed back and forth to each other like a technology round of hot potato, moving faster and faster until they're all lit up like a nuclear Christmas tree.

I love my job.

By the end of breakfast, everyone understands their mission for the day and what needs to get done in preparation for tomorrow's meetings. As my phone vibrates in my pocket, I grab my stuff, say my goodbyes, and head out to find a quiet place to take this call.

"Tell me." My mind is going a million miles a minute, racing with thoughts of Samantha mixing with those from my stimulating breakfast.

"Morning to you too, boss."

I sigh, knowing I need to reel it in. "Good morning, Michael. What did you find out?"

"She received a package a few days ago."

My heart sinks. *Samantha, Samantha, Samantha. What are you doing, baby? Honesty. Remember?*

"What kind of package? Do you know what's in it? Did you talk to her?"

"From the security footage it looked to be the size of a shoe box. She didn't mention the package. Therefore, I don't know what's in it. I assume you don't want me to ask her about it."

"No. I'll address it when I get home tomorrow. I don't want to upset her any further by discussing it over the phone." I slip back into my hotel room, deciding I need a few minutes to regroup before continuing my day. "Did she seem upset when you talked to her?"

"We didn't really talk much. You know how she is when we spar. She gets pissed she can't kick my ass. So, yeah, a heart-to-heart wasn't likely to happen." He lets out a punch of air. "But she did seem a little somber. I'll see if I can get her to hang out with me tonight if you want."

"Everything else on the security footage looks okay? Nothing out of the ordinary? Nothing suspicious from Lydia? No Todd? She's safe?"

He chuckles. "Man, how much coffee did you have today?"

"It's not that...I just..." I pace to the window and look out over the Vegas strip, wishing more than ever I could have convinced her to come with me. "I hate being away from her. Her inner demon gets the best of her when she has too much time to think."

"And you're not here to ground her, reassure her."

"Yeah, that too." Most definitely that. If I could touch her, hold her, look into her eyes, I could chase away those evil demon, self-doubting thoughts of hers.

"She's safe, Joe. Nothing seems out of the ordinary, except for possibly the package. But even that could be nothing. It could be wedding stuff. It could actually be a pair of shoes."

"Maybe, but my gut is telling me otherwise. Plus, she wouldn't have shoes delivered to the office."

We talk for a few moments more before I have to head downstairs. It's going to be a long day. I was excited after my breakfast, but reality is bringing me back to the here and now.

And the here and now is telling me to get my ass back home.

Samantha

A horn blast startles me. I look around to be sure I'm not the offending party. The light is still red, and I'm not the only one not moving. So, yeah, I don't know what the honking was about. I can't even determine who it was that honked in the first place.

I check the clock on the dash and sigh. *Come on, come on, come on.* I urge the light to change. I'm late to meet Joseph's mom for an early dinner before meeting Jace and my mom for our joint therapy session. Now, that appointment I wouldn't mind being late to, but I don't want to cut my visit with Fiona short. She's been more than supportive during this whole drama with my mom and Jace. Not to mention her guidance and support during the wedding planning process.

At the time of my high school graduation last year, I'd finally realized I wanted nothing more than a future with Joseph. A future that would eventually make me an official member of Joseph's family. The support they all showed me after my father's death astounded, humbled, and endeared them to me. Though I was still trepidatious, I think if Joseph hadn't asked me to marry him, I would have asked him. The idea of not being in his family for the rest of my life was unbearable. They became my family. Joseph's dad, Hugh, could never replace my father, but he's come pretty darn close. Fin and Matt are like brothers to me. And Fiona, well, she's more than my future mother-in-law. She's become my confidant and strongest supporter, besides Joseph.

A break in traffic gets me to the restaurant only a few minutes late. I spot Fiona the moment I enter. "Ah, Sam, aren't you a sight for sore eyes." Fiona gives me a warm smile and an even warmer hug. Pulling back, she grasps my shoulders, taking me in. "You look beautiful, but tired. Are you working too hard and not getting enough sleep?"

I laugh. "Are you saying I look like crap?"

"No!" she adamantly exclaims. "Tired. That's all." She sits, motioning me to do the same. "You have a beauty that comes from within, so no matter how tired you are, you'll still shine like no other."

Jeez, she's gonna make me cry. "Fiona, now you're going overboard." It's obvious where Joseph gets his silver tongue from.

Thankfully, the waiter interrupts us for my drink order, and, since I'm short on time, we order dinner as well.

Once he leaves, her focus is back on me. "How are you, really?" The tenderness on her face and in her voice allow for nothing but the truth.

Not all the truth, though. I can't tell her about the letters. If Joseph wants her to know, that's up to him to tell her, but I can't imagine he'd want his parents to know. I'm not even sure if anyone besides Michael knows. I take a sip of water and reply as openly as I can. "I'm tired, and I miss him." My eyes start to well up with tears.

"It's hard to sleep when he's not there beside you, isn't it?"

"How'd…"

She merely smiles and pats my hand at my surprise. "I can't sleep when Hugh is away either. Honestly, once the kids were old enough, I started traveling with him whenever I could. It was easier on both of us." She looks off as if remembering something fondly. After a moment, her gaze meets mine. Her eyes are dancing with memories. "I think it was good for our marriage too. They say absence makes the heart grow fonder. And in some cases, I'm sure it's true. But for us, the quiet time we had together, away from our normal routine, was far more valuable to our marriage."

Fiona and Hugh have a great marriage, much like the one my parents had. She's blessed, and I know she values it even more after seeing how my father's death has impacted my mother.

"What else do you know was good for your marriage?" I'm anxious to hear all the sage advice Fiona has to share. After all, hers is a living example of what a successful one looks like.

She lights up, welcoming the opportunity to share. Before Joseph even proposed to me, Fiona told me how much she and Hugh enjoyed having me around. I was the daughter they never had. I doubt any of her sons would ask her for such advice, and she's relishing every moment as much as I am in hearing it.

The dinner with Fiona was wonderful, relaxing, and filled up those empty holes in my heart left by my mom's absence, as well as my dad and Jace's.

On the other end of the spectrum, this session with Mom and Jace only seems to deplete the warmth Fiona instilled and replace it with dank, darkness.

"Sam, I'd like to start with you this time. Give you a chance to voice how you're feeling, tell your story since your father passed."

I open my mouth to speak, but nothing comes out.

"Why don't you start with your relationship with Jace?" Dr. Weston gives me an encouraging smile, looking between Jace and me.

Dr. Weston isn't messing around. We didn't ease into the issue of my own flesh and blood cutting me off at the knees when my dad died. I thought we'd only be dealing with my relationship with my mom since he's her therapist and not mine or Jace's. Apparently, he feels differently.

Jace is as flustered and as surprised as I am to be the topic of discussion. "I thought we were going to focus on Mom and her recovery," he asks.

"This is part of Eleanor's healing process. She needs to understand how your father's death impacted the two of you. She needs to hear it from your perspective, in your words." Dr. Weston types on his tablet before looking at me expectantly.

"How can she not know how his death impacted us?" My eyes dart to my mom. She's silently looking out the window as if I'm not even here. "Our father died, and you abandoned us too." I thought I'd cry, but anger seems to be the driving emotion at the moment. "It doesn't take a genius to figure out that it sucked."

Dr. Weston doesn't bat an eye. "That's a good start. Let's narrow down the *sucking* and discuss specifics. Tell me about you and Jace."

Jace's sorrowful blue eyes meet mine. I don't look away, I don't hide. It's time to give him a chance. A *real* chance. "Jace has apologized. Many times, in fact. He wants to make amends, but I haven't really been open to him." I face Jace on the couch we're sharing. "I want to make things right with you. I'm afraid. I don't want to get hurt again." I hastily swipe at my tears. Next to Joseph, Jace is the most important person in my life. He's my family, and based on the fact that my mom hasn't even acknowledged my presence—he's going to be my *only* family.

He grabs my hand and pulls me into a hug. "I'm not going anywhere. I swear, Sam. I'm here to stay. I'll do anything to be a part of your life again. Give me a chance. I won't let you down. Not this time."

The anguish and sincerity in his voice knock down my defenses. "Okay."

He pulls back with a hopeful smile on his face. "Yeah?"

"Yeah."

Dr. Weston is pleased with our interaction and encourages us to be patient with each other, as reconciliation doesn't happen overnight. It's a process that will have hiccups along the way, but open communication and forgiveness will make it a smoother road to travel together.

He moves on to the topic of my mom. "Jace, I'll ask you the same question in a moment, but I'd like to continue with Sam." He motions to me. "Please tell your mom what this last year and a half has been like for you."

I really don't want to go there. I've worked hard to push down these emotions of inadequacy, of not being enough for my mom to want to stick around and be a parent. Mom sits across the room, facing Jace and me. Her gaze hasn't left the window since I walked in the door. Jace was already here when I arrived, so I have no idea if she speaks to him when I'm not here.

"I feel like an orphan. Abandoned by my family. Dad didn't have a choice when he died." That's not true. "I guess he did have a choice. He chose to protect me, and in doing so, he was shot. His choice was selfless." I've tried so hard not to think about that day, not to second guess what I could have done differently. *If* I had done anything differently, would it have made a difference? "But, Mom, your choice to leave me was selfish. You left me alone to deal with the fallout of Dad's death, not only emotionally, but everything. The money. The house. Bills. Everything fell on my shoulders. Even taking care of you."

"Eleanor, how do you feel about what Sam's shared?" Dr. Weston asks.

"Sam, I'm so sorry." Jace takes my hand and holds it tightly as both he and I wipe at our tears.

Mom, on the other hand, can't even look at me. She wipes at her tears with a tissue, but remains silent. That's all I've gotten from her for over a year now. Not. One. Word.

I wait, glancing at the clock, and when five minutes have passed and her tears have ceased, I reach my breaking point. I squeeze Jace's hand and give him a nod and a quick smile. "Jace, I'm willing to talk with you whenever you want. Call me, come over. Whenever."

More tears slip down his pain-ridden face as he looks at me with regret. "I'd like that. I'll call you tomorrow."

I turn my focus to my mother for a moment before looking to Dr. Weston. "I'm sorry, but I can't do this anymore. If my mother truly wants to make amends, then I'll come back, but until then, I'm done."

With a succinct nod, he replies, "I understand. I appreciate you trying." He shakes my hand as I stand to leave. "I'll be in touch," he says before turning his focus to my mom.

Jace and I hug, and then I slip out the door. I don't know if he'll stay. Perhaps she'll talk to him. At the moment, though, I'm finding it difficult to even care.

Tears block my vision, making it nearly impossible to find my way. I manage to exit the building, only progressing a few steps before I hear him.

"Sweetness."

"Oh, God, Joseph." I all but crumble to the ground. Joseph's quick reaction saves me as he sweeps me into his arms.

"I got you." He holds me tightly, one arm below my legs and the other around my back, anchoring me to his chest.

I hold on to him for dear life, giving in to the grief, and let go.

His lips press to my head as he whispers, "Christ, baby. I got you. Shh, I got you."

Joseph

I don't know what the hell happened in there, but I'm angry as fuck to see Samantha hurting so deeply. I cut my meetings short, leaving my team in Vegas to do what they've been trained to do: seek, find, acquire. I've never been so thankful that I listened to my gut and came home to meet her at the care facility where her mom has been staying.

Once we're sitting in the back of the SUV with Victor at the helm and Michael in tow, driving her car, we head home. I hold her for the entire ride with no desire to ever let her go. Her crying has stopped, and I can feel her drifting off to sleep.

The forty-five minute drive feels like a lifetime. I don't try to wake her once we pull into the garage. Victor grabs her purse that I leave on the seat as I slip out with her cradled in my arms.

Michael parks in her space and grabs her belongings from the car. I stop cold when I see a box tucked under his arm.

"What the fuck is that?" I whisper with clenched teeth, determined not to wake Samantha.

"It was on the hood of her car," Michael replies with concern written all over his face.

I tremble with rage at the idea of her being alone, coming out in the condition she was in, and finding that box sitting on her car. A person can only take so much. I'm worried she's reaching her tipping point, and this box might put her over.

"Fuck," is all I can manage.

With a knowing look to Michael, Victor hands over Samantha's purse and leaves us to head up to our penthouse. I have no doubt Victor is heading to Fin's for a tumbler or two of Fin's cherished 1939 Macallan.

I manage to settle my girl on our bed without waking her. I turn on a lamp in the sitting area of our suite, in case she wakes up and is confused about where she is. Shutting the door behind me, I head back to Michael, whom I know is waiting.

I find him in the kitchen, eyeing the package and drinking a beer. Without even looking, he hands me an opened bottle of Heineken. He pulls a knife out of his front pocket.

"We can't open it." I move toward him, placing my hand over his.

He scowls. "Why not?"

"Because it's not addressed to you or me," I state the obvious. "But also because she needs to trust us not to hide anything from her." I take a long pull on my beer.

He sets his knife down and leans back against the counter. "What if it's a bomb?"

I grimace at the thought. "Do you think it's a bomb?"

"No." He drinks his beer, his eyes studying me. "She needs 24/7 protection." He points his bottle at the box. "Whoever delivered that followed her tonight, left it, and I imagine they stuck around to be sure she found it."

"Shit."

"It's escalating. The first two came to the office, but this one was delivered personally."

"You know about the box?"

We both whip around to see Samantha standing in the living room.

"Wait? *'First two'*? That sounds like there's been more than two." She moves closer and stops, waiting for a reply.

I close the distance between us. "There was a box on the hood of your car tonight. That makes three."

"What?" She steps back, fear written all over her face. "No, that can't be." Her head shakes. "No."

"Baby." I pull her into my arms, hold her tightly, and kiss her temple over and over again. She's shaking. "It'll be okay, Samantha. I've got you. Michael's got you. We won't let anything happen to you."

Calmer, she looks up. "So, you know about the first box, the second delivery?" Her eyes bounce between Michael and me.

I cup her cheek. "I knew something was wrong. You've been off for days. Michael checked the security footage and saw Teddy hand you a box."

"Oh." She steps out of my arms. "That makes sense." She turns and walks down the hall toward our bedroom.

I glance at Michael, who simply raises his eyebrow at me, but remains silent.

Samantha comes back a moment later, stopping in the living room with an identically sized box in her hands. "I didn't want to tell you about this over the phone. I didn't want to ruin your trip. That conference only comes once a year, and I know you had big plans for it."

"I understand that, but you should have gone to Michael. That's why I left him here, to be sure you remained safe and had someone to rely on if you needed it."

"We agreed I'd tell you first." She glances at Michael, who's still in the kitchen watching us, before meeting my eyes. "You didn't like it when I went to him first about the office betting pool."

I grip the back of my neck and squeeze. "You're right. I'm sorry. From now on, if you can't tell me, you tell Michael. What matters is not who hears it first, but that you tell someone and don't have to deal with this on your own."

"Okay." She glances between me and Michael. "Where's the other box?"

She's calm, no longer upset. Is it because she's truly okay, or is she only worn out from earlier? I point to Michael. "It's in the kitchen."

With a nod, she gives me the box in her hands. "I guess you'd better open this first."

I take the box from her, grab her hand, and join Michael in the kitchen.

"Before you open it," she says. "I want you to know that even though I'm confused on how the item in that box could be there, I don't believe what the letter says."

Fuck. What the hell could be in this box? "Okay." I kiss her forehead. It's good to know her faith in me hasn't been broken.

I start to open the box, but freeze when Michael hollers, "Stop." He looks around the kitchen. "Let's be smart about this. Sam's fingerprints are already on the box and its contents, right?" He looks to Sam, who confirms it with a single nod. Michael finds what he's looking for and pulls out box of Ziploc baggies. "Put this on your hand before you touch anything on the inside."

With the box on the counter and my right hand in a large baggie, I awkwardly open the box, revealing my blue tie. "Hey, I've been looking for this."

"You have?" Samantha's worried eyes meet mine.

"Yeah, I haven't seen it in weeks. I can't even remember the last time I wore it."

"You're sure it's yours?" Michael chimes in.

"It has his initials on the back," Samantha says. "And his is missing from the closet. I checked."

I turn it over, and sure enough, JPM is stitched into the back, like all of my custom ties. "Yep, it's mine." I drop it and look at Samantha, her blue eyes locking on me. "I bought it because it matches your eyes. I only have one this color, like I only have one of you."

A single tear drops down her cheek. "Joseph." She snuggles into my side.

"Only one of you, Sweetness."

Michael clears his throat. "That's really touching and all, but could we move this along? I'd really like to get this other box opened sometime this century."

He's right. "I'm sorry your tie got tainted by all of this," I say to Samantha as I reach in to pull out the note. Her response is lost on me as I fume at the words on the page. "What the fuck?"

"It's worse than the first one, huh?" Samantha says.

I read it again before showing it to Michael. As he reads it, I finger her chin, guiding her face to mine. "It's total bullshit. You know that, right?"

"I know."

"There's nobody but you."

"I know."

"There sure as fuck wasn't anybody with me in Vegas."

She places her hand on my chest, soothing the beast in me. "I know."

"You know?" I need her reassurance.

Her smile is unexpected but wholeheartedly welcomed. "I know, Joseph." She pats my chest. "I trust you. I believe you. I don't know how she got your tie, but I'm sure there's a logical explanation. We just haven't thought of it yet."

"God, I love you." I hold her against my chest, ignoring Michael's eye roll. "Are you okay if Michael opens the other box?" I ask Samantha.

She waves her hand. "Please, have at it."

We exchange a quick look in agreement, then watch as he slowly opens it. Michael dons two baggies, one on each hand, and lifts out a pair of black Mack Weldon boxer briefs.

I recognize them instantly as the brand I exclusively wear. I grip the counter. *What the hell is going on?*

Samantha gasps.

Michael scrutinizes me. "I take it you recognize these?"

"I recognize the brand and style, but I have no reason to believe they're actually mine." I point to the crusty-looking white stuff along the front. "What the hell is that?"

"Oh my god!" Samantha exclaims.

Michael turns them around so he can see, then looks back to me like I'm an idiot. "Really?"

Realization dawns. "Even if those are my underwear and even if that cum is mine, there is no way that proves anything other than someone managed to get a pair of my dirty underwear." I point to the other box. "And my favorite tie. Whoever the fuck this is has proven themselves to be quite resourceful, but none of this proves I know them or have ever had sex with them."

Michael agrees. "It's cir-*cum*-stancial at best."

"Seriously? Tell me you did not make a cum joke at a time like this?" I suppress a smile, nearly giving in to it.

"Hey, if not now, when?" Michael retorts.

"Grow up, you two," Samantha barks. "It's entirely too soon for cum jokes."

I groan at my stupidity. "You're right." I motion back to the box. "What's the note say?"

Michael places the underwear back in the box and carefully slips the piece of paper out from under it, holding the note so we can all read it.

This is proof of what I do to him.
He comes for me like he'll never come for you, Sweetness.

Sincerely,
The ONE Joseph calls "Baby"

I catch her right before she goes down. "Samantha!"

Eight

TAKE ME IN THE NIGHT

Samantha

ARMS, LEGS, BODIES INTERTWINE. NEEDFUL MOANS, *gasps, and cries for more.*

"Joseph, you're mine." An unfamiliar voice cackles in the air.

A deep, "Baby," in response scrapes against my skin like sandpaper.

No! I protest, but nothing comes out. I am silent. Mute.

A sultry "What happens in Vegas, stays in Vegas" runs on repeat.

Silence it. I need to silence—her.

"Samantha," he calls.

It's not true. He's mine. Not hers.

More moans. More gripping and pulling. More—

"Baby, wake up!"

I bolt up, nearly tumbling from the bed before a tight embrace stops my downfall. My heart pounds. My throat is dry. I frantically look around the room for something…anything. I lock on him. His familiar green eyes melt my fear. "Joseph."

"You were dreaming." He nuzzles into me. His lips caress my face as comforting arms pull me tightly against his strong body. His warmth and smell surround me like a soothing cocoon. "Are you okay, baby?"

Baby?

Visions from my dream flash before my eyes. Arms. Legs. Bodies intertwined. *His* body. But not with *mine*.

I pull away on a groan, shaking my head, rolling over to extricate myself from this bed and his arms. "Don't call me that." I stumble to my feet, swaying slightly, catching on to the corner post at the end of our bed.

Joseph slowly rises from the bed. "Don't call you what?" He cautiously moves toward me, his hands flexing at his sides, concern written all over his face.

I step back as he moves forward until I bump into the couch in our sitting area. Joseph quickly steadies me with a hand on my hip, shifting forward, allowing no room between us. His naked body presses against mine. "What don't you want me to call you, baby?"

My head shoots up to meet his worried gaze. "*That*. Don't call me *that*." But as soon as I say it, I realize how stupid it is. I slump against him. My forehead hits his chest. *What the hell am I doing?* "Oh, god, Joseph. I'm letting her in my head."

His arms wrap around me. "I know it's hard to read such words and not let them affect you." His voice is gravely, tired.

I hug him back. My hand captures the back of his neck, trying to get him closer.

He runs kisses along my neck and shoulder. "But that's *my* word for *you*. No one else. I've *never* called anyone else 'baby.' Only *you*. It's *your* word."

A whimper escapes at his claim over that one simple word, making it ours again. I lift my head needing to feel his love. "Kiss me."

"Baby," he moans as our lips touch, gently, tenderly at first. His tongue sweeping, prodding, asking for admittance, which I gladly grant on a gasp of air, intensifying our kiss with penetrating need.

His hands sweep down my body, firmly holding me against him, grinding his hard cock between us. Our moans mirror the other's in need and intensity. Hands grasping and pulling, my pulsing desire demanding more. Demanding everything.

With graceful precision, Joseph lifts me off my feet and onto the back of the couch. My legs wrap around him as he buries himself deep inside me in one long, hot thrust of his hips.

"Christ, Sweets." He stills. Our eyes lock. "This is always, ever, just you and me."

He pulls out and pushes in again. "There's no room for anyone else."

His hands hook under my knees and pull my legs over his forearms as he locks his hands around my back. With each thrust he goes impossibly deeper, impossibly harder, and impossibly tenderer—all at the same time. His words, his face, his mouth, his hips, his entire body, filling me with his love.

Each thrust is punctuated with "baby," "oh, god, baby," "fuck, yes, baby" to take back the word she tried to steal from us.

I hold on. I hold on so damn tightly, I don't even know if I'm breathing. If I *can* breathe. The tingle starts at my toes and slowly glides up my legs. My nipples harden, my insides contract, and a moan that must have come from the depth of my desire blasts from my lips as that tingle reaches my core. My head falls back as ecstasy erupts, consuming me in wave after wave of tremors.

He thrusts and thrusts, then grinds out his release as I continue to shake and tremble in his arms.

Over and over again, we make love throughout the night. One or both of us wakes and reaches for the other, igniting our passion, our need to reconnect. I feel powerful. I feel loved. I feel solid in our commitment. By the time the first morning light streams through the bedroom windows, I am sore, spent, languid, and more confident than ever in our future.

Joseph is mine. He's not going anywhere. I give him what he needs as he so intuitively gives me what I need. We are a team, a unit, a rock-solid force that won't be put asunder by a few letters and items of clothing that any maid could have picked up.

Dreamily, my head falls to the side, finding Joseph watching me with a mischievous grin. I roll toward him. "What's that grin for?"

He props up on his elbow, leaning over me. "I was watching you

93

wake up. It's like I could see the light radiating from you. And when you smiled, I knew in that moment that my girl was going to be okay."

I run my fingers through his sex-wrecked hair, my smile growing with every second his gaze lingers on me. "I'm going to be okay, because *we're* going to be okay."

"Damn straight." He kisses me softly, then rolls out of bed, throwing me the TV remote. "Don't get up. I'm bringing you breakfast in bed. We're playing hooky today." He pulls on a pair of pajama bottoms, and with a wink, he disappears down the hall.

I guess I'm playing hooky today.

Surprisingly, it doesn't stress me out about the schoolwork I'll be missing. That's what study partners are for, right?

With a yawn and a noisy stretch of my well-sexed body, I turn on the TV and welcome the day at home with my man.

Joseph

The first time I saw her, I knew she would be mine. Clichéd? Yes, but that doesn't make it any less true. We've come so far and only have three more months until that premonition comes to fruition. Three months, then no one can give me crap about calling Samantha *my wife* before she actually is—because she will be- my wife—and I will be her husband. She'll even be that much closer to coming to work for MCI as a full-fledged employee and not as an intern or as my PA.

I can't fucking wait.

That is my end game, my ultimate goal, my telos. But before that happens, I have to figure out who the fuck is messing with us. It's not only her they're targeting. Hurting her may be *their* end goal, but they're using me as a means to achieve it. I can't help thinking of what Fin told me weeks ago, after my happy hour slip up of letting those drunk tourists get a little too close for comfort. There are women who will want to get close to me because of my job and may enjoy the added challenge because I'm not interested in anyone except Samantha.

A week has brought little to light on who is trying to get Samantha to leave me. We haven't brought anyone else into the fold, besides Michael. For now, it's best to play it close to the vest as we don't know who could be watching, who could inadvertently let information slip in front of the wrong person. The fewer people who know the better. Besides, someone claiming I'm cheating on Samantha and providing "proof" in the form of soiled underwear is not something I relish sharing with anyone—especially not my family.

My cell phone chimes with a message.

Michael: *I'm coming up.*

I request Teddy hold my calls as Michael enters my office and takes a seat, letting out a telling sigh.

"I don't like it when you're stressed, Michael. It means I should be worried."

He smirks with a shake of his head. "I think you'd worry no matter how I'm feeling."

True. But I would feel a little more at ease about it if he wasn't concerned.

"I heard back from my contact at the forensics lab. He's emailing me a complete report, but I figured you'd want to know his initial findings."

I nod, not sure I can speak over my pounding heart.

Leaning forward, his eyes lock on mine. "The first letter has yours, Sam's, and a third set of fingerprints. There's no match in the system. I'll reach out to a different contact who has access to additional databases. If this person is in the system, we'll find him or her."

"Okay. And the second letter?"

"The second and third letters only have fingerprints from Sam and the same unknown contributor. So that's good that they match. Maybe we're only looking at one person here."

I sit back waiting for more.

"The tie came back with DNA matching the sample you provided. No other contributors were found. It's safe to say it's your tie."

No surprise. I was fairly certain it would come back with my DNA on it. "And the boxer briefs?"

He shifts in his seat. "There were two individual contributors to the fluids found on the underwear."

"Two?"

"Yes. Male and female."

Ah, fuck. My head hits the back of the chair, and my eyes lock on the ceiling. "It's mine, isn't it?"

"Yes." That's as solemn of a yes as I've ever heard.

I lift my head. Waiting. *Say it's Samantha's DNA. Please, God, let it be hers.*

"The female contributor is unknown."

"Fuck!" I lean forward, my head resting on the edge of my desk.

"Have you been with anyone else besides Sam?"

I shoot up out of my chair and round my desk as he stands, rock solid, no give. "What the fuck?" I bite, ready to take his head off.

He glares at me. "I have to ask. It's my job. I need all the facts to be able to help you, to find out what's really going on here. I also need to be sure you're not being a dick to Sam."

I back down. He'll protect Sam to his last breath, and I wouldn't have it any other way. "I haven't looked at or touched another woman since the day I met Samantha nearly two years ago." I sigh in resignation. "Except the Tiff thing."

His brow arches. "Not even before Sam was shot? When you were trying to leave her alone, let her graduate from college?"

Moving to the leather couch, I plop down. "No one. I wasn't interested."

Michael sits in the adjacent chair, surprise written all over his face. "What were you going to do all those years before she finished school, become a monk?"

I shrug and hold up my right hand with a smirk.

He relaxes back in his chair. "Jesus, that's a long time to go without pussy, man."

"She's worth it. I'd still be waiting for her, if that's what she wanted." And that's the truth of it. If I can't have her, I don't want anyone else.

"Then I guess I'm adding Tiff to the list of suspects. She could have easily snagged your underwear while you were smashed out of your gourd." Michael stands.

"You think so?"

"I don't know, man. It's possible. I'd rather start with her than dig up older partners." He pauses before he gets to the door. "But you'd better start thinking who else in your past might have a reason to want to hurt you or Sam. The female DNA may have been added later. It could be anyone's."

"I assume you mean sexual partners."

"Start there, but anyone who had access to your house in college could get a pair of underwear—male or female—so, I wouldn't limit your thinking to only women you had sex with."

"Jace." It's out of my mouth before I even have a chance to think on it.

Michael stops in his tracks and turns. "Really?"

"No, not really. But he, more than anyone else, had the easiest access over the past four years." I sigh on that thought. "No matter what's happened with his family—with me—I don't think he'd do something like this. But he had a lot of women coming and going. I never had a negative run-in with any of them." I tug at the seam of my pants. "Except Tiff."

"Then I say we start with her, but not rule anyone else out just yet." With that he exits my office, closing the door behind him.

And opening up a whole other can of worms.

Nine

ONE WOMAN ONE MAN

OCTOBER

Samantha

WALK INTO THE LOBBY OF THE CRESCENT HOTEL
where I'm meeting Jace for lunch. It's not a normal hangout for either
of us, but it's close to home, and he had business in the area. This will
be our second meeting since the failed counseling session with Mom.

Michael accompanied me the first time. Today it's William, his
hand barely touching my back, not guiding me, just sticking close. Both
Michael and Joseph insisted he remain in constant contact with me
when out in public and on the move.

We reach the hostess, and William takes over, ensuring the proffered table meets our security needs. Luckily, once he's comfortable with
our lunch accommodations, he'll back off and sink into the background,
observing from a safe distance.

"Sam?" Jace's familiar voice comes from behind me. I turn to see
him giving William the once-over and extending his hand. "I'm Jace,
Sam's brother. I assume you're keeping my sister safe?"

William shakes his hand. "William. And yes, sir, your sister's safety is my only priority."

Only priority? *Only?* That strikes me as an overly pointed reply, as if to say he'd throw Jace in the line of fire if it would save me.

"I'm glad to hear it." Jace's face softens as his gaze lands on me. "Hey, sis."

"Hey."

He kisses my cheek and wraps me a quick hug. "It's good to see you."

"You too," I respond and look to William. "Are we ready to sit?"

"Yes," he replies, then nods to the hostess, letting her know we're ready.

We sit, order drinks, peruse the menu, and talk about nothing in particular. William long forgotten, I look at the man sitting across from me. He's changed over the last few years. His black hair is shorter, definitely more GQ-business-man-of-the-town kinda style. His features are more chiseled, more defined. But there's still a hint of sadness in his eyes, particularly when he thinks I'm not looking. He's matured, in a good way. He seems more…manly…more grown up—more like Dad.

My heart pangs at the thought. *God, I miss Dad.*

After we order, Jace scans the restaurant and stops where I believe William has taken up residence. "What's really going on, Sam? Why do you have protection? Michael was with you last time, and I assumed he drove you and decided to come in and eat, but now you have a complete stranger guarding you."

"He's here to be sure I'm safe." That's probably more than I should say, but Jace knows I haven't had protection following me around since my dad's murderer was killed—by Michael and me.

His blue eyes look into my matching pair, pleading for more—asking me to trust him. "You can't tell *me*, or you're not telling *anyone*?"

"No one." Shaking my head, I open my mouth to say more, then close it. There's nothing more I can say, really.

With a gentle smile, he drops it. "Fill me in on the wedding. Is there anything I can do to help? Either planning or paying?"

"Paying?" I never would have expected that offer.

"I know Joe and his family are loaded." He lays his hand across mine, resting on the table. "If Dad were here, he'd be paying for the wedding and the reception. I'd like to help."

I'm not sure Joseph would have let Dad pay for anything. Maybe something as a token of respect, but when it comes to money, my family can't hold a candle to the McIntyres. "I appreciate the offer, but it's covered."

Disappointment spreads across his face. I swallow around the lump in my throat, unsure if I'm ready to be this vulnerable with him. "There is one thing, though."

"Yeah?" He looks hopeful. So hopeful.

"I need someone to give me away." The lump in my throat bites as my eyes sting with impending tears.

His hand squeezes mine; his jaw clenches, and his eyes mist as he fights his own emotional battle. "Are you asking me to give you away?"

The rawness in his voice undoes me, and tears start to fall. All I can do is nod as I swipe at my face, clear my throat, and try to keep the flood of emotions at bay.

"God, I'd love to." His voice cracks on his reply. He bows his head for only a moment, and then sits up straight with a huge, beaming smile. "I would be honored to give you away, Sam."

I'm flooded with relief. I wasn't worried he'd say no. I was worried I wouldn't have the courage to ask, or that he wouldn't realize the importance of me asking *him*. I'm beyond thankful because he gets it. He didn't make light of it, and he said yes. With a teary smile, I manage a simple "Thank you."

We both work to fill the next few minutes with light-hearted conversation in order to get our emotions in check. What I really want to know is if he's happy. Food arrives, and after a few minutes I bite the bullet. "Sooo, tell me what's going on with you? I know you're looking to move to MCI. Is that what you really want? Are you not happy at Solengers?" I don't want him to make the move in an effort to get closer to me and Joseph. I want him to love where he works.

"I like Solengers. It's a great firm. I've learned a lot in my short tenure, and I'm sure I could learn a lot more from them." He fidgets with his silverware, lining it up, smoothing out the tablecloth, and positions his water glass precisely so. I don't know if he's stalling, or if this is a new idiosyncrasy he's developed. The old Jace never cared where his silverware was placed on the table, as long as he had the means to get the food from his plate to his mouth as quickly as possible.

Satisfied, he looks up. "I want to work at MCI. It's something Matt and I have been talking about for years. You know, before Dad died." His shoulders rise, and he tilts his head. "It would be nice to be back with the guys. I've missed them." His eyes pin me. "I've missed you."

Yeah, the waterworks are back. "You know you don't have to work at MCI to be a part of our lives, right?"

"It would help."

I can't deny that. He'd be right in the thick of things with his old buddies, working day in and day out with Matt, Fin, Joseph, Victor, and Michael. "The Six Pack reunites!" I tease.

He lays his hand next to mine, our fingers barely touching. "If it will make you uncomfortable, I won't, though. Making things right with you and Joseph is my top priority. I don't want to push, and I don't want to fuck it up." The depth of his words shines brightly in his eyes, and I know he means them.

I move my hand to link our pinkies. It's a little awkward with him sitting across from me, but I manage. Just as I used to manage when we were kids. He didn't always want to hold my hand, but he'd let me link pinkies with him, giving me that little boost of connection I often needed from him. He was my big brother, my protector from a world I often found moved too fast and was a little too loud for my liking.

He smiles at our joined hands. "I'm sorry, Sam," he all but whispers.

His heartache is too much. I can't take any more crying. I cup my hand over our joined ones and squeeze. "I know." My voice is low. "I forgive you, Jace. Let's move on from *I'm sorry*, okay? I need time to get to know you again, to learn to trust you."

That's going to be harder than forgiveness, as I don't think I've ever truly let anyone in besides Joseph. All those years I thought of Jace as my best friend, my confidant, he truly wasn't. I kept him and everyone else at arm's length, not relying on anyone except myself. "Baby steps. And this right here is the first of many to come."

"Baby steps," he agrees.

I pull my hands back and pick up my fork. "I think you coming to MCI is an excellent step as well."

"Yeah?" He's relieved.

"Yeah."

Baby steps.

One foot in front of the other.

One pinkie-hold at a time.

Moving forward.

Forgiveness.

Trust.

Family.

Joseph

I hang up with Samantha—the joy and hope in her voice was contagious as she imparted the details of her lunch with Jace—when Teddy comes on the line. "Mr. McIntyre, there's a Jace Cavanagh here to see you."

"Really?" Did he come home with Samantha? She just arrived. I'm sure she would have told me if they had returned to MCI Towers together.

"Is he related to your wife?" Teddy whispers.

Pride wells in my chest each time he calls her my *wife*. "He's Samantha's brother."

"Oh. I…didn't…never mind." He's obviously surprised.

There's been no mention of Jace or their mother to Teddy. No reason to, really. Maybe if it wasn't such a fresh wound for Samantha, their existence would be more common knowledge.

"You can send him in, Teddy."

"Of course."

I rise to meet Jace as Teddy opens the door and steps inside, allowing Jace to pass. "Can I get either of you a drink?" Teddy offers.

Jace crosses to the sitting area. "None for me, thank you." He seems happy. Maybe he felt their lunch was as successful as Samantha did. I can only hope, for her sake.

"Thanks, Teddy. Please hold my calls." I shake Jace's hand. "This is a surprise. Everything okay?"

"Yeah." He takes a seat on the couch, and I sit in a chair facing him. "Actually, no…or I don't know…that's why I'm here. I want to know what's going on. Is Sam okay? Is she in danger?"

I cross my leg over my knee, pulling at the crease of my slacks—a Fin tactic all the way—giving me time to consider how to respond. "Why do you ask?"

Jace leans forward, his arms resting on his knees. "Seriously, Joe? Don't bullshit me. I know I've fucked up in the past. I haven't been around, but I'm here now, and I'm not going anywhere. Is she in danger? Has something happened? Why does she have a bodyguard sticking to her like glue?"

I smile, and that only seems to piss him off. I hold up my hand to stop whatever he's about to say. "I'll tell you." I chuckle. "It's good to see you getting all protective over your sister. It's a good sign."

He relaxes and sits back on the couch. "I've been an ass to you both, but even at my worst, I never wanted anything to happen to either of you. Learning about the kind of danger she was in from our father's killer was hard to hear after the fact. I don't want to miss out on anything, even if it's bad news. So, tell me what's going on, and what can I do to help?"

It only takes me a second to decide whether to bring him in or not. He is Samantha's brother, after all, and he also knows Tiff. Maybe he can be of help in that regard. Put some feelers out and see what he turns up. I'm not stupid, though, so I call Michael and ask him to join us. From a strategic perspective, when it comes to catching bad guys, Michael is the pro.

After Michael joins us, I fill Jace in on what's been happening. Even though I'd rather keep the details private, if we expect Jace to be able to help, he needs details to work with.

Jace finishes reviewing the photocopies of the three packages received. He holds the latest letter in his hand. He's been quiet most of the time. He hands it back to Michael and chugs the rest of his bottle of water before he speaks. "Has Sam seen all of this?"

Michael and I both nod.

"And the underwear? She's seen it? Knows the DNA results?" he asks.

"Yes. Unfortunately, all but the last package she opened up on her own. And I've shared the DNA results with her as well. We don't have any secrets between us."

Jace runs his hand over his face. "I can't imagine how she must be feeling." He looks at me. "How would you feel if some guy was sending you these things about Sam? Items of her clothing with her…DNA on it. Letters telling you how sex with *him* is so much better than sex with you? How would you feel? I'd be pissed and hard-pressed to listen to reason."

I can't deny the same thought hasn't crossed my mind. If the roles were reversed, I'm not sure I would be as open and supportive as she's been. I like to think I would be, but the thought gets my blood boiling to the point where all I see is red. "Jace, I'd rip his head off."

He looks at me and laughs. "Yeah, you would." He sobers. "But she's not the one being accused of cheating. You are."

"Yes, I am." I square my shoulders, waiting for the accusation.

Jace waves me off. "Relax, man. I know you're not cheating on Sam."

"You do?" It's my turn to be surprised. I thought for sure his over-protective instincts would accuse first, question later.

"Joe, I know you, man. You've never been a horn dog. Even before you met my sister, you were never one to sleep around. Your career was more important than chasing pussy. But after you met Sam, your grumpy ass didn't even know other women existed." His eyes meet mine for a moment before he looks away. "And I saw the look on your face when you realized what happened with Tiff wasn't a drunken dream about the girl you love, but the harsh reality of what I did to you both." His eyes close for a beat or two, then his shame-filled eyes lock with mine. "I saw the devastation in your eyes, the pure remorse as it ate you up. You, Joe McIntyre, are not a cheater. You are a one-woman man, and like I told you after my dad's funeral, Sam is a one-man woman. You were destined for each other. I know you would never cheat on her."

I let out a shaky breath, emotion tight in my chest, as I look at my future brother-in-law sitting across from me. "You have no idea how much that means to me." Maybe there is hope for me and Jace to move past the Tiff thing after all. I reach out and pull him into a hug. "It's good to have you back, brother."

He pounds on my back. "It's good to be back, brother." He pulls away and rubs at his eyes, shakes his head, and laughs at his emotions. "You have no idea."

No, I don't have any idea. But I can see his self-imposed exile has been difficult, probably in ways we can't even imagine.

We spend the next thirty minutes or so discussing how Jace can help narrow down the suspects, starting with Tiff. By the time they both leave, we have a plan of action that gives me a sense of peace I haven't felt since the first letter arrived.

Now I need to head home to the only true peace I know.

My girl.

Joseph

Silence greets me as I enter our penthouse. The lights are dim, but I can smell food cooking. I relinquish my armor—my jacket, tie, and briefcase—in the entryway and grab a water in the kitchen. I check the oven and the timer—all good—and go in search of Samantha.

I'm not surprised when I find her asleep on our bed. She hasn't been sleeping well since all of this began. Her nightmares are back, but they've morphed into a combination of her father's death and me with another woman. I cringe at the thought. It'll never happen. I'd never cheat on my girl. It's more than that, though. It's not even a battle. It doesn't even cross my mind. I truly see no other woman in a sexual way. I only have eyes for her. My dick only wants *her*. I know she knows it, but deep down her insecurities still linger. Her subconscious is struggling and beating her up in her dreams.

Toeing off my shoes, I slip into bed, curl up behind her, wrap her up in my arms, and revel in the warmth and peace that engulfs me.

Warm, soft hands traverse my body as I slowly come awake to the realization that I'm hard as stone, and Samantha is lying naked beside me. She's managed to get my shirt unbuttoned. Her hot, wet mouth is sucking on my nipple, and her hand inside my unzipped pants strokes my cock. I flex into her greedy hand. "Christ, Sweets." What a way to wake up.

I shuck my clothes. Her hands and mouth never leave me. I'm shaking, on edge, ready to blow.

I'm not going alone.

She squeals when I lift her on top of me as I roll to my back, finding heaven in her mouth before I slide my way home. Slow thrusts as she grinds against me, her moans and gasps challenge my control. My name on her lips nearly has me blowing like a rocket.

I'm not going alone.

Rolling us over so I'm on top, still buried to the hilt, I grind against her, hitting the spots that send her sailing. Her hands grasp and pull. Her head, thrown back, allows my mouth to ravish her delectable neck. She chants my name over and over again. My heart is pounding, pounding, pounding in time with my cock. Deep. Deeper. And deeper still.

She squeezes, contracts, and moans. And when her release wraps around me, and her fluids coat my cock and seep down my balls, I shoot over the edge, growling, filling her. Filling her. Filling her.

Spent, I collapse and roll to my side, gripping her ass to stay inside her. My mouth finds hers, and we kiss, our bodies entwined, connected, until we are both out of breath and ready again.

Never enough.

Over dinner we catch each other up on our days. Her lunch with Jace, details she didn't share earlier, a phone conversation with Margot that gave no hint of a relationship with Fin, much to Samantha's dismay, and plans with Sebastian to join our next happy hour. He's missed the last few due to his schedule. I fill her in on a few business meetings, and then the unexpected and very productive meeting with Jace.

"Wow. He really is trying, isn't he?" Her surprise matches mine.

"Yeah, he is. Are you okay with this?" I try to read any emotions that play along her face, but she seems okay.

"What? You meeting with him, him knowing our dark, dirty secret, or him helping out with our dark, dirty secret?"

I try not to flinch. "I'd rather you not call it our 'dark, dirty secret,' but, yeah, all of that."

Her brow bunches on a head tilt. "But it *is* our dark, dirty secret, Joseph. We're not sharing it with your brothers, whom you share everything with."

I grab her hand, lacing our fingers, my lascivious stare eating her up. "Not everything." I've never shared details of our sex life. They know the extent of my love for her, but the rest is none of their fucking business. A blush creeps up her neck. She fidgets in her chair and bites the corner of her bottom lip. So fucking sexy.

"I'm glad to hear you don't share *those* details." She sits back, pulling her hand from my grasp. "But that's not what I meant. We're in trouble, someone's after me—"

"Us. They're going after you through me. *Us.*" We're a unit, my tone holds no leeway.

"Okay, *us.* My point being, we're keeping it a secret from the people you trust the most. If I were being threatened with kidnapping or bodily injury, would you hesitate to confide in them?"

She has a point. "I prefer to keep it secret because of its malicious sexual nature."

"I know." Her voice so soft. "I don't disagree with your desire to keep it private, nor do I disagree with you bringing Jace on board."

Thank God. My shoulders relax, and the knot that was forming in my stomach unwinds. "Good."

"What's the plan?"

"Jace is going to reach out to Tiff. Play up the whole falling out with us over your father's death and what happened between her and me. He's going to work on getting a DNA sample, but of course, a confession would be good too."

"Well, if anybody can charm the pants off a woman, it's Jace." She takes her half-eaten plate of food to the kitchen, setting it on the counter.

"He's working with a bit of a disadvantage, though." I join her in the kitchen, pointing to her plate. "You need to finish that."

"I'm done." Her intonation is flat, not open for debate. "What disadvantage? He's sworn off women?" she teases, scraping her plate into the trash.

"Yes."

"What?" Her head whips up.

I take the plate from her hands before she drops it. "He's been celibate for a year. He feels it's what's giving him his clear head and edge in the office. He's written off women for the immediate future, at least."

"Wow. I never saw that coming."

I chuckle. "You and me both."

Ten

CRAZY LOVE

Samantha

'M LATE. I'M NEVER LATE. I'M ABSOLUTELY ALWAYS on time or early. Never. Late. I throw the box at William, "Hold this," and slip into my Creative Coding class, knowing William will either follow or stand sentry at the door. I can't think about which, and I most definitely can't think about the box that was delivered to me moments ago as we walked to class.

William nearly tackled the guy as he approached me. After the third degree, checks of the delivery guy's credentials, and pictures taken of all of it, I was left holding the box. I stared at it as if it might give its secrets away by the mere fact I was giving it a death glare. When nothing happened, and with William's quiet reminder of the time, we jogged the rest of the way to class.

I settle at a desk near the door, easy in, easy out. My professor gives me a nod and glances at the door as if she's waiting for William to follow. When he doesn't, I get a questioning look before she turns her attention back to the projector and her lecture. As it was when I had FBI protection my last few months of high school, nobody asks me about my protection, but it's obvious someone gave my teachers a heads-up. This time, I'm sure it was Joseph or Michael.

I pull out my laptop and wake up the screen, thankful I turned it on earlier. Soon, my brain focuses on the images, formulas, and statements on the professor's projected screen, and all thoughts of the box waiting for me fade into the background.

After two more classes and lunch, I take the box from William as we sit at a table in the commons area. Turned so he can't see the contents, I unwrap it to reveal the same type of shoebox I've received two times before. I lift the lid and set it aside. I don't have to touch the contents this time to see what is inside. Side by side, possibly affixed to the bottom of the box to ensure maximum effect, is a picture of Joseph. Next to it is a letter. The same type of letter I've received before, but this time the punch is a little deeper seeing his face right next to *those* words.

"Sam?"

I look up into the blurry face of Michael standing over me. I blink a few times to clear my tears. The sadness in his eyes is too much. I place the lid on the box and hand it to him. "Take it to Joseph." I brush away my tears and look at William. "I'll be late for class."

He nods and collects our trash, disposing of it while Michael keeps watch.

"Come with me." It sounds like a plea, but coming from Michael it can't be. I can't stick around and watch tough-as-nails Michael go soft on me.

Shaking my head, I stand and gather my things. "Tell Joseph I'll see him at home." I walk away before I change my mind and melt into his concern and the idea of finding comfort in Joseph's arms.

Joseph

My two o'clock meeting is interrupted by a text.

Michael: *We have another package*

Luckily, I'm not the one presenting, nor am I key to this meeting. I make my excuses and exit the meeting with Teddy in tow. "Clear my afternoon."

"Yes, sir." He heads to his desk as I enter my office to find Michael standing at my desk, his back to me, looking down.

I stop and close my door. "Samantha?"

He turns. "She's still at school. She said she'd see you at home later." The Grim Reaper look he's sporting tells me this is worse than the others. How can it possibly be worse?

"How bad?" I set my laptop down on my desk, giving wide berth to the box, catching only a glimpse of the letter inside.

"Bad."

"Are you gonna make me look, or can you just tell me?"

His eyes lock on mine. "You need to see it the way she saw it."

"Fuck." I close my eyes, like I need the reminder that my girl is being inundated with this shit over and over again. I steel myself and move around to stand next to him.

Inside the box is a letter on the left and a picture of me on the right. It's close-up from the mid-abdomen up, looking down on me, like whoever took it was sitting on me. I'm in a bed, my head on a pillow, white sheets. It could be my college bed or any hotel bed—any fucking bed—it's impossible to say. It can't be too old of a picture. I look the same age, maybe a tad younger. My hair is a sticking out as if I, or someone else, has had their fingers in it. And my face...Jesus, my face... has a look of pure ecstasy. I'm coming—hard, by the looks of it. "Fuck me," I sigh.

"Yep, that's pretty much what it looks like." I'm getting no sympathy from him. He seems pissed. "Read the note."

I know this face well.
It's the one he makes when he fills me with his cum.

Sincerely,
Joseph's baby girl

"Goddamnit!" I'm about to lose it.

Michael grips my shoulder. "Calm down. I need to ask you some questions before you go all caveman."

I pace to the window, close my eyes and breathe slowly in and then out until I feel calmer. "Okay."

"Come look at the pic again, and tell me what you see."

I stomp to my desk and scrutinize the box's contents. "I see me. In a bed. White sheets. I've got fucked-up hair. And…" I clench my jaw as I look up, meeting Michael's gaze. "…and I'm having an orgasm."

He smirks. "Yeah, that's one sight I'll never get out of my head. Your come-face."

"Fuck off." I try not to, but he makes me laugh. "You're just envious."

Ignoring my comment, he continues. "Do you know where this was taken? When it was taken? Who you were with?"

The questions go on and on like an interrogation until my emotions have settled, I'm feeling numb, and his queries are exhausted. My best guess is this pic is from college and may or may not be my bed. I have no idea whom I was having sex with, but I'm positive I wasn't alone as I've never taken a sexual selfie in my life—plus, most of the time I jerked off in the shower, not in bed.

Thankfully, my sex life with Samantha leaves me with no need or desire for self-gratification. I want all of her pleasure, and I want to give her all of mine.

"Are we done? I'd really like to get home to my girl."

Samantha

I'm not a drinker, but after today, I need something to help me quiet the voice in my head. The one that shouts *he's cheating on you, and you're stupid enough to believe he's not when the evidence is staring you in the face.* It's a mean, nasty voice. I take a glass and an open bottle of wine to the balcony. I'm on my second glass when I hear the door open and Joseph step out.

His eyes roam over me and then the wine bottle. He sits next to me on the chaise, finishes off my glass, refills it, and then holds it to my lips. I take a sip, my eyes glued to him. His tongue licks across his bottom lip as he watches me, heat flaring in his eyes, causing wicked thoughts of his tongue to take flight. I nearly groan when he takes a deep drink and sets it aside.

His jacket, shoes, and tie are already discarded somewhere inside. His shirt is untucked and lies open, his every movement highlighting his taut chest and abdomen. "Samantha," he breathes as his lips brush mine. It's just my name, but it sounds more like *I'm sorry… I love you… Don't believe what you see.*

My sob is consumed by his mouth, tender and passionate, pleading and demanding. He tantalizes my senses, and my body explodes with need to consume and be consumed. I'm famished, starved for something my body knows only he can provide. My hands dwell under his shirt, pulling him closer, but when his bare chest comes into contact with my clothed one, he groans his disapproval, pulling away enough to remove the sweater I put on when I came home.

"Fuck, yes," he growls when he sees I'm braless.

His head dips, pushing me down on the lounger, his hands and fingers squeezing and pulling at my breasts. His tongue flicks over my nipples, making them hard before sucking them deep. With a pop, he releases one before he moves to the other. His hands grip the waist of my leggings, and in one clean motion, he relieves me of them, my panties, and my socks. I'm naked, and the cool October breeze sends goosebumps rippling across my skin.

Green eyes of fire look up at me with a quirked brow, asking *too cold to say outside?* When I don't object, his hands and mouth continue to lave me in his love. His kisses move lower, and my moans of pleasure merely feed his fire. He lifts my legs, pushing my knees to my chest, spreading me wide, and he dives in. There's no slow buildup of kisses down my thighs, around my pussy, teasing my opening. No, he dives tongue first, slipping inside me and kissing me like it's my mouth—long, deep, and probing.

"Oh, god, Joseph." I try to buck my hips, but I'm locked in place, only able to take what he gives.

The more I thrash, the hungrier he gets. His forearms rest on the back of my thighs, holding me open. His hands tease my clit and play with my breasts, working me into a frenzy. My cries echo around the balcony, turning me on even more thinking someone could hear us. I doubt they can see us, but my excitement ratchets even higher.

"I can't. I can't," I cry out, needing more, needing less, needing *him.*

"Yes," is all he manages before his entire mouth covers me, his tongue fucking me, his sucking on my clit in time with his fingers pulling on my nipples. In a move worthy of wrestler pinning his opponent to the mat, Joseph holds me down as I buck and shatter around him, crying out to him, to God, for mercy, for more, for *him.*

As my contractions abate, Joseph releases his cock, rubbing his head over my clit a few times before sinking inside. "Sweets," he groans. Kneeling on the chaise, my legs over his arms, his eyes latch on to mine, feral and hungry as he thrusts.

For leverage, I hold on to the sides, but it's of no use, I can't hold back my caveman. He needs this. He needs to claim me. He needs me to know I'm his, and he's mine.

"Look at my cock, baby."

My eyes break from his and lower to where we are joined. It's so hot watching him slide in and out of me.

"I'm covered with your sweet juices. This cock belongs to you. It only fits your hot and hungry pussy, only yours."

I clench around him. "Joseph." He's gonna make me come again.

"Watch, Samantha. Watch what you do to me. I only come undone for you." He wraps his arms tightly around my thighs, adjusts his thrusts, and when he hits that magical spot inside, I'm the one starting to come undone. "Fuck, I can feel you. You're so ready, baby." He presses his thumb to my clit, and I spiral out of control. "Yes, Sweets. Fuck, yes, take me with you."

On a scream I don't recognize as my own, I come so hard as he pistons deliciously in and out of me with quickening strokes. My mewling mixes with his as his orgasm overtakes him. My eyes never leave his as I relish the look of ecstasy on his face, the look of love in his eyes.

He has *that* look. My heart sinks.

The. Look.

That matches.

The one.

In the picture.

The look that was for somebody else.

Not me.

Eleven

GROW MY SHAME

NOVEMBER

Samantha

I HAVEN'T BEEN TO THE OFFICE IN WEEKS. IF TEDDY needs me, I talk to him over the phone or desktop share if he needs more guidance than words alone. But, honestly, I don't have much else to teach him. It's all just my opinion now. We've moved beyond my expertise as to what's best as Joseph's PA. Teddy is making his own rulebook now. I only guide when asked, and it's usually application-related. It's really my Microsoft Office skills that are needed. I'm his personal helpdesk, I suppose.

My life consists of going between school and home now. Fiona has been handling all wedding-related tasks, dealing with our wedding planner, Jackie, as needed. School is the perfect excuse as to why I'm too busy to deal with it properly. The reality is, as much as I try to deny it, I'm avoiding everything wedding-related. If I can't brush it off and change the subject, then I make any excuse to separate myself from the person asking.

We're six weeks away, and that means Thanksgiving is only a few weeks off, which also means tonight is our couple's wedding shower. I insisted that we keep the festivities down to only one. I don't have any family to invite or to host a shower. I don't have enough female friends to attend a non-family shower, and Margot can't afford to throw one, plus she's in Austin. It doesn't seem fair to put that kind of pressure on her. Therefore, Joseph and I requested that we have a couple's shower with family and friends. So, no girly, all white, tea and finger foods shower for me, which I'm totally fine with. Especially since I have no desire to be the center of attention, which goes against the whole bridal tradition of being doted on. I don't want that. At. All.

"Why are you frowning?" Joseph's voice startles me.

I turn from the bathroom mirror. He's watching me from the door, his brow hard-set in a line. I grab what I need for my clutch and skirt around him. "I can't shake the feeling we shouldn't be doing this."

"What? Having a wedding shower?" He follows, hot on my heels, his gaze hitting mine in my dresser mirror.

I slip my cell phone into my small purse as I step into my pumps. "No. Yes, but not just that."

His steps, never far behind, as I walk to the kitchen. "I'm not letting this bitch, or whoever it is, stop me from marrying you." His voice is hard and chockfull of emotion.

Grabbing a bottled water, I hand it to him before getting one for myself. "Maybe you should."

He hates this discussion. We've had it many times over the last few weeks, since the last letter and picture arrived. I can barely look at him without seeing that picture. I can't get it out of my mind. I haven't even let him touch me since that night. He's pissed and frustrated. "Don't fucking do this."

His anger grows, and I just become silent, resolved, and distant. I'm pushing him away, preparing for the worst. Each letter said it would get worse until I finally left him. Maybe it's time to heed that warning, at least until the person is caught.

Do I believe he's cheating on me? No, not really. But the doubt is so tangible, it's like a third person in the room. It sours everything. It's turned his touch into flinches of pain. It's turned his look of love and desire into a mask I can only see him using on someone else. He's pissed at it getting to me, and I'm helpless to see anything else but his face in that come-shot.

We silently board the elevator and meet Michael in the garage. He's driving us to Joseph's parents' house for the shower. William will be outside, along with a few other guys keeping watch, but they have orders to stay in the shadows since our friends and family don't know what's going on. Michael opens the door and stares at me when I remain mute, barely making eye contact with him.

I slip into the back of the SUV, and the door closes behind me as Joseph and Michael converse in voices too low for me to make out. But I don't miss the shortness in tone from either of them as they make their way around the car to get in.

Michael's penetrating glare in the rearview mirror does nothing to ease my nerves. "Sam," he says softly, too softly, with too much concern. He thinks I'm an idiot, too. I'm surrounded by testosterone-laden men who can't see that perhaps it's best to delay the wedding and lie low until things blow over. God forbid it make them appear weak by giving in to the threats. I, on the other hand, would like to get married without the threat of unspeakable packages already received, and those yet to be delivered, tainting everything in my path.

My path to the altar is littered with nasty letters saying how much Joseph loves another woman, fucks her better, comes for her harder, leaves articles of clothing covered in their sexual secretions as proof of their joining. And yes, let's not forget the lovely picture of Joseph in complete and utter rapture as he has sex with *someone else*. Nothing says *joyous wedding* like the proof of your betrothed's sexual exploits that don't include his bride.

Do I believe he's cheating? No.

Do I believe this whole episode is tainting our wedding? Abso-fucking-lutely.

Joseph squeezes my hand, and I fight to keep it securely ensconced in his. *This is the man you love. Let him hold your hand, for God's sake.* I take a deep breath and close my eyes.

"Please, Samantha. Let it go." His lips brush my cheek. "Let's just enjoy tonight with our friends and family as we celebrate." He tips my chin, and I open my eyes to meet his warm green ones. "I love you. Don't think about anything else but that."

I curl into his side. "Okay." I can do that.

He loves me.

He loves me.

He. Loves. Me.

Joseph

I can't stand how much this is affecting her, affecting our relationship. I thought it was tough after her dad died, but this arbitrary line she's drawn between us, keeping me at a distance, keeping me from touching her intimately, makes that time look like a walk in the park. She can't look at me without seeing that picture. I don't know how to fix that. I don't know how to wipe it from her mind. How to make her see me as I am now and not how I looked while having sex with some woman I can't even remember.

"You look tired, son." Dad claps me on the back and motions across the room. "Your bride doesn't look much better."

"There's just a lot going on, Dad."

"She looks like she'd rather be any place else but here." Fin hands me a beer.

"Thanks." I take a long pull, watching Samantha talking to Margot, Mom, and two of my aunts. "She hates being the center of attention."

Fin chuckles. "Then she's gonna love opening gifts in front of everyone."

"Gifts? We said no gifts. We don't need anything." And if we do, we can buy it for ourselves.

"Your mother is a traditionalist. You have a wedding, you have wedding gifts. It's not about whether you can afford to buy it for yourself or not. It's about everyone expressing their happiness for you—by buying you gifts." He shrugs with a laugh, his look telling me *get used to it.*

I wonder if Samantha knows there will be gifts.

Jace joins us, greeting my dad and Fin before eyeing me. "You look like shit," he teases, but I also see deeper meaning in his gaze.

"Thanks."

"You're welcome. How is she?" He scans the room until he finds Samantha.

"Distant." A single word that sums it up.

He looks to my dad and Fin, who are deep into MCI business, oblivious to the two of us. "I'm sorry, man. I know this has to suck. I'm making progress." He glances around and whispers, "Next week. She'll be in town."

I know exactly who the *she* he's referring to is, and I hope that means he'll be meeting up with Tiff when she's in town. A raised brow is all it takes for confirmation.

"Yes, we have plans to meet up."

"That's great news." Maybe we can get this wrapped up before Thanksgiving. That will give me nearly four weeks to make Samantha forget all about it before we say *I do.*

Damn, that day cannot come soon enough for me.

Samantha

"Babycakes, what's going on? I don't think you could look more miserable if you tried." Sebastian pulls me from a group of Joseph's family members I've never met before.

"Shit, Bash, I'm trying. I really look that bad?" I thought I was doing a pretty good job of faking it. I actually meant many of the smiles and thank yous I've given in the last hour and a half.

He nudges me with his shoulder as we continue moving away from the crowd. "No, I can just read you. It's my job to pick up on patient cues even when they don't want me to see what's really going on."

I sag in relief. "I really don't want to be here. Can you just act like you're me, but be all friendly and social like you, which is not like me at all, but it's the me that needs to be here?"

He laughs. "I think you've cracked." His hand presses to my forehead, then he feigns taking my pulse. "Nope, nope no fever, heartbeat normal. Yep, you're all good."

If only he knew how *not good* I really am.

His stare pins me in place, waiting for an explanation. I sigh. "I'm just tired. School is busy, life is…busy. You know I don't like social situations."

"Psh, that's not true. You're great at social situations." He looks around the room. "You just don't like this big of a crowd." He wraps an arm around my shoulder and squeezes. "You like smaller, intimate gatherings like our happy hours, where you know everyone."

I nod. "And where I'm not the focus."

"Ah, yes. I hate to break it to you, but you're going to have more eyes on you than this at your wedding. You'd better get used to it."

"I wished we'd just eloped," I whisper more to myself than him.

He turns his concerned look on me. "Do you really?"

"Yeah, I think I really do." There's no *thinking* to it, truly. Maybe if we were already married, the office betting pool wouldn't have had a chance to even start. The woman trying to get me to leave maybe wouldn't have even tried. All this heartache could have been avoided.

I look around the room at Joseph's family, our mutual friends, and Jace—my only family—and I'm hit with guilt. Would I really want to do this without all of them by our sides, cheering us on, congratulating us, supporting us every step of the way? "No." I turn to face Bash. "I wouldn't want to do this without you…" I motion haphazardly over my shoulder to the rest of the room. "…or them."

His devilishly handsome smile is enough to know I'm right. "I would have been really mad at you if you'd run off. You deserve the big wedding."

I don't know about deserve, but I'm getting it whether I do or not. "Come on, let's go see my husband-to-be." Joseph needs a little reassurance that I don't hate him.

Joseph

My girl curls into my side, and my chest nearly collapses into itself, tight with emotion. She came to *me*, seeking *my* touch, *my* comfort. Sebastian smiles at me, standing with her between us. I don't know what he said, but I'm thankful that whatever it was prompted this. I smile and shake his hand. "We've missed you at happy hours."

He nods. "I got a suck-balls rotation this round. I'm trying to swap a few shifts to see if I can make it next week."

"Maybe we could swap days, occasionally, to something that works for you. We'd at least get to see you a few times a month," I suggest.

"That'd be great. Let's see if I can make the next one, then we can discuss it with everyone."

Samantha looks up and presses into me. She likes that suggestion, and that I'm working to fit her *Bash* into our tight-knit group. But really, everyone loves Sebastian. He's a great guy. He cares for my girl—in a way I'm not threatened by—and he's funny as shit with hysterical stories from his ER patients. We'd do the same for anyone else in our group if they had a continual schedule conflict.

I steal a kiss and relish the fact that she doesn't pull away from me.

It's not long before my mother calls the two of us to take a seat in the chairs placed in front of the fireplace, facing the room filled with our guests. *Shit. She's gonna hate this.* I squeeze her hand, letting her know she's not in this alone—I'm right here beside her—not letting her go. Ever.

Fuck. Now I just want to take her to my old room upstairs and see if she'll let me kiss and hold her some more. I don't even care if we have sex—I just need to reconnect with my Sweets—feel her safe, secure, and at peace in my arms.

Fuck me running backwards with a dog in my arms, this is gonna be a long-ass night.

Margot kneels beside Samantha, writing down each gift and who it came from. I guess that's the job of the maid of honor? Or maybe it's just a best friends thing. My brothers take turns handing us gifts that Mom has stashed in some other room, hence why we didn't know there were gifts—even though we agreed there wouldn't be any. Samantha and I take turns reading the cards, telling Margot and the room whom it's from, and opening the gift.

To my complete and total shock, we have a china pattern and thus far, we've received twenty-four complete place settings. Who the hell needs twenty-four place settings of china? We can't even seat twenty-four people in our penthouse. We can seat sixteen at our dining room table and four at the breakfast bar. I guess four lone diners could sit on the couches or eat at the coffee table. Huh, maybe we do need twenty-four. Who'd have thunk it?

Fin, being the ass he is, even though we have a completely good coffeemaker, bought us the exact same contraption he has. Great, now I'll have to get a second degree just to run the damn thing. Samantha, on the other hand, is ecstatic, jumping up to hug Fin so fast she nearly trips over the monstrosity. Christ, that thing is ugly. *I wonder if it does dishes?*

I'm so busy giving Fin a hard time, I miss what the next gift is or who it's from. I simply hear a gasp from beside me, and when I look to Samantha, she's turned as white as her sexy bride-ish looking blouse. "What—"

She slams the box shut, clutching it to her chest like it's a bomb about to go off, protecting everyone as she nearly hurdles over any obstacles or guests in her way. She runs out of the room—and I mean runs—flat out, as fast as she can, fifty-yard-sprint kind of run. I catch sight of Michael's back as he rounds the corner and barrels up the stairs after her. Without a second thought for our guests or any explanation as to what happened, I bound up the stairs behind them in time to see Samantha slam the bathroom door shut. Michael skids to a halt as he grabs the doorknob, only to find it locked.

He looks at me solemnly, glancing over my shoulder. "Let me know if you want me to break it down." He pats my shoulder as he passes. "I'll keep everyone away." He stops at the top of the stairs, blocking Fin, Jace, and I don't know who else from coming up.

Ignoring them, I turn to the door, checking again to be sure it's really locked. It is.

I press my forehead to the cool surface. "Samantha, please let me in. Let me see what's in the box. We're a team. Remember?"

In response, all I hear are her soft sobs. Fuck. "Please, baby, let me in."

The sound of running water fills my ears, muting any other noises. She must have turned on the faucet. I press my ear to the door, closing my eyes to concentrate on what's happening on the other side. A deep, muffled voice fills the void, but I can't make anything out. Then it's gone, only to come back a few seconds later. Another sob, loud enough to breach the water barrier she's erected. Then the deep voice again. A loud clang has me pulling away momentarily before I catch myself and resume my listening stance. Only this time, over the din of the water,

I hear the worst sound imaginable—the sound that sends me back to that day I told her I slept with someone else—the sound that fills me with so much regret and helplessness—the sound of the woman I love retching.

I look to Michael. "I have to get in there."

With a quick nod, he's by my side. He stills and listens. "Is she—"

"Yes." Fuck. Yes, that's the sound of my girl vomiting over whatever is in that goddamned box. "I have to get to her, Michael. Now."

I move aside, giving him room as he prepares to kick the door in.

"Stop!" Fin elbows his way past William, who took Michael's place as guard. "Did it even cross your mind to pick the lock? Aren't you the ex-FBI-military-extraordinaire?"

Michael pats his pockets. "Didn't come prepared to pick locks at a wedding shower."

"Then it's a good thing one of us is prepared." Fin hands me the master key.

I move to insert the metal key into the hole to pop the lock, but stop. "Fin, I need you to stay back."

He looks offended but nods and steps back.

"Michael, I need you to get that fucking package and ensure no one sees it."

"On it."

That's all the confirmation I need. I pop the lock, push the door so hard it bangs against the wall and hits me on the rebound, but I move on, not letting it slow me down. Samantha is slumped over the toilet, still throwing up. I glance at the open box lying on the floor and get a glimpse of a video and the sound of my voice coming from inside the box. Motherfucker!

Michael picks up the box. I turn my attention back to my girl and block everything else out, knowing he'll take care of it.

I kneel beside her, gather her hair in my hands, relieving her of her valiant attempt at keeping it out of her way. I hold it with one hand and gently pat her back. "It's okay, Samantha, I've got you."

She vomits again and again.

Her body finally gives out—gives up—and I'm able to get her cleaned up and tucked against my chest on my old bed, in my bedroom. The one I wanted to bring her to earlier, under totally different circumstances. She's cried herself out and has fallen asleep. I text Michael and ask him to send Sebastian to meet me in my room.

With a soft knock, the door opens and Sebastian peers in. I motion him forward. He quietly closes the door behind him and walks silently to my side of the bed. His eyes rove over Samantha.

"I need you to watch her. Stay with her. I need to step across the hall, and I don't want her alone if she wakes up while I'm gone. Can you do that?" I ask, knowing he would never say no.

"Of course. Is she sick?" His concerned doctor eyes study her face.

I slowly extricate myself from her grasp. She moans and frowns in response but doesn't wake up. I move us away from the bed and quietly explain. "We've been getting disturbing mail. I don't know what was in the box she opened, but it was enough to upset her to the point of making her sick." I look at her resting peacefully on the bed. "If she wakes up, call for me." I move to the door, not giving him a chance to ask questions. "I'll only be across the hall."

I step into the adjacent room, not surprised to see Fin and Michael standing there arguing. Once I get the door closed, Fin is all over me. "What the fuck is going on?"

I hold up my hand. "Fin, I need to talk to Michael, alone."

He flinches as if I slapped him. It's not like me to keep secrets from Fin. "I can help."

On a sigh, I sit on the bed. "I know you can. And you will, but right now, I need you downstairs getting rid of all these people. Tell them Samantha is sick, thank them for coming, smooth over ruffled feathers, and get them the fuck out of the house. I'm gonna take Samantha home soon, and I'd rather not have to carry her through a house full of guests."

"And then we'll talk?" he confirms.

"And then we'll talk. Tomorrow."

He wants to protest. I can see it in the tension of his body and the bite in his jaw, but he simply nods. "Tomorrow, brother."

"Tomorrow." I stand and hug him, fighting to keep my emotions in check. "Thank you, brother."

As soon as Fin leaves, I turn to Michael. "Show me."

He hands me a note.

Why haven't you left yet?
Is this not proof enough?
You'll never be able to satisfy my Joseph, not the way I can.

Sincerely,
Joseph's cock riding baby

Rage courses through my body, and my fists clench, needing to hit something—someone. Michael grips my hand, forcing me to release the note before pushing me down on the bed. "If you think that's bad, you're really gonna hate the video."

"Michael." I don't even have the words.

He grips my shoulder. "We're gonna find this motherfucker, and when we do, we're gonna take them down, rip them apart limb from limb. Whatever it takes."

"Show me."

Sitting beside me, he pulls out an old iPhone. There's a still of me on the screen. He hits play.

I come alive on the screen. My eyes are closed, and from the movements, it's obvious I'm having sex with the woman taking the video.

"That's right, baby. Make it feel good." My voice echoes in my ears—so familiar.

The me in the video moans and thrusts in time with the woman who's moaning too.

Then I open my eyes, staring into the camera with pure pleasure on my face. *"I'm coming, baby."*

127

The video ends.

Fuck me and my life.

I stand abruptly. "I need to get Samantha home."

"I'll have William pull the car around back. We can go down the back stairs and through the garage."

"Fine. Let me know when we're ready." I open the door and stop. "Michael, I'd like you to move into the penthouse. I know that's a hardship, but I'd feel better having you close."

"Not a problem, brother," he says with conviction, and he means it. He'd die for Sam.

It had better not come to that.

"Thank you, brother."

I slip across the hall to collect my girl and take her home. Tomorrow we will face this shitstorm together, but tonight I need to hold her, comfort her, and love her in any way she will let me.

Twelve

HAVE A LITTLE FAITH

Samantha

WARMTH SURROUNDS ME AS I SLOWLY WAKE. HIS hand skims my hip, his breath on my neck, and the tender graze of his lips across the bare skin of my neck and shoulder has my nipples hardening.

"Keep your eyes closed. Stay in half-slumber. Don't think." His raw voice sends chills skating down my body.

A soft kiss behind my ear.

"Let me love you."

Kiss on my neck.

"Don't turn me away."

Kiss. Kiss along my shoulder.

"I need you."

Kiss on my ear.

"I miss you."

His tender words lull me in and keep me in a peaceful place, not asleep and not fully awake. I linger, welcoming that space where nothing exists but the two of us.

"I love you."

He moves over me, whispering across my skin his words of love and comfort. His hard, heated parts, rubbing, seducing my softer, needful ones. Warm breath and hot tongue soothe and tempt in sync with his knowledgeable hands, pulling and teasing, opening and filling. His body surrounds me, cocoons me, fills me and fills me, taking me flying—higher and higher.

Our love. Our souls. Our bodies burst like a phoenix, consumed in flames, fed by the hunger of our passion, our sorrow, our need, our joining. Burning and burning until we are reduced to ash and are reborn.

I leave the thoughts of yesterday and the vision of that video where it belongs, in the past. Showered and dressed, I head to the kitchen to start breakfast. Peace and calm is my motto for the day. It's Sunday, after all. If peace can't be found on a Sunday, then there is no hope.

"Princess." Michael's presence halts me in my tracks.

"Michael?" It's not that unusual to see him here early in the morning, but it is on a non-working day.

He chuckles. "It looks like we're gonna be roomies for a while."

"What?"

Joseph ensconces me from behind, nuzzling into my neck. I can feel his smile against my skin. "I asked Michael to move in. Temporarily."

"Temporarily?" I repeat, turning in his arms.

My Caveman nods with a shrug, not wanting to elaborate.

Peace and calm.

"Okay." It's not like it's a hardship. I love Michael, and it's not the first time we've spent more than our fair share of time together. It's too bad it always seems to be when I'm in danger, which they obviously feel I am. "Pancakes?"

"Hell, yeah!"

Joseph

Michael and I meet with Jace before the others show up. It's family meeting day. It's time to bring in the big guns and stop fucking around. Privacy be damned, except for the picture and video. They'll be aware of their existence, but they don't need to see them.

Jace is pacing the floor, having finished viewing the video. "Jesus, I can't unsee that."

"Welcome to my world," Michael mutters.

"Hey, this is no cakewalk for me. It's humiliating as fuck," I bark.

They both turn to face me, stunned.

Jace is quick to make peace. "Sorry, man."

"Yeah, me too. I know how hard this is on you and Sam," Michael replies with sincerity.

Now that that humiliating show and tell is out of the way. "Anything we need to discuss before Fin and Victor get here?"

Michael grabs a seat across from my desk. "We may need to let Victor see the copies of the picture and video. He has expertise in this area. He may see something we don't." Michael's already overnighted yesterday's package to his forensic buddy.

"I leave that up to your discretion, but under no circumstances are my bothers to see them. The letters are bad enough."

"Matt's still out of town. I can bring him up to speed when he returns," Michael offers.

I nod my agreement before ushering them out of my office to wait for the others' arrival. My need to check on Samantha is strong, more than normal. She seems fine, better than fine. I'm not complaining, but I don't think she's dealing with the events of yesterday, and I don't want to leave her alone too long.

We find her in the kitchen, making lunch for everyone. She may not like social gatherings, but she sure enjoys feeding the Six Pack when we're all together. Sebastian is coming over too; he's going to keep her company while I fill in Fin and Victor. I'm not looking forward to it. It's a total clusterfuck, and I'm quite sure neither of them will fail to remind me of that fact.

"It smells good, Sweets." I kiss her cheek and then her temple, giving her a side hug as she stirs the large pot of gumbo on the stove.

"I hope it tastes good."

I tip her chin, searching her eyes for any signs of sadness. "I have no doubt it'll taste even better." A slow kiss on the mouth with a suck on her bottom lip has her leaning into me like she hasn't done in weeks. "God, I've missed you." I breathe between our lips.

She drops the spoon, letting it stand in the pot, turning into me, wrapping me into a welcoming hug. "I'm sorry," she whispers against my chest.

"Shh, none of that, Sweetness. You're with me now. That's all that matters." With my cheek pressed to the top of her head, I hold her tighter, never wanting to let her go.

A throat clears from behind us.

Fuck off. I don't give a shit who it is, and I don't bother to turn to see.

Another "ahem" has Samantha pulling away, but I stop her. "I'm not ready," I say, my voice low, only for her to hear.

She looks up, a sweet smile lighting up her face, and I'm lost in her blue eyes. She pats my chest, nodding behind me. "I think we have an audience."

On a groan, I turn to see Fin, Victor, Jace, Michael, and Sebastian staring back at us with stupid grins on their faces. *Fuck me.* "Can't you see we're having a moment here?"

Fin laughs. "When *aren't* you having a moment?"

I try to smile back, but if he only knew how rare this was lately, he'd leave us the fuck alone.

Samantha kisses my cheek. "Do you want to eat or have your Boy Scout meeting first?"

Fin and Victor say, "Eat.

Michael, Jace and I say, "Meeting."

"We need to get this over with," I say to them. A nod to Michael has him prompting them to follow him to my office.

Sebastian comes around the breakfast bar. "I guess it's just you and me, cupcake."

My girl smiles. "Now you made me want cupcakes."

"Damn, that does sound good," he agrees.

I'm quite sure he means an actual cupcake and not *my* Samantha, whom he calls *cupcake*. But either way, it sure as hell puts one delectable image in my head of losing myself in my Sweets' pussy. *Shit. Concentrate.* "You two don't have to wait for us to eat, if you don't want to." I kiss her quickly—trying not to think of her other parts I'd like to be kissing— and thank Sebastian for keeping her company with a silent nod, then leave to apprise Fin and Victor on the crap that's been consuming much of our lives for the past few months.

"Why in the hell did you keep this to yourself?" Fin steams as Victor glares daggers into Michael and me.

Yep, pretty much the reaction I expected.

"What could you have done differently that we haven't already done?" I challenge.

Fin steps forward. "Supported you." He clamps on to my upper arm. "Make sure you knew this was bullshit, and we don't believe a word of it."

"Is this why Sam hasn't been to the office?" Victor seems to have calmed down a tad.

I turn on a silent nod, running my hand down my face, not able to admit she can't look at me without seeing that damn photo, and now that fucking video making it even more ominous, more real.

"Brother?" Fin's concern pulls at my gut.

"She's been pulling away, wanting to delay the wedding," Michael steps in.

"What? She can't possibly believe it's true. You'd never cheat on her." Fin's outrage and the depth of his unwavering belief in me tightens the vise in my chest.

"She won't… We haven't…" I turn to face them, avoiding Jace, as I know this is awkward for him, being Samantha's brother. "She can't see me without seeing that fucking picture, and now she has a video to remind her." I stare at the door, like I can see her on the other side. "Today was…unusual." She's her old self today—my girl.

"And we interrupted your moment." The sorrow in Fin's voice is evident.

A curt nod is all I can manage.

"Does she believe you're cheating on her?" Victor asks.

The weight of the last few weeks hits me hard, and I slump down into the couch, my head back, and press my palms over my eyes. *Keep it together.* I still can't find my voice to answer them.

Jace steps up this time. "She doesn't believe it. She trusts Joe." I can feel his eyes on me. "She can't get the images of him with someone else out of her head. She's never been confident in her ability to hang on to him—"

I growl and lean forward, my arms resting on my knees, my hands buried in my hair. "Fuck!" It's one thing to know it. It's another thing to hear it from someone else's mouth. "I'd never cheat on her. She's my world." My voice cracks. It's killing me how much this is hurting her—hurting us—bringing these fucking doubts to the surface that have long since been buried.

The couch dips as Jace and Fin take a seat on either side of me, their hands clasping my shoulders. "We know," they chime in unison.

I look at them, surprised, not so much that they believe me—that is huge, trust me—but that they're so in sync. Jace has been apart from us for a long time, it's good to see him slip back into our fold so seamlessly, as if he never left.

I clear my throat and hope I can keep it together. "Yeah, so she feels we should delay the wedding until things blow over. Not because she believes I'm cheating, but because she believes maybe the threat of even worse packages will stop if we don't get married." I stand at the windows with the image of Samantha walking down the aisle to marry me. "All of this is ruining the wedding for her, 'tainting it,' she says. I won't lose her. I won't let them win by delaying the wedding." Pure menace rages through me for whomever is behind this emotional blackmail.

"We won't let that happen, brother," Fin says, always so sure of himself and his ability to fix my problems.

A soft smile and moment of peace, believing what he says is possible. "Let's talk strategy, then."

Michael takes over, laying out our plan. I glance at the door again, hoping, praying the warm, open woman I left a few minutes ago will still be there when I return.

Samantha

"You're such a troublemaker, Bash." I push his shoulder, and he falls over on the couch laughing.

"I can't help it. If you don't want people knowing you're having sex in the on-call room, then don't have sex in the on-call room." He shrugs. "It's fair game. We may eat at the hospital and sleep there, but that doesn't mean it's okay to have sex there. Seriously, it's our place of business. You don't have sex where you work."

God, if he only knew.

"What? Why are you blushing?" He sits up, looming over me. "Cupcake, is there something you need to confess?"

I push against his chest, laughing. "No. I don't have anything I'd like to confess."

He squints at me. "*Like to confess?* That means you do, but you're not saying." His eyes widen. "Oh my God! You've totally had sex at MCI!"

"No!" I jump up and head to the kitchen. "That would be so wrong." I can't keep a straight face.

Bash follows me. "But kinda hot," he murmurs behind me.

"Really, really hot." I sigh as I stir the gumbo and turn off the rice.

"Holy fuck, Samantha Lilian Cavanaugh, you've totally had sex at the office." He leans against the counter, facing me.

Shaking my head, I suck in my lips. I'm not admitting anything. But I can't keep a smirk from spreading, despite biting my lip to keep my mouth closed. I bang the spoon on the pot, place it in the spoon holder, and close the lid. "I wish they'd hurry. I'm really hungry."

"I can't believe you're not going to answer me. After all the stuff I've told you." He feigns indignation.

I scoff. "Uh, you're the one who says sex talk is off limits. It goes against our *friend-agreement* or some shit like that."

"That was when you were still a virgin, and before I knew you were having sex at the office."

"I never said that."

He chuckles, his face all handsome and lit up. "Babycakes, you don't have to say it. Your body is telling plenty."

He's enjoying this way too much. "Oh, hush. Stop looking, then." I can't get away with anything. All these men around me read me like an open book, like I have a digital banner running across my forehead, advertising my inner thoughts. It's frustrating. Except when Joseph does it, it's kinda hot that he can read me so well.

Bash leans in, whispering in my ear, "Okay, I'll stop. Don't be embarrassed. It's great you two have such an adventurous sex life. I never would have thought of you taking such a risk." He kisses my cheek and pulls away, his teasing gone, but his eyes still twinkle—enjoying this way too much.

"What risk? He has a lock on his office door." I wink as I leave him gawking at me from the kitchen.

The guys finally come out of the office. Joseph looks worn out and leery as he approaches. I meet him halfway. His hands grip my hips like he needs me to ground him. I rest my arms on his shoulders as his forehead touches mine.

"Sweetness," he says so softly it sends chills across my skin.

One hand sinks into his hair, and my other cups his cheek. "I'm here, Caveman."

His eyes close on deep exhale. "Say that again."

Oh, Joseph, you're breaking my heart. I brush my lips across his. "I'm here, Caveman." Kiss. "I love you." Kiss. Kiss. Kiss.

He pulls back, his eyes red-rimmed, but sparkling green. "Besides your orgasms this morning, that's the best sound I've heard all day."

"Well, then, I guess I'll have to be sure to tell you again and again." I kiss his cheek and take his hand. "Now, let me feed you so you have the stamina to pull more of those sounds from me later."

He pulls me back around. His lips crash into mine with a deep rumble in his chest. "Fuck, you made me hard."

I press against him. "You're making me wet."

"Christ, I've fucking missed you." He breathes across my lips.

"The sooner we feed the guys, the sooner they'll leave."

With a gleam in his eyes and a panty-dropping smile on his lips, he pulls me to the kitchen. "Come eat, you assholes, so you can get the fuck out of our house. The caveman needs his woman."

Well, that's one way to call people to come eat. Too bad he doesn't remember he's asked Michael to live with us. Though, I don't think that will stop Joseph from throwing me over his shoulder once his belly is full.

My Caveman needs me. How can I say no?

Thirteen

EXTINGUISH MY FLAME

Samantha

TWO YEARS AGO TODAY I WAS HAVING Thanksgiving with Joseph and my family, our little budding romance not much more than pure attraction and burning lust. My father was still alive and deeply and endlessly in love with my mom. Jace was still a manwhore, and my best friend and overprotective brother.

In a blink of an eye, a shot of a gun, a strike of a single bullet—everything changed. My father was dead from the bullet that tore through his heart and into my shoulder. And, as if that very bullet continued to ricochet through my life, it tore my brother and mother from me too. That one action took everything from me, yet it also gave me everything. It gave me Joseph, though we admittedly had a rather rocky and unconventional start. It also gave me my second family in Joseph's brothers—Victor and Michael fall under the umbrella of *brothers*—and his parents.

Even without Mom, I feel at peace today. Jace is back, full force, one hundred percent in my life. It's a work in progress, but I'm hopeful our relationship will be better than it was before. We're more honest with each other. I don't pretend I don't need anybody, and he doesn't disappear on me.

He's making strides with Joseph too, not only because he's back in my life, but because he believes in Joseph's fidelity and is sticking by him to help figure out the Tiff angle in the emotional blackmail scheme we're in the middle of.

Jace is joining us for Thanksgiving at the McIntyres', but he called Joseph a few minutes ago, sending Joseph striding out of our bedroom to talk to him. "Sweetness," Joseph calls from the living room.

"Coming." I'm running late. I have to stop and pick up a few last-minute items from the grocery store. I rush from our bedroom. "Sorry. I'm ready."

Joseph motions to his cell phone. "Jace has an update. I've got Michael on the line, as well."

"Hey, guys."

Their voices greet me via the speaker on Joseph's cell.

"Jace would you mind repeating what you just told me?" Joseph pulls me down to sit beside him on the couch.

"I met with Tiff," Jace shares.

My eyes lock on Joseph's. He nods as if I need the confirmation that Jace's words are true.

"I only had to push her a little. She folded like a house of cards." Jace clears his throat. "Joe, are you sure want to talk about this with…"

Me. He doesn't want to talk about Tiff with *me* on the phone. I squeeze Joseph's hand. "It's okay, Jace."

A few beats pass before he continues. "Someone named Lydia reached out to Tiff."

"Lydia? MCI's Lydia?" I ask.

"Yes," Michael chimes in.

Wow. She really did hate me.

"Tiff doesn't know how Lydia found her, but Lydia convinced Tiff that you two needed your lives turned upside down—that you didn't deserve to be happy. Lydia played the bitch card, and Tiff bought into it hook, line, and sinker, providing the boxer briefs and video from the night she raped Joseph."

"No. No. No," I whisper. This can't be happening. All of this is from his rape.

"Can you guys give us a moment?" Joseph puts the call on hold. "Samantha, look at me."

My blurry gaze locks on him.

"This is good news." He seems so happy, and I'm devastated.

"What? How can proof of your rape be good news?"

His beautiful smile reveals the dimples I love so much. "Because we know where the underwear, pic, and video came from. We know who's behind this. It's all a scam concocted by Lydia."

I touch his face. "Joseph, you amaze me that you can see the positive in such devastation."

He kisses me quickly before taking the call off hold. "Okay, we're back.

"Everything alright?" Jace's concern is evident and so very welcomed. It's good to have him back.

"Yeah. What else?" I don't want to dwell on the details around Joseph's rape, at least not with Jace and Michael on the line. It makes me sick to my stomach to even think about it.

"I didn't let on that I was in cahoots with y'all. I figured it would be better to keep her on the hook in case Lydia contacts her again. We don't want her to give up that we're on to them." Jace pauses for a second before he continues, a bit sheepishly, I might add. "I, uh, was able to get a DNA sample."

I don't want to know how he accomplished that without making her suspicious.

"I sent the DNA sample off to my guy, but we're going to assume that it's her DNA on the boxer briefs."

Lovely. My stomach rolls at the thought.

"Fin, Victor, and I tracked down Lydia late last night. She no longer works for MCI—Fin was more than happy to fire her ass." Michael chuckles.

"So, it's done then? It's over?" Joseph's hope is contagious, but I have doubts.

"How did Lydia even know about Tiff?" I ask.

"That's a very good question." Michael goes on to advise after threatening Lydia with charges being brought against her, she admitted she was not the mastermind behind all of this. "Supposedly a woman named Bonnie was the one who approached Lydia after she was transferred to Accounting."

"Bonnie? Who the fuck is Bonnie?" Joseph's happy bubble just broke.

I give him a consolatory smile and kiss on the cheek. It was too good to be true. Nothing this nasty wraps up this easily.

Michael continues. "Lydia was out drinking with a few coworkers the evening she was removed as Joseph's PA. She was complaining about not working for Joseph any longer. This Bonnie chick approached her in the bathroom after overhearing Lydia's bitch session. Bonnie convinced Lydia the two of you needed to be taught a lesson. Lydia was all too willing to help."

"I'm sure she was." I don't like to hate people, but I'm pretty sure what I feel for Lydia right about now is hate, pure and simple.

"I should have fired her for her lecherous behavior instead of giving her a second chance." Joseph's happy bubble is definitely gone.

"I doubt it would have made any difference. She would have been bitching about being fired instead of transferred. Whoever Bonnie is probably had her sights on MCI employees, waiting for an opportunity. I doubt her finding Lydia that night was a coincidence," Michael interjects before continuing to share the details of his Lydia discovery. "Lydia was the middle man dealing with Tiff. Lydia swears she has no idea what Bonnie did with the underwear or the video. She said she partied more with Bonnie than anything else."

"Any idea who Bonnie is?" Joseph asks.

"No, but we'll work to get video footage from the places Lydia said she met Bonnie and see if anything comes of that. We also have her cell number. Victor's looking into that, but we assume it's probably a burner phone. I'd also assume Bonnie is not her real name. I'll let you know when we have more." Michael sounds confident we'll figure this out. I find some level of comfort in that, at least.

We hang up with the promise of seeing them later at Joseph's parents' house.

"I guess that's both good news and bad news." I get up from the couch. Despite this latest news, we really need to get going, otherwise we're going to be late for Thanksgiving dinner, well, lunch.

My caveman rakes over my body from head to toe. "I think it's all good news. It's not resolved, but we know more now than we did a few days ago." He stalks closer. "Maybe we can skip Thanksgiving dinner this year." He pulls me into his arms. "Have a little feast of our own." His mouth latches on to my neck on a growl. "Yes, I could savor you for hours, Sweets."

All but panting, I pull back. "Nuh-uh, we're not missing Thanksgiving." I pat his chest. "You'll have to cage the thought. Until later."

On a sigh, he releases me. "Okay, but I'm not swearing I won't whisk you off to my old room for a little dessert afterwards."

My heart leaps. "I look forward to it, Caveman."

Joseph heads to Fin's and will meet me at their parents' house in a few hours. William and I take the elevator to the basement. "Why aren't you spending the holiday with your family?"

He smiles sheepishly. He's a nice-looking guy, tall, big—like Victor—brown buzz-cut hair and pale green eyes. "My family's in Tennessee. I promised Mr. McIntyre I'd see this job through until we catch whoever is threatening you. I mean to keep my word, even if it means I miss a few holidays."

"I hate that you have to work today, but I'm grateful to have you here, protecting me."

"It's my honor, Sam." He opens the door to the SUV, helping me in, before he rounds the front of the car to the driver's side.

Joseph's not crazy about it, but I've asked all the guys to call me Sam. Maybe once we're married, I'll be okay being called Mrs. McIntyre, but I haven't earned that name yet, and being called Ms. Cavanagh only makes me think of my mother. She's the last thing I want to think about today, or most days, for that matter.

We hurry through the store, picking up the last minutes items Fiona needs. The crowd is not bad, but they don't have many cashiers working, so the checkout line is taking a while. I pivot from foot to foot, like I have ants in my pants.

William eyes me with a raised brow. "Problem?"

"I, uh, need to go to the bathroom."

He looks around, trying to hide his smirk. "Okay, we'll find the restroom." He starts to pull out of line, but I stop him.

"Look, we're next. You check out, and I'll run to the bathroom and meet you back here." I squeeze my legs together.

"No. I'm not leaving you unprotected."

I grab his arm, trying to communicate with my eyes that I'm in dire straits here. "I don't have time to argue. I'm gonna pee my pants." I fidget, glancing behind me. The lady next in line only smiles and points to the back of the store. I give her a silent thank you and turn back to William. "Okay, I'm going."

I take off in a near run, having no idea if he's following me. Why is it that the closer you get to a bathroom, the more urgently you have to go? I barge through the door, find the nearest stall, lock it, and barely make it to the toilet.

As I finish and sigh in total relief, a manila folder slides under the stall door.

Holy shit! In my haste to see Bonnie or whoever the hell is stalking me, I stumble over my panties, still down around my ankles, and slam into the stall door. By the time I get situated and out of the stall, the bathroom door closes. I rush out the door, only seconds after whoever was in there with me, but all I see are shoppers and their carts, busy finding what they came for, not paying me any mind, having no idea of what went down in the bathroom. I scan their faces, looking for anyone familiar, but it's to no avail. Whoever it was is gone.

I reenter the bathroom and wash my hands, peering over my shoulder to the envelope lying on the floor behind me. I keep staring at it as I dry my hands and collect my purse. With a resolved sigh, I pick up the envelope.

It's addressed to me, no surprise there.

I have two options. I can wait to open it with Joseph at his parents' house—not my favorite choice—or I open it now, so I can be prepared.

I open it.

And nothing could have prepared me for what I find inside.

Nothing.

There's three pictures.

And a note.

Jesus, those pictures.

I force my emotions down. I can't afford to get upset now.

My hands are shaking, making it difficult to put it all back into the envelope and stuff it in my purse.

Don't think. Move.

I exit the bathroom.

Don't think. Move.

I head to the nearest exit, glance over and see William busy checking out. He doesn't see me.

Don't think. Move.

Outside, I hail a cab.

Breathe. Close your eyes and breathe.

The cab stops at my destination. I pay and get out. I don't have long.

Don't think. Move.

I ride the elevator, unlock the door. Quiet. Empty. Hurry.

Don't think. Move.

I grab an overnight bag, haphazardly throwing items inside. Hurry. Keys.

I run to Joseph's office and grab the keys I need. Hurry.

Don't think. Move.

With a final look around our penthouse, I close the door and take the elevator, sending Michael a text.

Me: *I need you. Don't bring Joseph. Find me like you always do.*

I unlock the door. Cold. This doesn't feel like home. I drop my bag at the entry and walk to the nearest couch. My phone chimes.

Michael: *Fuck, Sam. Why'd you have to ditch William? I'm coming. Don't move.*

Me: *I'm safe. I'm not going anywhere. No Joseph.*

Michael: *I heard you the first time. I understand.*

I turn my phone off. Even if Michael succeeds in leaving Joseph behind, there is no way Joseph won't call me. I'm not sure I'm strong enough to reject his call—but I need to.

The envelope in my purse is taunting me. I take it out and throw it on the coffee table. Maybe the taunting won't be as loud over there.

There's no knocking; only Michael opening the door alerts me to his presence. Of course, he has a key. He always has a key.

"Princess." He approaches me slowly, assessing. His eyes land on the coffee table. "When did that arrive?" He stops in front of me, standing between me and *it*.

My chin starts to quiver. *Dammit, I was doing so good too.*

"Oh, Sam." He's at my side before my first tear falls. He pulls me into a hug. He's big and strong, but he's not Joseph. He's not my home, and that makes me cry even harder. "Shit," he murmurs into my hair. Feelings are not Michael's favorite thing.

I pull myself together enough to speak. "Someone slipped it under the bathroom stall at the grocery store."

He doesn't seem surprised. William must have told him about my pee emergency. "Did you see who it was?"

I shake my head.

"Did you open it?"

I nod.

"It is worse than the last one?"

My tears start to fall again.

"I'll take the fact that you ran away as a yes."

"I didn't run away. I ran home." I look around. "Well, almost."

He smiles. "Thank you for that. It's easier to protect you at MCI than anywhere else."

I don't have a death wish. "That's why I came here."

He eyes the envelope. "I need to open it."

Taking a deep breath, I sit up, allowing him to extricate himself from my side.

He pulls plastic gloves from his pocket and slips them on. "I came prepared." He opens the envelope and tips it up, letting the contents slip out. "Fuck."

"Yep." I can't look away as he picks up the first picture—I should—but I can't.

It's a picture of a woman lying on her back, legs spread wide, held open by strong, powerful hands. A beautiful man with dark hair and emerald eyes feasts on her with a look of pure desire in his eyes—my Joseph's eyes.

He picks up the next picture. This one is basically the same—same woman—except it's from a different angle where I can see the woman's face, smiling at the camera, looking into my soul—laughing at me—as Joseph eats her out with his eyes closed, and I can nearly hear him growling in pleasure. The window is open behind them with a beautiful view of the Las Vegas strip all lit up at night. *Loving Vegas!* Rings in my ears as an echo from the second letter.

I point at the pic. "That's Veronica Hamm." I can't believe it as I say it. I'd hoped the face I saw in the pictures in the bathroom was a mistake, but now that I see them again with the shock worn off... It's her.

"Who's Veronica Hamm?" Michael points a gloved finger at the woman's face. "Her?"

"Yep."

"How do you know her?"

"It's a long story. She used to date Jace, and now she doesn't, because of me." I laugh, but it's humorless. "Jokes on me, huh."

"It looks like we found our Bonnie." He sets it down and pics up the last picture. "Holy shit."

"Yep."

"That's Lydia."

"Yep."

The third and last offering is a picture of Lydia on all fours with Joseph fucking her from behind. Again, Vegas is in the background, and if you look closely enough, you can see Veronica's reflection in the window flipping me off as she snaps the picture.

Michael points it out as he notices Veronica's reflection.

"Yep. It's icing on the fuck-you cake she's worked really hard to deliver."

"Fuck. This girl has to be crazy."

"Nope. She really doesn't like me. She never has, and I don't know why." I'm not sure it matters anymore. She's obviously gotten what she wanted. To take away the man I love—to leave me feeling like I'm nothing. Nothing at all.

"Sam, I'm so sorry."

The pity in his eyes is more than I can take. "Read the letter."

He loves my pussy.
He can't get enough of my taste or the way I feel around his cock.
He's mine. LEAVE. NOW!

Sincerely,
Joseph's favorite meal
P.S. I let Lydia get a feel of his massive cock as he pounded her from behind, watching me the entire time. See, I'll share my Joseph—just not with you.

Michael puts everything back in the envelope, sets the discarded gloves on top, and slumps back into the couch. "I don't know what to say. I want to tell you it's all bullshit. That those pictures aren't real. And there's a very good chance they aren't. But given that it's this Veronica chick and Lydia, both of whom have a connection to you and Joe, I really don't know anymore."

"You understand why I don't want to see him, then?"

He huffs. "Oh, I understand, and I don't blame you. But, I also know Joseph. I believe in my gut he would never cheat on you. I can't explain anything in that envelope, but I promise, I will work night and day to find the truth. Not what Joseph says is the truth, but the *actual* truth. I can promise you that."

Fourteen

I WON'T GIVE UP

Joseph

IT'S BEEN AN HOUR SINCE MICHAEL DROPPED everything to find Samantha. I don't know how he does it, but he always seems to know where she is. I assume he still has a tracker on her after all this time. He's not taking any chances. I'm thankful for that.

I'm home, pacing. I told my family to proceed with Thanksgiving without us. I made Fin promise to stay there and make sure we don't ruin dinner for them. The last thing I need is Dad and Mom up here in my business—my sexual business—my love life, my future, my world.

"William, sit the fuck down. Or better yet, go to Fin's and get a bottle of his Macallan," I bark, pointing to the front door like he doesn't know where it is.

It's okay for me to pace, but his pacing only agitates me further.

"Yes, sir." He exits quietly. These ex-military guys move with such stealthy precision—it's unsettling at times.

I text Fin so he doesn't freak out about one of his precious bottles missing. I'm sure he has his stash plotted out to the ounce on some multicolored spreadsheet somewhere. His reply is instantaneous, "Take what you need, brother."

149

Always there. Always supportive. Always has my back. That's Fin.

My phone dings again.

Michael: *Sam is in penthouse 2C. Another package was delivered. Send William down, and I'll come up as soon as I get her settled.*

Relief floods me knowing she's safe and close, but not nearly as close as I want her. I promised Michael I'd give him time to deal the situation before I barged in, possibly making it worse.

Me: *I sent William on a Macallan run. I'll send him over as soon as he gets back. Tell her I love her. She's not answering her phone.*

Michael: *Good, you're gonna need it. Have a couple of glasses to calm yourself down. I can hear your pacing from here. She turned her phone off. I'll tell her.*

Me: *I'm dying here. I need my girl. I need to know she's okay.*

Michael: *You're gonna have to trust me. This is bad. Really fucking bad. She's not okay, but she's safe. I'll always keep her safe.*

"Fuck!" I set my phone on the breakfast bar before I throw it across the room. How can anything be worse than that video? I can't imagine what's in this next package, but if Michael says it's bad, then it's probably horrific—like worst nightmare horrific.

I change into a t-shirt and workout pants. It's gonna be a long day, and I need to run to work off some of my agitation. In the living room I find Jace and William pouring tumblers of the only scotch whisky that passes my lips, thanks to Fin's good taste.

"I hope one of those is for me." I flop down on the couch facing the door. I don't want to miss a second of scrutinizing Michael when he enters.

"They both are, if you need it, but I was hoping to join you." Jace hands me a glass before sitting across from me. "Have you heard anything?"

"William, Michael is with Samantha in penthouse 2C. He'd like you to go down there so he can come here to fill us in."

"On it, sir." He swiftly departs.

"Your mom sent over food. I left it on the counter, not knowing if you'd want to eat it while it's still relatively warm." Jace takes a sip of his whisky.

I, on the other hand, swallow it in one sweet-burning gulp. "Thanks, but I think I'm good with this for right now."

He refills my glass. "Don't get shit-faced, brother. You're gonna need a clear brain when Michael gets here."

"Funny. Michael told me I needed to get a couple of drinks in. Do you know something?"

He laughs. "No, I know my sister. She never would have asked for Michael instead of you unless it was something really bad and incriminating against you."

"Fuck," I hiss and take a slow sip this time.

"You don't have any idea what's happened?"

"Another package was delivered. Samantha ditched William at the grocery store and came here, and asked Michael to meet her, sans me."

"That completely blows."

My sentiments exactly.

Except for the calming music Jace turned on a few moments ago, we sit in silence while we wait for Michael.

We both jump up when the door opens. Michael looks worn out, like he's been up for two days straight instead of the five to six hours it's actually been. It's still early afternoon. His white button-down is rumpled and untucked, and I don't miss the smear of mascara on his chest.

"She's been crying?" I point to his shirt as I sit down on unsteady legs.

He pulls at his shirt, examines it, and then shrugs. "Yeah." In the kitchen he grabs a beer and then joins us in the seating area.

I wait. Impatiently.

He opens his beer, tossing the lid on the coffee table, and sets a manila envelope on his knee. After a long drink, he looks at me. "This was delivered to her in the women's restroom at the grocery store."

"Fuck. Is she okay? Did she see them? Did they hurt her?" Questions charge from my mouth like a runaway train.

He holds up his hand. "How 'bout you let me tell you, then you can ask questions?"

Testy. A testy Michael is not good. I simply nod. Otherwise, I might have to punch him.

"She's fine. Physically. She didn't see anyone. No one hurt her."

"Why did she ditch William?" Jace asks.

"I think once you see what's in this envelope, you won't ask that question." Michael looks to me. "I need to show you these in private." He points at Jace. "I'll explain why after." He gets up, taking his beer and the envelope, and heads to my office.

I finish off my scotch and follow, dread eating me up as I go. I close the door behind me and face Michael.

"You're going to need to sit down." He motions to the couch.

After I sit, he hands me a set of gloves that match the ones he's already wearing. I slip them on as he pulls something out of the envelope and sits on the coffee table in front of me.

"There's no way to warn you, other than to say it's bad. Really, really bad."

I nod my understanding. What is there really to say other than let's get it the fuck over with!

He was right to warn me. There's no way to prepare for what I see. I stare at it in disbelief. "I see it, but I don't believe it. There is no way that's me." I point at the woman's pelvis. "I've never been with a woman with a tattoo. I have no idea what that one says, but I'm pretty sure I'd remember, with it staring me in the face in that position." I hand it back to Michael. "Don't look so fucking pissed. It's not me."

Silently, he hands me the next picture. Same position, same woman, except her face is showing. "I've never…wait." I stand and then sit again. "Son of a bitch! That's the woman from the happy hour. The one Fin was questioning me about. She's a British tourist."

"Do you know her name?"

"No." I shrug and hand him back the pic. "I only talked to her for a few minutes. She and her friend wanted a selfie with me. That's the night

Samantha stayed home, upset because of the whole betting pool thing. Remember?"

He groans. "Don't remind me. That's the day I stuck my foot in my mouth and hurt her feelings."

"It's a sensitive issue for her. And this shit right here is not helping." I catch his gaze. "She thinks I've cheated on her, doesn't she? Because of these pics."

"Let's finish with the contents before we jump into what she's thinking. I need both your and Jace's feedback on these pics. It's quite a puzzle, and it seems each of you may have input to help pull it all together."

I hold out my hand. "Hit me."

He lays the third pic on my hand. "Ah, Christ." I close my eyes and turn my head. "That's Lydia." I try to hand it back to him.

"I'm sorry, man, but I really need you to look at these pics in detail and tell me what you see." He pushes my hand away.

Drawing a deep breath, I look at the pic again. But instead of looking at Lydia, I look at the guy. "That's not me. That's not my body. It may be my face, but this dude is skinner than me."

"What else do you see?"

"Uh…shit is that Vegas?" I look up. "Holy fuck, Samantha thinks I cheated on her in Vegas." I drop the pic and storm out of the office.

"Jace, don't let him go," Michael yells.

Jace jumps in front of me, holding me back. "Joe, just wait. Wait." He looks behind me at Michael.

"I've got to see her, Jace. She thinks I cheated on her."

"Joe, we need to finish this. It's going to take the three of us to figure this out. Until we do that, she's not going to see you. I promised her I'd find the truth. I intend to do that, but I can't do it without your help. Don't make her suffer longer than she has to. Come back to the office, and let's finish this. She's going to need real proof this time."

My head falls forward. He played the Samantha's suffering card, knowing there is no way I'd knowingly cause her any more pain. I back down.

"Jace, grab the Macallan and join us." Michael squeezes my shoulder as I reenter my office.

Michael collects the pictures, gives Jace some gloves, and repeats the same process he did with me, handing Jace one photo at a time.

Jace glances at the first one and then at me, his brow raised.

"Jace, I swear to you. *That* is not me." I point to the guy in the photo.

He shakes his head. "This is taking our relationship to a whole different level." His gaze bounces between Michael and me before landing back on the pic. He squints. "This guy is too skinny to be you."

"See, I told you," I say to Michael.

"Hey, do you have a magnifying glass?" Jace asks, looking closer at the photo. "That tattoo looks familiar."

"I think I have one—" I start to say.

"I don't think you'll need it once you see the next picture." Michael hands Jace the second photo.

"No fucking way." Jace looks at the photo, to me, and back to the photo. "Joe, do you know who this is?"

He says it like he knows who it is. "Who?"

"You don't recognize her?" He holds up the pic to my face.

"Wait." I look at Michael. "How does he know who it is? I only met her that one time at the bar. Jace wasn't there."

Michael smiles. "Now we're getting to the meat of it. Jace, tell Joe who it is."

"You really don't recognize her?" Jace asks me again.

"No! I saw her that one time in the bar, but you weren't there. She's a British tourist, but I never got her name, and I sure as shit didn't do to her what those pictures lead you to believe." This is insane. What the hell is going on?

"British tourist?" Jace frowns at me. "I can't believe you don't recognize her. You gave me such shit for dumping you and Sam to go home with her." He shakes his head, staring at the picture. "I can't believe it's her." He looks up at Michael. "Why would she do this? Besides the shit that happened with Sam, she's the sweetest girl I know."

I'm crawling out of my skin. "Who the fuck is she?" I nearly scream.

Jace's big blue eyes look at me with pure sadness. "It's Veronica. My Veronica."

The name takes a moment to come back to me. "Veronica Hamm? The one who hurt Samantha?"

He nods. "Yeah."

"Fuck. Wait. So, you're saying the British tourist isn't a British tourist at all and was Veronica? How did I not recognize her?"

He shrugs. "Even back then you only had eyes for Sam. I guess what she looked like didn't really register for you, only what she did to Sam made a lasting impression." He sets the photo on the table and looks at Michael. "Is there more?"

Michael hands him the last pic.

Jace studies it for a second, not even flinching. "Who is this?"

"It's Lydia, my old temp PA."

"The one you fired? You fucked her?"

"Christ." I stand up and pour myself three fingers of scotch. "Fin actually fired her since she was transferred to his department. And no, for the hundredth time, I didn't fuck anyone. I haven't had sex with a single solitary person in over two years except Samantha and that bitch Tiff. Which I still don't remember, but we're being technical here, so there." I set down the bottle harder than I should and take a large gulp from my tumbler, when I'd rather drink it from the bottle.

I turn to them. "Look at that guy in the picture. You've both seen me practically naked. That guy is not me. He's a different body type than me, close, but smaller and probably shorter, but my thighs are bigger. My chest is wider, and my guns are definitely bigger than that guy's."

Jace looks at the picture again. "Shit. Did you see the reflection?"

Michael nods.

I lean against the wall, not really wanting to look at Lydia getting nailed by some guy who's been digitally altered to look like me. "What?"

Jace holds up the pic and points to the window. "Veronica is there, taking the pic, and giving us the finger."

"Sam thinks she's giving *her* the finger," Michaels speaks up. He's been rather quiet.

"Michael, what do you think?" I resume my seat on the couch.

"I think Veronica Hamm is Bonnie. I think she's the mastermind behind all of this. What I don't know is why or how she got ahold of Joe's blue tie, or if these pictures are doctored." He holds up his finger. "We'll get back to that. Here." He hands me the note that came with the photos. "You need to read this before we get into the other details."

"Motherfucking bitch from hell." I hand the paper to Jace. My eyes lock with Michael's. "You don't believe me. That those pictures aren't me."

The look of guilt tells me all I need to know.

"Actually, I believe you, Joe." His response is not what I was expecting. "To be honest, I didn't initially. At first glance, those pics are awfully incriminating. The photo from the fourth package was you. The video from the fifth package was you. The underwear and tie are yours. This next set of photos are good—whoever doctored them is really talented. But mostly, when I look at you, Joe, I see a man who's so in love with one woman, that there is no way in hell you'd cheat. I know you, man, and even if you did cheat, you wouldn't keep lying about it. You'd fess up. Shit, man, you even fessed up to sleeping with Tiff, and she's the one who raped you. You don't even remember it, yet you still owned up to it like you cheated."

He stands before me, his hand outstretched. I take it, and he pulls me to my feet. His hand holds mine tightly, and his other grips my shoulder. "You listen to me." His brow is pinched, and his eyes stare at me like he's pissed off, but his words tell me otherwise. "You did not cheat. You. Were. Raped. Whether you remember it or not. That's the truth of it. I don't know if you still harbor any guilt about it. But you need to let that shit go. Understand?"

"Yeah." I nearly choke on my reply. That's the most Michael's ever said to me about the Tiff incident. He's always made it clear he believed me, but still, the level of his support is moving. "Thanks, brother."

"Don't mention it, brother." With a squeeze of my shoulder, he releases me, moving back to his chair.

"All this stuff doesn't help, does it?" Jace motions to the photos and letter on the table.

I sit back down. "No, it doesn't help having it thrown in my face over and over again. The worst part, though, is how it's impacted my girl. I'll endure any hardship if only to save her from all of this."

"You need to remember that, Joe. She's really upset. I know she wants to believe in you, but her self-doubt and lack of confidence in being able to compete with all of this is eating her up. She doesn't want to see you. She made me promise that if she remained at MCI Towers, where we can keep her safe and under our watchful eye, then I have to keep you away. If you force her to see you, she'll run. She's proven herself to be quick on her feet and calculating. I have no doubt if she wanted to, she could evade our protection like she did today, or before when she plotted to meet up with Daniel's killer. She's smart. We all know it, and she's not afraid to put herself in danger if she believes it's for the greater good."

"Okay, I'll agree to it for now, but I don't know how long I can go without seeing her. I also have one condition. I need to go to her tonight. Even if it's only to talk to her through the door. I *have* to speak to her. I *need* to do this."

Thankfully, he agrees, and we spend the next few minutes filling Michael in on why Veronica hates Samantha so much, and what Veronica did to her in high school.

"Jace, you had no idea?" Michael asks in disbelief.

"No. You know I'm a self-absorbed prick. I had no idea any of the girls I hung out with were bitchy to Sam. Joe filled me in. I still can't believe it. I was so oblivious. Veronica has always been so sweet and quiet, maybe a little standoffish with the other girls. But I had no idea she was plotting against Sam. Veronica was never catty like that in front of me. But the whole blowjob set-up thing—that's a level of spite I couldn't ignore. I cut off all ties with Veronica that Thanksgiving. The last time I saw her was at Dad's funeral."

"You didn't tell me she was there." I'm not too happy about that.

"She didn't approach Sam or me, so I figured it was harmless. Plus, I didn't want to upset Sam by bringing it up."

Understandable. "What are you thinking, Michael?"

He collects the evidence and puts it back in the envelope. "I think I need to get these to my forensics guy, but I want to show Victor first. Then we need to find Veronica and get a confession out of her, or prove it's not you in these photos." He stands. "We need concrete proof to show Sam."

"We'd better fucking hurry. We get married in less than four weeks." I glare at them both. "Don't even think it. There is no way in hell I'm not marrying my girl."

Fifteen

YOU ARE THE REASON

Joseph

MY ALCOHOL-INDUCED CALM HAS PASSED, AND now the need to see my girl is overpowering. I'm done waiting. I send Michael a text telling him I'm on my way. I take a couple of Advil, grab a water, and head to the penthouse below ours.

She's only one floor away, but it feels like a continent at the moment. A floor, a door, the width of our clothing, a single breath between us seems too great a distance.

I knock, knowing it won't open, praying she'll at least listen if nothing else. There's shuffling on the other side, a few murmurs. Then I hear Michael. "She's here. She can hear you."

On a thankful sigh, I lean against the door and speak into the crack that separates us. "Sweetness." My voice breaks, and I have to take a couple of deep breaths to keep my shit together.

With steadier emotions, I try again. "Those pictures...the guy in them. It's not me. I know all the evidence tells you otherwise. But it's not me, and I'll prove it to you. Don't give up on me—on us. Give me time to find Veronica and get to the bottom of it."

Her sob breeches the barrier between us, and it guts me.

"Sweetness, please let me in. Let me hold you. Comfort you."

More sobs.

"I'm sorry. I'm so fucking sorry."

She wails.

Shit! "No. I'm not apologizing because I cheated. I didn't. Those photos are not me. I understand why you think they could be real, but I promise you they aren't. I'm sorry for hurting you, for making you doubt me, for everything that Veronica's done to you."

"Us," she croaks from the other side.

I gasp on my own sob. "Yes. Us. What's she's done to *us*."

She spoke to me. She thinks we're still an *us*. There is hope, and I'm not letting go of it. "I'm here. I'm not going anywhere. You cry, and I'll sit here and comfort you." I slide down the door, sitting sideways, my lips pressed to the crack, and I swear I can feel her breath slipping through and feeding my soul.

"Joseph," she cries with such anguish. Her voice is even with mine, confirming she's on the floor too.

"I'm here, Samantha. I promise you I'll always be here. Until my dying day, I'll always be here."

Her crying stops only to start up again. Hours pass and eventually she falls silent as do I, afraid if she's fallen asleep, my voice will wake her up.

My ass is numb, and I'm sore from sitting in the same position, but I don't dare move. Her cries, her words, her silence are the only company—only comfort—I need.

I start to doze. My head falls forward, and I catch myself. I've ignored offers from William to get me something more comfortable to sit on. I'm not going anywhere. I'll sleep right here on this cold hard floor. It's as close as I can get to her. I need to be here if she needs me.

At some point, I must have fallen over. I open my eyes and blink at Michael, who is staring down at me. He throws me a pillow and comforter. "She fell asleep. I put her in bed, but she insisted I give you those if you're going to stay out here all night."

I sit up, smiling. "She still cares."

Michael laughs. "Of course she cares, jackass. You don't cry your eyes out over someone you don't give a shit about." He throws something at William. "The key to 2D. He's gonna have to go to the bathroom eventually. Maybe you can drag him inside once he falls asleep."

"I'll fire you if you do." I crack my neck and smile at my comforter and pillow. My girl is looking out for me. It's a good sign.

Day 2

Joseph

I wake on the hard floor, wrapped in the comforter, my head on the pillow and a smile on my face. Things don't seem so bleak today. My girl spoke to me last night. She made sure my camping out at her door was as comfortable as possible, and she still considers us an *us*. That's huge.

Stretching out my aches, I get to my feet and spot Victor in a chair outside the other penthouse door. "Good morning, lover boy. Breakfast and coffee are inside, if you'd like some." He stands as I approach.

I shove the comforter and pillow at him. "Take care of these, will you? I'll need them later."

"Yes, sir." He chuckles, finding this way too humorous.

First stop, the bathroom, then breakfast, and then attacking my plan to woo my girl and prove my innocence.

Samantha

When my father died, I thought I knew what darkness was. When I broke up with Joseph, believing he slept with someone else that same night, I didn't think I could sink any lower. I was wrong. I should know better than to tempt fate, believing it couldn't get any worse. It can always get worse.

I'm not going to say this is the worst—that I can't go any lower—the whole fate thing has me skittish. So, I'll just say—it sucks. I'm feeling emotionally hung over, and in desperate need of my Joseph fix.

He couldn't have been any sweeter last night. He didn't force his way in. My Caveman honored my wishes, my request that he not try to see me. He kept his word, comforting me from the other side of the door in a way that only Joseph can do with a simple turn of a phrase. He might be a caveman, but he's a romantic beast.

Flowers. He sent me the largest arrangement of flowers I've ever seen. There have to be six dozen roses, at least. William sets it on the coffee table and hands me the card.

> *My Sweets,*
> *I love you more with every passing moment.*
> *Don't let the doubt in.*
> *Check out the newest song in your music library.*
> *You are the reason for everything I do, for everything I am,*
> *for everything I will be.*
>
> *I love you,*
> *Joseph*

I pull up my music on my phone, and there in my library is a new song, "You Are The Reason" by Calum Scott. I hit play, and by the end of the first verse I'm crying.

I send him a text as I continue to listen.

Me: *You break my heart in the most amazing ways.*

Joseph: *If I'm breaking your heart, then I'm doing something wrong, Sweets.*

Me: *You're doing everything right, Caveman.*

I wipe my tears and lie back on the couch, his card held to my chest. As I listen to his song again, my phone chimes.

Joseph: *I'll be at your door after dinner. I'll bring my blanket and pillow. You don't have to say a word. I need to be close to you. To feel you near.*

That night and the two that follow, Joseph shows up after dinner. He sits outside the penthouse door, talking to me through the crack. Sometimes I answer, but most times I don't trust myself to not break down. I love him, and I know he loves me. I don't know how we move past this. How can I marry him after seeing those pictures? Those pictures that don't make any sense to me. How could he cheat on me with Veronica, of all people, and that bitch Lydia?

He wouldn't! But...I don't know what to believe. My heart and my eyes don't agree, and I can't bear to look at those pictures again—to study them—to pick them apart—to see if I can tell truth from lies. So, I don't. I stay sequestered the Friday after Thanksgiving through the weekend. The only time I feel alive is when Joseph is sitting outside my door at night, telling me he loves me and that he'll prove his innocence.

Proof. I need proof, and that's what he's promising. So, I wait each day for him to show me he's not a cheater—that it's all a scam—concocted by one of my brother's ex-sluts and my fiancé's bitter ex-PA, all in an effort to get back at me for a wrong they believe I've done them, when in fact, I've done absolutely nothing.

But sometimes life and people don't care much about truth or what's right. Sometimes life throws a tantrum, and those in its wake just have to hold on, ride it out, and pray—pray—for mercy.

Sixteen

I WILL WAIT

DECEMBER

Joseph

DAY 5

MONDAY. THANK GOD. THE WEEKEND WAS torture without my girl. I welcome the distraction of work and an office full of people and meetings. I've avoided my parents for as long as I can, with Fin running interference. Matt is finally back in town. I don't know where the fuck he's been, but I've been a little busy with my own shitstorm to worry about him.

I enter Dad's office and close the door, finding Dad giving Matt the third degree. Fin sits on the couch, busy on his phone, but it's a ruse. Taking a seat next to him, I silently ask what's going on with a single look. All I get is a shrug and a raised eyebrow.

Matt looks uncomfortable, like he'd rather be anywhere else than here.

"You requisition a company plane to fly to Sin City for a week and don't even bother to call your mother to let her know you won't be home for Thanksgiving!" Dad's voice is getting rougher the redder his face gets.

I feel like I'm fifteen and about to get grounded, waiting for my turn on the chopping block.

"Actually, we only spent two nights in Vegas. We went skiing for Thanksgiving," Matt tries to clarify, like that's going to make a difference.

But then it registers—what he said. I elbow Fin. "Uh, Vegas?" I ask loud enough for them to hear me.

All eyes zoom to me.

"You have something to add, Joseph?" Yeah, Dad using my full name is not a good sign.

I stand and clear my throat. "Who were you in Vegas with?"

Matt scowls and looks away. "What difference does it make?"

"Bear with me." I look at Fin to see if he's caught on to my train of thought, but the crease in his forehead tells me he hasn't. "Who were you with in Vegas?" I ask again with an edge to my voice.

Matt avoids eye contact like his life depends on it.

In a heartbeat I'm in his face. "What's. Her. Name?" My body hums in agitation for what I believe is coming.

Dad steps forward, pushing us apart. "What's going on, Joseph?"

Ignoring my father, I glare at Matt.

"Spit it out Matt, before he pummels you." Fin joins me at my side, facing Matt.

"Lydia." Matt steps back as if I'm going to attack him.

But that's not the case, not at all. I'm filled with elation.

"Who else?" Fin asks, finally catching on.

"Some chick you don't know." Matt frowns at us walking to the sitting area, putting the couch between us.

I nearly laugh. If I wanted to get to him, that couch would not stop me. "Her name?"

"Joe, what the hell is going on?" Dad moves toward Matt, looking between the three of us like he doesn't know who he needs to protect and who he needs to scold.

"Just…" I hold up my hand to the man who gave me life. "Give me a second, then I'll explain."

"Matt," Fin barks.

"Bonnie. Her name was Bonnie, for fuck's sake. Jeez." Matt looks at us like we're crazy.

I try to catch my breath. "Thank, God." I collapse on the couch, my head in my hands. "Someone get Michael and Victor in here. Now!"

Samantha

The bed seems particularly empty this morning. Melancholy oozes from my pores. The sun coming in from the bedroom windows is entirely too chipper. But I'm glad it's Monday. I need the distraction of school to eat away the hours between now and when Joseph comes this evening.

William escorts me to the car. I'm in a daze. I can't get my mind off the last thing Joseph said to me last night, and every night since those damn photos showed up.

I'll prove it to you. I'll prove my innocence.

Proof. I keep saying I need proof.

But what does that mean?

What kind of proof do I need?

Do I need some sort of forensics report stating the pictures are fakes?

Couldn't that be doctored as well? Who's to say Victor or Michael won't have one of their contacts provide a fake report? I'd never know the difference. It's not like I'm an expert in photographic forensics. I don't know what I'm looking for. I don't know what verbiage on the report would satisfy my need for proof.

How far am I willing to take this until I'm convinced Joseph didn't cheat on me?

How long am I willing to live without him? A month? A year? Forever?

Am I going to cancel the wedding? Why? Because some bitch sent me a photo that may or may not be real? I know Joseph. *His love* for me is real. *That's* what matters.

Dizzy with a wave of nausea, I grip my stomach and lean forward. *What the hell am I doing?*

"Stop! We have to go back."

"Are you okay? Are you going to be sick?" William's concern is evident.

"No. Turn around."

Damn downtown. It takes three rights to make a left with all these one-way streets. Finally. Finally, we pull into the garage. As soon as we're parked, I jump out and run to the Alpha Tower elevators. "Come on."

"Sam?" The sound of William's pounding feet get closer until he catches up with me.

I glance over. "Don't tell him I'm coming."

He smiles. "No, ma'am. I wouldn't dare."

I walk laps in the elevator. William simply stands back, watching me in amusement.

When the doors open, he steps in front of me. "At least let me get out first."

I nod. I've broken all kinds of protocols already. And if I have my way, I'm about to break some more.

With his okay, I rush to Joseph's office.

Teddy stands when he sees me. "Sam. God, he's going to be so happy to see you."

I hope so. "Hi, Teddy." I motion to the door. "Can I?"

He smiles. "I wouldn't stop you for the world."

I return his smile, but a rush of fear stops me from opening the door.

"Go on," Teddy whispers from behind me.

I subdue my emotions on a deep breath and slow exhale, and then open the door and step inside.

Joseph rises to his feet. "Samantha."

As soon as I see him, my emotions crash into me. Tears prick my eyes, and I cup my mouth to stop a sob from escaping. Five days. It's been five torturous days.

What the hell was I thinking?

Joseph rushes to me. "What happened?" He collects me against his chest as soon as I'm within reach.

I can't answer him. The dam has broken free, and there's no stopping it now.

"Nothing. Nothing happened. She… needed to see you," William says.

A mass of noise and shuffling pass by us, and then silence. Except for my sniffles and stunted breaths, I hear nothing else.

Joseph whisks me off my feet and sits with me on his lap. "Christ, it's good to see you, to hold you in my arms." His lips brush my forehead as his warm breath skirts my face. "Tell me what's going on."

"I believe you." I look up, meeting his eyes. "I believe *in* you."

"Thank fuck," he sighs, his relief palpable. "What changed?" I start to pull back, but he stops me. "Please don't. I need to hold you."

I cup his cheek. "I'm not going anywhere. I just need to see you."

He situates us so he's holding me as close as possible while still making eye contact. "Better?"

I smile my reply, but when I see his fatigue-worn eyes, my chin starts to quiver. "I've missed you so much."

He runs his hand down the side of my face. "I was there. I was always there."

"I know." I bite my lip and close my eyes to stop from crying.

"Hey." He taps my cheek, and I open my eyes. "Don't hold it in. If you need to cry, cry. I'm not going anywhere. I'll wait forever to hear what you have to say."

"I'm so sorry. I feel like I'm always apologizing for being a step behind, for not being confident enough in our relationship to trust you without proof." I run my fingers through his hair. *God, I've missed this hair.* "But you know what? I had proof all along."

"You did?" He truly seems perplexed.

I nod. "Your love. Your commitment to me for the past two years, even when we weren't together. Your eye never strays from mine. You don't ogle women when you think I'm not looking. You don't tolerate threats. You simply remove them—hence, Lydia. You've never been a playboy even in your most single of days before me. You're a one-woman man—and I'm *it*."

"Yes, yes you are." His smile, even tired, is still devilishly handsome.

"I don't know if you can forgive me, but I pray you will. And if you'll still have me. I'd like to marry you in three weeks."

His lips crash into mine. *Oh, god, I've missed these lips.* But he pulls away on a groan, ending the kiss too soon. "Sweets, there was never any chance of you not marrying me in three weeks." His desirous stare and growled words send a chill through my body.

"God, I've missed you, Caveman."

Seventeen

STILL YOURS

Joseph

WE MANAGE TO MAKE IT TO THE PENTHOUSE before we launch at each other. Five days. Five fucking days without my girl. "Never again," I hiss as our mouths collide in a needful, hungry kiss. She moans, latching on to my hair and the back of my neck, trying to consume me, keep me from pulling away. No way am I stopping. Not now. Not ever.

I lift her off her feet, and she wraps her legs around my waist as I cup her bite-worthy ass. To the soundtrack of our moans and lustful kisses, I make my way to our bedroom and drop her on the bed. She giggles on a bounce as I free my cock and relieve her of her panties. "Thank god for skirts."

She squirms as I gather the material over her hips and settle between her thighs. All thought of removing shoes or any other articles of clothing is lost in a single thrust, sheathing my rock-hard cock in her warmth. "Fuck." My eyes lock on hers, telling me everything I need to know.

"Kiss me," she pleads, lifting her legs, spreading, welcoming me to sink in deeper.

170

And I do. I anchor my forearms under her shoulders, and my hands are lost in her hair. My lips brush hers tenderly as I grind my hips, burrowing as deeply as I possibly can. She clutches me to her, pulling, as if she's trying to absorb me into her body. "Kiss me," she repeats, but I know what she really means is *fuck me*.

"Sweetness," I breathe before the caveman takes over, consuming her mouth as I drive my cock into her over and over again, setting a relentless pace.

Ravenous, my girl asks for more. "Harder. Faster."

"Fuck." She's gonna unman me with her moans and need for me to claim her, to take her, to love her even in this heated mania.

My phone starts ring.

"Ignore it," I command myself and her, kissing her harder.

Her phone starts to ring.

I growl and pound harder. "Stay with me…"

A door slams as shuffling feet and low murmurs come from the entryway. "Joe!"

"Christ. Fuck. We're not done. Don't move." I pull out on a groan and stalk to our bedroom door. "Fifteen minutes. You better be dying!" I bellow and slam the door, locking it.

Samantha giggles from the bed, closes her legs and starts to pull down her skirt.

"No. No fucking way are those assholes stopping me from making love to you." I climb back on the bed and still her hands.

"It's okay. We can do this later."

"*Do this later?*" I hover over her on all fours, my eyes searching hers, watching her trying to calm her breathing. "No, Sweets. You came back to me, and not even the end of the world could stop me from being with you." I settle between her thighs, rubbing my cock through her wet folds. "Now, where were we?" I pull back and push into her deliciously slowly.

Her back arches. "Oh, god."

I pull out and push in again slowly, ever so slowly. "Was this where I was?"

"Nearly," she mews.

Out and in a little faster, a little deeper. "Here?"

"Almost," she moans, her eyes begging for more.

Ah, fuck, my sexy girl. I thrust. Deeper. Harder. Pumping. In. Out. In. Out.

She moans, clutching me to her. Her whole body shaking, begging for release.

"How about now, baby? Is this where I was?"

"Yes! Oh, god, yes!"

My mouth consumes hers, plunging, teasing, sucking as my body rides her like the best damn seesaw I've ever been on. Back and forth. Our hips rocking together. Back and forth. Her knees come up. Her feet lock below my ass and squeeze with each thrust.

"Fuck. Just like that, my Sweets."

Harder. Deeper.

Faster. Faster.

"Joseph." She's warning me, praising me, telling me she's coming.

"Yes. Come for me, baby."

And she does. Christ Almighty, she does. Gripping my cock with the most glorious pussy I'll ever know, she shatters, calling my name, begging me not to stop—like I'd ever stop. She comes undone and takes me with her.

I groan my release with quick thrusts, bury my face in her neck, and nearly weep—so thankful to have her back in my arms, in my life—asking me to fuck her and never stop.

Never stop.

My girl.

Samantha

I'm panting, trying to recover with Joseph's dead weight pressing me into the mattress, or maybe it's me still clutching him to me—with my arms and legs—like he'd float away if I let go. A deep breath, a steady exhale, I slowly loosen my grip—not completely—but enough for him to lift his head.

His lips and warm breath kiss along my jaw, nip my chin, and down the other side. "You okay, Sweetness?"

"Yeah. You?"

The green eyes I love so much come into view. A slow smile ticks across his lips. He thrusts his hips, reminding me we're still joined. "I couldn't be any better." His mouth moves lovingly over mine with slow brushes of his tongue pushing my lips apart, languidly kissing me until he starts to harden and twitch inside me. He pulls back on a groan. "I guess I need to go see what the guys want."

Dazed, I simply nod.

He smiles, then presses his mouth to mine softly. "Hurry, come join me."

I whimper when he pulls away, sliding out of me.

Before I can close my legs, he dips his head and lays a gentle kiss above my clit, his tongue sweeping out and pressing ever so tenderly.

I gasp and nearly bow off the bed.

He does it again and again, holding my legs open, pinned to the bed. His fingers plunge inside slowly, caressing that tender spot that makes me want him even more.

I clutch the comforter, close my eyes, and pray he doesn't stop.

He doesn't.

Thank god.

Thirty minutes later, we walk into the living room. Joseph sits on the couch and pulls me next to him with my legs flung over his, one arm behind my back, while the other rests over my legs. Michael, Victor,

Jace, Fin, and Matt are scattered around the room, talking, getting drinks from the bar, food from the kitchen, and completely oblivious to us joining them.

Fin quirks a smile when he spots us. "Nice of you to join us. Enjoy yourselves?"

Joseph squeezes my leg. "Fuck off."

"I'll take that as a *yes*," Fin teases, offering to get us drinks.

Once everyone has settled, all eyes focus on Michael, who looks to me and then Joseph. "So, you told her?"

My love's hand kneads my leg as if to soothe his response. "No, not yet."

Michael's eyebrows arch as if to say *why the fuck not?*

I meet Joseph's gaze, his eyes hopeful, if not a little sad. "Right before you came to me, we discovered that it was actually Matt in the pictures with Veronica and Lydia."

Holy shit! I seek out Jace and then Matt to see how they're handling this news. "Matt, you were in Vegas?"

He simply nods, obviously embarrassed.

"But how…your face?" I stumble, looking to Joseph.

"They were doctored," Victor speaks up. "With Matt and Joseph looking so much alike, it's easy to do."

"Not you?" I whisper to Joseph's blurry face.

He swipes at my tears. "Not me, baby."

"Oh, god. I'm so sorry," I bawl.

Joseph pulls me to his chest, my face buried in his neck. "Shh, Sweetness. None of that. You believed me before you had proof. There's nothing to be sorry for. Anyone would have doubted with the evidence stacked against me."

That only makes me cry harder.

"Asshole! I can't believe you fucked her!" Jace's voice breeches my meltdown.

Matt backs up, hands in the air, not wanting to fight Jace. "I didn't sleep with her, brother. She wasn't interested. I didn't even know who she was. If I'd known Bonnie was actually your Veronica, I never would have done anything with her. I swear."

Jace halts his advance. "You didn't sleep with her?"

"I swear. The only thing that happened is what you saw in that picture. She didn't even touch me. I thought she had some crazy kink and only wanted to watch, take pictures." Matt lowers his hands and slowly moves toward Jace. "I swear, brother, I didn't know it was Vee. *Your* Vee"

Vee? *His* Vee? "Jace?"

He glances at me. "Leave it, Sam." He's hurt, really hurt.

"I swear," Matt reiterates.

Jace simply nods, grabs his glass full of what I assume is Fin's favorite indulgence, and sits in the nearest chair, brows drawn, not open to further discussion.

We take a break and devour the Chinese food Fin ordered. Jace joins in, alcohol having mellowed his anger. Matt, a little self-conscious, is quiet but not closed off. Michael and Victor keep exchanging glances like they have a secret, which they usually do. Fin watches everyone, calculating who is gonna freak out next. Me? I keep looking at Joseph, finding him looking at me with a beaming smile. My heart soars but flutters a little each time I think about how I doubted him. Reading me like he always does, he simply touches me, gives me a squeeze, or a kiss—each time telling me he forgives me—he loves me—and to stop beating myself up.

Once dinner is cleaned up, we reassemble in the living room. I reclaim my seat next to Joseph, who can't keep his hands off me—not complaining.

This time it's Victor who speaks. "After the revelation this morning, Matt agreed to call Lydia and ask that she and Bonnie meet him for an early lunch under the ruse that he had gifts for them as a thank you for their time in Vegas."

None of us misses Jace's scoff from across the room.

Victor gives him a sympathetic glance before continuing. He points to Matt. "Needless to say, Matt didn't show. However, the ladies did."

Joseph leans forward. "Tell me you have them."

"We have them."

"Holy shit," Fin says.

"No. Fucking. Way," Joseph punctuates before meeting my gaze. "We have them," he whispers, pulling me closer.

"What does this mean?" I ask.

Michael moves to sit on the coffee table in front of me. "It means it's over, Princess."

I lean forward. "But we can't hold them. It's not legal." I glance around the room. "Have they broken any laws?"

Joseph takes my hand, moving closer. "Lydia broke her Non-Disclosure Agreement by sharing information she acquired while employed at MCI. Her NDA applies while she was an active employee, and for three years after she leaves the company either of her own accord or released. She shared information with Veronica that breached that agreement. Additionally, though Veronica did not blackmail us to extort money, Lydia and Tiff colluded with Veronica in acquiring defamatory information with the sole purpose of causing emotional distress to a VP at MCI and his fiancée. We may not be able to bring criminal charges against them, but we can sue the three of them in civil court for emotional distress and defamation of character. Even if we don't win, we could tie them up for years and bankrupt them for life."

Holy shit. Joseph as a hot lawyer nearly trumps Joseph as a hot VP—nearly. My panties just got wet.

He smirks as if he can read my mind.

"But...w-we can't hold them," I stutter, overwhelmed by Joseph's hot lawyer persona.

"We're simply providing accommodations for them while we negotiate their surrender," Victor offers.

I look to Michael, the only one in this room with recent law enforcement experience. He simply smiles. "We have it handled, Sam. We need to know how you want to move forward."

"How *I* want to move forward?" I look at the men in this room. All of them are watching me as if I have jurisdiction on how this should play out.

"Michael, you should share the additional information you have on Veronica before any decisions are made." Victor looks at me, Jace, and then Joseph, trying to impart some secret meaning that I don't understand.

Michael scowls. "I wanted to know what she wanted to do first before this information skews her decision." He's looking at me, but I know his bark is for Victor.

"What information?" Joseph asks.

Silently, Michael refills Jace's glass of Macallan, pours one for Joseph, and hands the bottle to Fin, then pours me a glass of FAT Bastard Merlot. "You're gonna need this, Princess."

His sad eyes have me on edge. I sit back, curling into Joseph's side, and take a sip of my wine.

Michael resettles on the coffee table. It's disconcerting he feels he needs to be this close to me. I grab Joseph's hand, take another drink, and wait.

Fin refills his glass. Victor and Michael stick to beer, which I don't think either have touched. Another reason to be concerned—they feel they need to keep their faculties sharp—which should be comforting, but it only means things aren't as *wrapped up* as they want me to believe.

Michael leans forward, his muscular arms resting on his knees, his hands steepled, and his eyes on me. "Do you remember those unidentified fingerprints my forensics guy found on the evidence?"

"Yes, you were going to send them off to another contact who has access to additional databases. Did he get a hit?" I reply.

He smirks. "Yeah, he got a *hit*."

My pulse ramps up, and Joseph must sense it as he squeezes my hand and pulls me closer.

"We didn't find the contributor because we were looking for perps—someone with a criminal record. When no match could be found, we broadened our search to include victims." Michael glances at Jace.

Shit.

"We found a match in a closed case from a few years ago. Three years to be exact. The perp was a single father who abused his kids when he got drunk—and he was drunk a lot."

Victor clears his voice.

Michael looks down for a moment before straightening up, squaring his shoulders. "Abuse is too kind of a word for this scumbag. He raped his kids. The daughter from the time she was eleven to sixteen, and the son from the age of ten to thirteen. The abuse stopped when the young girl fled from their home, taking her younger brother with her. They were homeless for a year. Living out of her car, working odd jobs, and going to school. No one knew they were homeless. Not teachers. Not friends—though they had few of those."

With each passing moment—each excruciating word—my heart breaks for these kids. "Who are they?"

Michael takes a deep breath before answering, "Veronica Hamm and her brother Spencer."

"Holy shit," I gasp, glancing at Jace. He's as shocked as I am.

"They were eventually caught stealing food from a local grocery store. One thing led to another, and charges were brought against the father. He was found guilty and is currently serving time. Veronica turned eighteen shortly after her father was sentenced and was released from the system. Her brother ran away shortly after Veronica was removed from the foster home they resided in and before she could make arrangements to be his guardian. He hasn't been heard from since."

Jesus.

Jace sinks into the chair as if he wishes it would swallow him whole.

Michael turns to him when he continues. "When reading her file, I noticed something interesting. Veronica was interviewed by a social worker when she was first taken into custody. The social worker asked why she didn't go to live with her grandparents in Oklahoma or go to the authorities to report her father. Veronica said she couldn't bear to leave the only person who showed her and her brother any genuine kindness. The social worker surmised Veronica was probably in love or highly infatuated with this person to the point where she was willing to endure her father's wrath, and then homelessness, in order to remain close to this special person in her life."

"Don't say it," Jace pleads.

"I'm sorry, brother." Michael genuinely looks upset. "The name the social worker wrote down was Jace Cavanagh."

I gasp. I should have seen it coming, but that was one surprise I didn't anticipate. I thought Veronica was only an easy lay to Jace. But it looks like she meant more to him than he ever let on, spending time with Veronica and her younger brother, obviously doing things other than just sex. And he meant more to her. "I took you away from her."

Jace sits up. "No, Sam. She hurt you for no reason, and I cut her from my life. *I'm* the one who took me away. You didn't do anything wrong."

I stand up, handing Michael my wine glass. "Then why does it feel like I did?" I feel dizzy, like I can't breathe. I walk to Joseph's office before anyone can stop me. I need a minute to think.

SAY YOU WON'T LET GO

Joseph

JACE AND I FOLLOW SAMANTHA INTO MY OFFICE. The news of Veronica's past is unexpected. It's hit all of us hard, but none harder than Jace and Samantha.

"I took you away from her, so she wants to take Joseph away from me." She's facing the window and doesn't even turn around as she speaks. "I'm so sorry, Jace."

"Fuck. *You're* sorry? I'm the one who hung out with them. I had no idea." Jace plops down on the couch.

I stand close to Samantha, wanting to comfort her but getting the feeling she needs a minute to process this before I overwhelm her with my need to make this right, to make it better for *her*.

When she finally looks at me, the sadness in her eyes draws me to her. I cup her cheek, moving in close. "Tell me what you need." It's a simple phrase, and by the way her shoulders relax, it's what she needed to hear.

"I want to help her. She's had enough heartache in her life. Maybe she needs someone to give her a break." She glances at Jace before returning her focus to me. "Give her some money. Find her a place to live.

180

Pay for her to go to college—if she wants—get her help, but let's not take anything else from her. She's endured enough."

I may have suspected she'd want to let her go, but I didn't anticipate her wanting to bankroll her. "Are you sure?"

"Jace, are you okay with that?" She wants to make this right for Jace, too.

His head comes up. "We need to find Spencer. He was such a great kid." His voice breaks as he looks away.

"We can do that. We can do all of that," I confirm. "What about Tiff and Lydia?"

On a humorless laugh, Samantha steps back. "Sue them, or threaten to sue them. Make them sign something that's legally binding keeping them from doing anything like this in the future. Do whatever it takes to make it go away." Her hand waves in the air. "Just make them go away."

We rejoin the others in the living room. No one is surprised to hear Samantha and Jace want to help Veronica and her brother. Though, I'm not sure they were prepared for the level of support we're suggesting.

"We could fund Veronica and her brother through MCI's scholarship program," Fin suggests, much to Samantha's delight.

"She needs to sign the same legal document, saying she won't try something like this again in the future or try to get more money out of you," Victor steps in. "Helping her is one thing, but making a dependent out of her is another."

Samantha nods. "She's obviously smart, smart enough to stay under the radar for a year while living out of her car, taking care of her brother, working, and still going to school. She's a survivor. I think she needs an environment where she can do better than merely survive. I want her to have the opportunity to thrive and make a future for herself and her brother."

"Veronica was smart enough to pull this whole emotional blackmail scheme together too. Don't forget that." Michael brings us back to reality.

Samantha's smile grows larger. "Even more reason to give her something productive to focus on. A bored, under-utilized brain is a dangerous one. Let's give her a chance to find a better use for her talents."

Michael nods. "Okay, Victor and I will talk to them and make the deal."

"I want to talk to them." I have things I need to make one hundred percent clear.

"Is that smart, brother?" Fin sets his glass down and moves closer. "It might be better to let someone less emotionally impacted by this situation handle it."

I chuckle. "You think I'm going to go all caveman on them?"

Fin's smirk tells me he understands my need to confront those who have caused us so much pain. "Don't say or do anything that will give them cause to sue *us*."

"Understood." I'm capable of keeping my emotions in check, particularly when it comes to protecting my girl and our future.

"What about you, Sam? Do you have something you want to say to them?" Michael asks.

She shakes her head. "No, I trust Joseph to say what needs to be said to Lydia and Tiff. As for Veronica, her past doesn't excuse what she did to me, but it changes the way I see her, and I want to help. I doubt she's in a place to hear anything I have to say. Maybe someday she'll be more open to it. But for now, giving her a chance is all the closure I need."

With a kiss, I leave Samantha with Fin as the rest of us leave to wrap up our loose ends; and give Matt, Jace, and me a chance to find closure with three women who have impacted our lives in substantial, yet different ways. I don't envy these women the shitstorm of testosterone they're about to encounter.

Samantha

While Joseph is gone, Fin helps me move my stuff from my temporary penthouse lodgings back home. I didn't have much, so we manage to get it done in one trip. Afterwards, we sit on the couch and watch one of my dirty little pleasures—okay, not so dirty, but definitely a pleasure—*Outlander*. I got Fin hooked on it when I was living with him for a few months after my father died and before I graduated high school. It could have been awkward living with the brother of my kinda boyfriend at the time—now my fiancé—but it wasn't. Fin reminds me enough of Joseph to make me comfortable. Add in protectiveness like a brother, a heart like a lion, and a wicked sense of humor and, well, I plain love the guy.

We've finished two episodes and started another when Fin pauses the show. It takes me a second to realize he's not getting up to go to bathroom. He's sitting here staring at me.

"What?" I resist the urge to wipe my nose to check if I have a bat in the cave.

"Are you sure you're okay? Do you want to talk about it?"

Talk about it? "Hmm...other than feeling bad for doubting your brother, I'm not sure what else there is to talk about." Is *he* wanting to talk about it, or maybe he wants to talk about Margot? "Do *you* have something you want to talk about?"

"Me?" He frowns. "No, I want to be sure you're really okay and not hiding from us."

I smile. "Us? Are we an *us* now?" I can't resist teasing him.

He shakes his head and laughs. "'Us' as in your family. Us."

It never gets old or fails to shock me how Joseph's family has adopted me so fully into their lives. It's as if they've known me my whole life, like I was always their little sister—well, except for Joseph, of course—that would be wrong.

"I need time to let everything settle, sink in, and I need time with

Joseph to be sure he forgives me. As hard as this all was on me, it had to be even harder on him being accused of such things. Especially when the one person he's supposed to be able to rely on—above all others— doubted him." I shrug my shoulder like it's no big deal, but the depth of my shame is immeasurable.

"He knows. He doesn't blame you. You haven't had many people stand by you no matter what. He understands. We all do."

"Shit, Fin, you're going make me cry." I blink my eyes, and an idea takes root. "Fin? Would you help me do something?"

He perks up. He likes tangible things he can do, conquer. "Anything."

I hop up. "We need a tattoo parlor."

"A tattoo parlor? What? Now?"

"Yes, before he gets home."

"Fuck." He stands. "If I get punched for this, you're gonna owe me big. And I mean B-I-G, big."

I smirk. "You mean like keeping a certain brunette a secret?"

He narrows his eyes at me. "I used to like you, Sam. Now, I'm not so sure."

That makes me laugh so hard, I have to sit back down until I compose myself. "Oh Finley, you crack me up. You love me. You know it. I'm the sister you never had."

"I never wanted a sister. They're too much trouble," he says dryly.

My eyes round on a pout.

"Ah, fuck, Sam. I'm only kidding. Of course I love you. You're the best damn thing that's ever happened to my family—to Joseph. Don't cry. Please."

I smile deviously. "See, now *that* is much better."

He chuckles. "You're evil, Sam, pure evil."

"Nah, I like to give my fiancé's brothers a hard time, especially when they take naked pictures with women who try to blackmail me to leave Joseph, or when they sleep with my best friend and don't bother to let me know."

"Fuck, Sam." He's all pouty now.

"You don't have to talk about it, but if you break Margot's heart, I'll break you. Understand?"

"Fair enough."

"Excellent. Now, let's go get me a tat."

Joseph

I get home to a quiet house and a note from Samantha letting me know she had to run an errand. Fin and William are with her, and she'll be home as soon as possible. I text Fin to confirm she's alright. His reply was quick and cryptic, but didn't set off any alarm bells.

Heading to my office, I use the time to catch up on emails.

Two hours later, I'm getting out of the shower and find her standing there watching me with love and want in her eyes. My cock twitches with the idea of getting her all wet with my dripping body before getting her all wet where it matters most.

"Hey, Caveman." She bites her bottom lip, trying to hide her smile. She's up to something.

"Hey, Sweetness." I casually dry off, taking my time, watching her watch me. It's hot as fuck seeing her antsy with anticipation as her skin pinkens and her eyes roam my body like she wants to lick me from my toes to my head. She doesn't even focus on my cock, which I might find disappointing if she wasn't burning my abs, chest, and face alive with her wanton gaze. "How was your errand?"

She licks her lips before her eyes lock on mine. "Good. It was good." She fidgets with the material of her skirt, rubbing it between her thumbs and fingers.

She's definitely up to something. But it's going to have to wait. "I need to show you something." I hang up my towel and kiss her quickly as I pass by to slip on workout pants. I run my fingers through my damp hair, turning to find her staring at my ass. "Are you hungry?"

She swallows. "Yes." Her eyes still roam my body like she's never seen me bare-chested before.

"For food?" I try not to laugh; obviously the three orgasms from earlier were not enough to satisfy my hungry girl.

"What?" Her eyes lift to mine.

"There you are." I smirk. "Are you hungry for food?"

She crosses her arms, feigning indignation. "What else would I be hungry for, Mr. McIntyre?"

My brow arches. "You seem to be eating me up with your eyes, Ms. Cavanagh. I want to be sure it's food you're wanting."

Her blush is fucking adorable. "I…uh…both."

I chuckle and take her hand. "Come on, let me feed you. Then I'll show you what I need to. Then I can feed your *other* hunger."

"Okay," she whispers.

So fucking cute.

She sits on the kitchen counter as I feed her leftover Chinese and tell her about my visit with Lydia and Veronica. "Lydia was a total bitch, not an ounce of remorse. I left her in the hands of Matt, Michael, and Victor. They'll scare the pants off her. She'll sign what she needs to and be out of our lives."

"I'm surprised she didn't play all nice, still trying to get in your pants." She sucks a noodle from my fingers. "That's what I'd do."

"No, you wouldn't." I kiss her Peking Duck-flavored lips.

"No, I wouldn't. I don't have the balls to hit on someone. I could never." Laughing, she takes a bite of my pancake.

I'm struck dumb by the truth of her statement. I put down the food and wipe my hands. I wait for her to finish her bite before cupping her face as I stand between her knees. "I'm a lucky man." My voice hitches on the power of what I feel for her.

"What? No. I'm the lucky one," she insists.

I smooth out her furrowed brow with my thumb. "You're the sexiest woman I've ever seen, the way you come undone for me, the way you look at me, the hunger in your eyes, and the shyness of your blush—so fucking sexy. But you wouldn't have made a move on me if I hadn't sought you out first, would you?"

"No. Never." Her eyes beseech me.

"Even if you knew how much I wanted you, if you were positive I wouldn't turn you down?"

She adamantly shakes her head. "No."

"Why?"

"Because if you really wanted me, you'd make a move. If you don't, then it's only an idea you're toying with in your head. I don't want to be anybody's toy. I want to be somebody's everything, the somebody who compels you to make the first move. Not a knee-jerk reaction where you give in to being hit on, not a compromise, not a second choice, not an 'oh, why not' decision. I want you to know without a shadow of a doubt that you want me and are willing to take a chance, make an effort. I want a man with the confidence, the will to go after what he wants, not wait for it to come to him."

Fuck. Me. "I came after you."

She beams. "You did."

"But you weren't an easy catch."

"No, I wasn't. I'm still not. You have to work for me, Joseph. Not because I'm confident and believe I deserve it. But because I don't."

"Samantha." I press my forehead to hers. "It kills me when you say stuff like that."

"I need to be sure you understand what you're getting into with me. I don't know if I'll ever be that confident. I may always have doubts, and it's not a reflection of your character, but of mine. I couldn't love you more, Joseph. I don't ever want you to doubt that."

"I don't doubt it, baby. I've got confidence enough for both of us. If you run, I'll chase. I'll always come for you, because I know you're worth it."

She closes her eyes, nodding her head over and over again as tears slip free.

My lips brush her cheeks. "I'll always come for you, Sweets."

"I'm counting on it." Her voice is tight with emotions. She wraps her arms around my neck. "Please forgive me for my doubts. I know we said it earlier, but I need to hear it again."

I pull her closer. "I forgive you. I'll always forgive you. I'll always come for you."

"Don't let me go."

"Never. Never letting you go, Sweetness." I kiss her warm lips. "Come on."

It's now or never.

Samantha

In his office, Joseph pulls me into his lap. "I need to show you something."

"You keep saying that. You're making me nervous."

"I'm a little nervous myself." His fingers tip my chin so that I'm looking him in the eyes. "We need to finish this thing with Lydia, Veronica, and Tiff. I need you to trust me, give it a chance, let me show you what I see."

I have no idea what he's wanting to show me, but the knot in my stomach tells me it's not good. I can't speak. I simply nod.

Joseph wakes up his laptop, and a large monitor on his desk comes to life with a still of Joseph. "Shit. No." I try to get up, but he won't let me. "I can't watch this, Joseph."

His grip on me tightens. "Michael obtained the full video from Tiff. What you've seen is only some of it. This is the last copy. The only copy, and once you've seen it—I'll destroy it."

"So, the video and the come-face picture are for sure from when you were with Tiff?" Holy shit. I can't watch this. I can't watch him being raped.

"Watch it, and then ask me that question again."

"Joseph, please. Don't make me watch this."

His hand cups the back of my neck as his lips crash over mine, licking and sucking tenderly, passionately.

I know what he's doing, but I'm helpless to resist him. I don't want to watch her take advantage of him. I want to be what he needs. When he needs it.

He pulls back, both of us breathless. "I need you to trust me, Samantha. I need you to see this through my eyes, see what I experienced. We need this closure." He pulls me into a hug, whispering into my ear. "Please give me this. Trust me."

How can I not? This man gives me everything, forgives me for doubting him. I can do this for him. "Okay."

As the video starts, it's obvious Tiff is on top looking down on Joseph taking the video. They're in the throes of it, moaning, thrusting. Joseph tightens his hold on me. We watch for another minute before he pauses the screen—his face frozen with a look of pure ecstasy.

"You know that look, Samantha."

"Yeah, that's you having sex."

"No, not just sex. And not sex with just anyone. That's *me* making love to *you*."

"What?" But he's having sex with Tiff. Even though I can't see her, I know it's her. They got the video *from her*.

"Watch." He resumes the video.

We watch in silence the most difficult thing I've ever witnessed—the man I love having sex with someone else.

He looks and sounds like my Joseph, the way he looks and sounds when he's with me. His moans become more coherent. He's talking to her, telling her to *make it feel good*. Shit. He's said those words to me. Tears slip down my cheek. I blink to clear my vision.

Then I hear it: "Samantha." The Joseph on the video called out to me. *Me.*

Joseph squeezes me. "That was you and me, Samantha. There was no one else in that bed with me besides you. Watch."

All of a sudden, I don't feel like a voyeur watching Joseph have sex with someone else. I'm watching with his eyes, seeing his moves, his face, his sounds he makes with me. *Me.*

In the heat of his desire, he looks into the camera. "I'm coming, baby." The look on his face is the one in the still photo—his come-shot. But the video doesn't end there. It continues, and he comes undone. "Fuck, Sweetness, I'm coming so hard for you."

The video ends.

Silence. The room is full of silence and my ragged breath.

"It was only ever you and me, Samantha. That's my drunken fantasy sex dream I had with you. I don't remember Tiff. I don't want to remember her, because what you saw is what I remember—what I cherish—you and me—making love."

He carries me to our bed, lowering me down gently like I might bruise. I sit in the middle of our bed and watch him undress. He's not giving me a show, like a strip tease, he's simply undressing—for me. When he's gloriously naked, his cock at full attention, bobbing against his tight abs, I'm in awe of him—as I am every time I see him—that he's mine.

Kneeling next to me, he slowly undresses me, his eyes caressing every bit of skin as it's revealed. My shoes. Gone. My blouse and bra. Gone. My skirt. Gone.

"What the fuck did you do?" His concern alarms me until I see his eyes are on my panties. Well, actually on the bandage sticking out from under my panties.

"Shit. I forgot about that."

"How the hell did you hurt yourself there?" His fingers gently glide over the top of the bandage. "Does it hurt?"

I lie back on my elbows. "It does hurt, to be honest. But Bowser promised it'll be better in a few days."

"Who the hell is Bowser?" Anger flares in his eyes, his jaw clenched tightly, staring daggers at me and then the bandage.

"It's supposed to be a surprise for you. But based on your reaction, I'm afraid to show you."

He takes a cleansing breath or two—okay five. His eyes soften. "What did you do, Sweetness? Please don't tell me you marked this beautiful skin with a tattoo."

Oh, no. He hates tattoos? Tears fill my eyes.

"Baby, please tell me you didn't."

I shake my head, unable to answer.

He sighs in exasperation. "Fin took you to a goddamned tattoo shop?"

I roll away, kneeling at the top of our bed, covering myself with a pillow. *He hates it. What was I thinking? So stupid.*

"Fuck. I'm sorry. Come 'ere, baby. Let me see." He moves toward me.

"No." I jump off the bed, pillow securely covering my front. "I'm sorry. I thought...I wanted to do something for you. To show you my dedication to you."

"Baby, please."

"No. It was stupid."

He stops in front of me. "Show me."

I shake my head. "You hate it. I'm never letting you see it."

"How do you think I won't see it?" He pulls the pillow out of my grasp.

"I'll get it lasered off."

"The fuck you will," he growls. He cups the back of my neck, tipping my head back. "I'm an idiot, Samantha. I'm sorry. I didn't...it's a shock that's all." He runs his hand down my neck and shoulder, watching as if he can see the trail it leaves behind. "You have such beautiful skin, unblemished, untouched, pure."

I scoff at that. "Untouched? Pure? Not anymore."

Anger flashes again. "You will always be pure to me, because your body only knows *my* touch."

"Caveman, that's exactly why I wanted to get this tattoo."

His nostrils flare. "Show me, Samantha. Let me see your gift."

He tenderly carries me back to bed, lays me down, and swiftly removes my panties. I'm naked except for the bandage. His lips reverently kiss around the dressing. "Show me."

"Okay, but don't touch it. I have to keep it clean and covered for forty-eight hours."

"I'll clean it and cover it back up after I'm done examining my present." His smile is earnest and gives me hope that he won't hate it.

"If you don't like it, they can turn it into something else, or I can have it removed."

"No fucking way. Show me." His impatience grows.

"Close your eyes."

"Samantha."

"Close your eyes, grumpy."

Finally, he does, but his hands remain on my hips, his thumbs caressing back and forth. I lift the corners and peel off the dressing, placing it on the nightstand. I look back at my man, his eyes closed, his jaw lax, his lips full and begging to be kissed.

"You're staring." He grumbles.

"No, I'm not."

"Can I open my eyes?"

"Yes." I take in a sharp breath, waiting.

He opens, zooming in on it before I exhale.

"It's green for your eyes."

He nods, staring. Then he slowly traces the tips of his fingers directly below the writing in a delicate, ornate green script highlighted in black, not too big, just big enough for him to read. Only *him*. "You did this for me?"

"Yes."

"I don't know what to say." His gaze is still locked on, examining, his fingers caressing circles around it.

"You don't like it." I grab the bandage.

His hand covers mine. "No. Don't cover it. I'm not done." The longer he stares, the deeper he breathes. Then I notice he's hard again, after having lost his erection, thinking I was hurt.

If he's turned on, he must not totally hate it. "Say something. Anything."

"I can't believe you did this—for me."

Yeah, that's not helping. I still don't know if he hates it or not.

But then he bends down, trailing warm kisses from hip to hip. He continues, moving lower until he's right over the tattoo. He blows across it, and I squirm, unable to remain still. His flicks his tongue below it, ever so close to where moisture now pools.

"Joseph."

His tongue flicks over my slit, delving in, finding my clit, and sucks.

"Oh, shit." I fist the bedspread.

"Does the tattoo mean this belongs to me?" His tongue rubs up and down over and over again.

"Yes." I want to spread my legs, but he has them pinned.

"Do you know how much this turns me on? To see you mark yourself with my name—the name you call me?"

"No, tell me."

"Fuck, Samantha. To taste you and see my name on you, like a brand, telling me you're mine. I think I could come right now if I look at it much longer."

I moan at the thought.

"I can't wait until I can touch it, kiss it, lick it."

"Oh, god, Joseph."

"I can bury my cock, balls deep, and see who you belong to."

"Yes."

He pushes my legs apart, kneeling between my thighs. His fingers slip inside. "Fuck, you're so wet." His fingers glide in and out. "Say it. I want to hear you say it out loud. Whose pussy is this?"

"Caveman's."

"Fuck, that's right. I never thought seeing a tattoo on you would make me want you even more, but the fact that you tattooed *Caveman's* right above your pussy is the hottest fucking thing I've ever seen." He pumps faster. "Are you gonna come for me, Sweets?"

"Yes."

"That's right. Whose pussy is this?"

"Caveman's."

"Fuck, my balls tingle every time you say that and I read it on your body. Come for me, baby, because I need my cock inside you. Now."

He bends down, his tongue lapping at me, focusing on my clit, his fingers working that magic spot. He sucks and licks me into a frenzy until I come undone around his fingers. It only feeds his hunger for more. His groans and sucks continue, taking me into another orgasm.

Before I recover, his thighs are spread, my legs swung over his thighs, his cock rubbing my folds, then he slides home. "Dammit, you feel so fucking good." His hands grip my hips, his thumbs on either side of his *Caveman's* tattoo. His eyes are glued to it, watching himself slide in and out of me.

"Do you like your gift?" I manage through choppy breaths as he pumps into me.

"Fuck, yeah. Tell me again whose pussy this is?"

"Caveman's."

"That's right. You're mine, Sweets. You have the tattoo to prove it, and in three weeks you're gonna have my ring and name." His eyes lock on the tattoo again. "So fucking hot, baby."

Nineteen

I GET TO LOVE YOU

Saturday Before Christmas

Joseph

MY HEART IS POUNDING, THUNDERING LIKE A champion racehorse at the starting gate, biting at the bit for the race to begin. It's been two years, four weeks, three days, and seventeen hours since I first laid eyes on Samantha Lilian Cavanagh. It was the Friday before Thanksgiving, my family out of town for the holiday. I took the standing offer from my then-roommate, Jace, to spend the holiday with his family. I'd met his parents before, many times, in fact. But the illustrious Samantha was known to me only through Jace's words and actions when he talked to her or about her.

Even then, she stood out in my mind as someone important. Important enough to be spoken of in awe by a man who chased women like a stud working for his next meal. Jace revered his sister, and though his actions didn't always equal his love for her, it was obvious, even to me, that she was the most important person in his life.

He wasn't wrong.

As soon as I saw her, my heart flipped. My jaw clenched. My cock sprang to life—but so did my soul. It's as if it recognized its other half, yawned and stretched from a long slumber, and jumped to attention. She was it. The one I had unknowingly been searching for, bettering myself for, making a future for.

She. Was. It.

My. Future.

My. Everything.

Now, I stand at the front of the church, my brothers next to me. Fin as my best man and Matt standing next to him. Margot as maid of honor stands across from Fin, who might possibly be his other half by the way he's staring at her. I want to scream at him that *this is my fucking day—pay attention*. But I don't have it in me, and it would be pointless if he feels even a miniscule amount for Margot what I feel for Samantha—it's a lost cause. He couldn't change his focus even if he tried. He's a goner.

The wedding march pipes through the biggest damn organ I've ever seen. The center doors at the back of the church open—and there—standing next to Jace—is my girl. My breath catches, and I have to fist my hands to keep from running to her. I told her I'd always come after her, but this once, I have to let her come to me. This one time.

She's all in white, her shoulders bare, her veil perched on her head like a crown, cascading around her as she walks, arm in arm with her brother—to me. Her dress hugs her curves like my body wants to do, flares at the bottom, and trails behind her.

Her face, dear lord help me, that face. Angelic and innocent, blue eyes I want to swim in, pouty lips I want to devour, bone structure I'd want as my muse if I was any kind of an artistic fuck. And that silken mane of auburn hair, curled and flowing around her, making my fingers twitch to sink in and hold on tightly, while I set those abundant breasts free from their confinement.

Holy fuck, I've got a hard-on the size of Texas for my girl.

Movement to Samantha's right has me meeting Jace's gaze. His brow is hooked with a smart-ass grin on his face. *You're a fucking pussy,* I hear his voice in my head.

Yeah, I am. And only for *her.*

They stop next to me, Jace impeding me from taking hold of my girl. The minister asks, "Who gives this woman to be married to this man?"

With a smile and dancing eyes, Jace looks at Samantha and then me. "I do." He then places her hand in mine and steps back. He grips my elbow. "She's all yours, brother. Be good to her." His eyes shine with tears.

I swallow around the lump in my throat. "Like my life depends on it, brother."

He nods, pats my back, kisses her cheek, and takes a seat.

Finally. I step closer, taking her in, that lump in my throat trying to steal my voice, but I manage to say, "You look beautiful, Sweetness."

Her face lights up like she thought I might possibly think otherwise. "You look like pure heaven."

I lean in to kiss her cheek, but she turns, facing me.

"Kiss me, Caveman." She tips her chin to me. "It's the last kiss you'll ever get as a single man."

Fuck me. Is it against protocol? I shrug at the minister and do as my soon-to-be wife requests and kiss the hell out of her. Clapping and catcalls erupt. The minister clears his throat, but I don't give a shit. This is a very important kiss, nearly as important as the one right after he pronounces us man and wife. This is my final goodbye to all that came before her, all that happened before this day, any doubts and fears she has for our future—I need to kiss out of her. And kiss out of her. And kiss out of her.

I pull away with a wicked grin. "That was *your* final kiss as a single woman."

She blinks, trying to catch her breath, and wipes at her lipstick—which must be magic as it didn't smear—and smiles. "I don't need any other kisses as I've only ever had yours. Single, married, pregnant, young, old, they're all yours."

Fuck. Me.

I'm the luckiest damn man around. I take her arm in mine and turn to the man of the cloth, who's watching us with brazen surprise. "You need to make this woman my wife, like yesterday," I command.

He simply smiles and begins…

Samantha

"I Get To Love You" plays through the ballroom speakers. Our friends and family surround us, but I only see my man—my husband—turning me on the dancefloor like Fred Astaire for our first dance.

Did I envision this day? Did I dream of my wedding as so many little girls do? No, I never did have that wedding fantasy of finding my prince in shining armor or being whisked away to his castle where we live happily ever after. I didn't have *once up on a time* kind of thoughts as a kid. I was never your average girl—I suppose I'm still not. I'd rather code than shop. I'd rather see a sci-fi movie than a romantic comedy. And I'd rather fall in love with one man—and only one man—than play the field, notching my belt with romantic dalliances before I found the one, or Mr. Good Enough.

I'm lucky. I know. I've hit the romantic jackpot. A jackpot I wasn't even looking for, longing for, or even knew was possible until Joseph Patrick McIntyre came into my life like a storm, turning it upside down and sweeping me off my feet.

"Do you take this woman to be your wife?" The minister asked Joseph.

"I do," he replied with tears in his eyes.

"Do you take this man to be your husband?"

"I do." I really, really do.

When the minister pronounced us *"husband and wife"* and told Joseph, *"You may kiss your bride, again,"* everyone laughed, except Joseph and me. The intensity of his stare, the need in his eyes, and the possessiveness of his embrace left no room for anything other than my love for this man—my husband. He kissed me like a new beginning, a breath of fresh air, a promise of happily ever afters, and a lifetime of hot, delicious sex. How can this be? How can I have come so far in two years and still feel like the same determined, ambitious girl who saw stars in her eyes, computers in her future, and didn't dare to dream that the VP of Product and Technology at McIntyre Corporate Industries would even know who I was, much less want a future with me?

"Mrs. McIntyre, I believe it's time to cut the cake." My dreamy Mr. McIntyre draws my thoughts back to our reception and our duties as the bride and groom.

I take his proffered hand, my smile blazing a path across my lips. *I can't believe I'm his wife.* "Husband, I don't think I'll ever tire of hearing you call me that. Though, I do so love *Sweetness, Sweets,* and *baby.* I hope you won't retire those."

He stops and pulls me close, our hands joined at my side. The back of his fingers caresses my cheek. "I have no intention of retiring any of those, Sweetness. I'm simply adding *Mrs. McIntyre* and *wife* into the mix. I believe my repertoire of lovenames is now complete."

"Hmm, and which one will you get tattooed on your cock?" I whisper.

His devious smirk has me blushing. "I've got it all planned. When I'm not hard and ready to fuck you senseless, it will simply say *Sam's.*" He kisses the corner of my mouth. "But when I'm hard as steel and aching for you, it will say *Samantha Lilian McIntyre's.*"

I snort on a laugh. "Oh God, I walked right into that, didn't I?"

He leans close and whispers into my ear as his erection pokes me in the stomach. "I need to bury myself inside my wife—soon. I've been hard since I saw you walking down the aisle."

"Joseph," I groan, my head falling to his chest. "You sure know how to wind a girl up."

His chest rumbles with a laugh. "Come on, Sweets. Let's eat some cake. We've only got an hour before we leave for the airport."

"Really?"

His emerald eyes flare. "It might not be what you want, but our first time as husband and wife will be a mid-air collision. I can't survive hours until we make it to our destination."

"You're not teasing me." *Please, can't we leave now?* I really want to ask.

"Mrs. McIntyre, I would never tease about a thing like that. Soon, Sweetness." His succulent lips take mine for too short a ride before he pulls away, leading me to cut our cake.

We transition from cutting the cake to bouquet and garter toss. Margot catches my bouquet, and Fin catches the garter. Now if that's not a telling sign, I don't know what is. They're still keeping their relationship a secret, but they do manage a dance or two beyond the wedding party's obligatory ones. Love is in the air, and I pray they get sucked in deeply, endlessly, and most definitely happily.

I don't bother with changing. Whatever I wear will only end up on the bedroom floor of MCI's corporate jet anyway. So, what's the point? I'll change on the plane, that is if I can manage after hours of mindless sex with my husband.

My husband. How long will it take before the novelty wears off?

Never.

Like my love for Joseph. It's endless. Timeless. Immeasurable. And steadfast. The latter sealed and made true by his unfathomable faith in me. He says I'm enough for him.

And.

I.

Finally

Believe.

It's.

True.

Twenty

PERFECT

Samantha

A WEEK ON A SECLUDED CARIBBEAN ISLAND HAS done wonders for my tan, not to mention my sex life. My husband's unquenchable desire for me is only matched by my limitless desire for him. If this wasn't a private island, we would have been arrested by now. I thought impromptu sex in Joseph's office was our thing. Apparently, we've progressed to beaches, the ocean, sun loungers, jet skis—yes, we fell in—hammocks, sail boats, catamarans, palm trees— yes, I have the bruises to prove it—and of course every room, surface, and piece of furniture in our cabana.

I use the term cabana loosely. It's more like a beach-front mansion made to look like a hut and blend in with its surroundings. It comes complete with full-time, very discreet—never see them unless you need something—staff. Our every meal, need, whim, desire, is fully provided for by little mice I've only seen twice.

Oh, and did I mention this very private secluded Caribbean island is now ours? Yeah, so Joseph was researching honeymoon destinations and ran across this gem that happened to be for sale. So, he bought it and plans to lease it to MCI for its executive employees to enjoy—namely

Joseph's family. It's like a high-end timeshare for the rich. The very rich McIntyres.

Pinch me. Seriously. Pinch me.

As if my Adonis can read my mind, he rises from the water like Poseidon. His abs glistening like cut diamonds, mask and fins dangling from his hands, water dripping from his torso—though, reluctantly, I'm sure—he whips his hair out of his eyes and blesses me with a panty-dropping smile. "Hi, Sweetness."

"Hey, Caveman. How's the water?"

"Lonely without you." He plops beside me on the double lounger. "How's the book?" He places a cool wet kiss on my shoulder and then my lips.

"Disappointing compared to our romance." Truly.

"Yeah?" He seems surprised.

"Yeah." I run my fingers through his hair. "No book boyfriend can compare to you."

"I'm glad to hear it." He shakes his head, spraying me with cold droplets.

I giggle and screech, but honestly, it feels amazing on my sun-heated skin.

"You were napping earlier when I spoke to Michael. Let's grab some lunch, and I'll fill you in."

Sitting on the covered veranda, the cool ocean breeze keeps the heat at bay, and Joseph, seated next to me feeding my body and soul, is nearly as perfect as it gets.

"As you know, everything is wrapped up with Lydia and Tiff. They've signed the papers. Tiff is still in Austin, and Lydia has moved home to Connecticut. Michael feels certain those two won't be a problem in the future."

"That's great news. I wish them well, but hope never to see or hear of them again." Though, I never did meet or see Tiff, and I'm perfectly fine with that. If I ever do see her—I'll punch her—no doubt in my mind about that. She raped my man. He may not remember it, but we all know it, and I will never forget or forgive her. She had better keep her ass in Austin.

He kisses my hand and feeds me a slice of mango followed by pineapple. "Oh, and I have news on how Veronica obtained my blue tie."

"Really? How?"

"Remember I told you about her pretending to be a British tourist that night you didn't make the happy hour?"

"Yeah."

"Michael checked the video feed from the bar. It turns out that was the last time I wore that tie. It was rolled up in my jacket pocket, hanging on the back of my bar stool. Veronica snagged it when I wasn't paying attention."

"Wow. So that's it, right? There's no more outstanding questions."

"Yep, that was the last loose end." He looks relieved. I know he has to be glad to have this behind us. I know I am.

"Did he have any more news on Veronica?"

"They've got some leads on her brother, Spencer. They haven't found him yet, but feel they're close."

"God, I pray they find him."

"Me too. As for Veronica, she's settled in her new place and has registered at UTA for the Spring semester. She's also going to counseling twice a week. Michael and Victor have been checking on her weekly and feel she's making progress, positive changes toward working through her past and making plans for the future. She wants to be a counselor for abused children."

"Wow. That's amazing. She'll probably be really good at it." I tear up at the thought of where she came from and the potential of where she can go if she chooses. "She'll be great for kids going through what she did. No one will understand them like she will. And she's smart and devious—they won't be able to pull the wool over her eyes. She'll know their tricks and help them navigate to their own healing."

"Sweetness." The look on his face has me turning toward him.

"What?"

"You."

"What about me?"

"Do you hear yourself?"

I frown, not understanding what he's saying; of course, I hear myself. I'm the one speaking.

He pushes his chair back and pulls me into his lap. "Do you not see how amazing you are?"

"What are you talking about? We weren't even talking about me. We're talking about Veronica."

His look is indulgent and tender as he tips my chin to look in my eyes. "Veronica did lots of nasty things to you to hurt you, yet you don't hold it against her. You've gone out of your way to ensure she has a future. A future that you're rooting for, like a proud parent or a good friend. You don't think that's remarkable?"

"What kind of person would I be if I couldn't see past the hurtful things she did? Accurate or not, from her perspective, I took away the only light in her life when Jace cut her off. Was that my fault? No. Would it have happened if she had been nice to me? No. But she felt threatened and acted out the only way she knew how to protect what was precious to her. Jace." I touch Joseph's cheek. "I would do anything to protect you, my husband. Love is fierce and territorial."

"But *you* wouldn't have used your body to get what you wanted."

"No. But I also wasn't raped when I was eleven by the man who was supposed to protect me, keep me safe, and show me how a woman should be treated. She doesn't know how to use her body except as a weapon. I'm hoping through therapy she'll learn."

He pulls me into his chest, holding me tightly. "You're remarkable, Samantha. You make me want to be a better man, a man who deserves you and deserves to be a father to the children we'll have—especially a daughter." His teary eyes lock on mine. "Our daughters will know how a man should treat them. And our sons will know how to treat a woman, starting with their sisters and their mother. I promise you that."

I swallow my emotions. "Daughters? Sons? Plural? Exactly how many children do you want, Mr. McIntyre?"

His hand slides up my leg as his eyes move down my body. He

fingers his tattoo hidden under my bikini bottoms. "As many as this sweet body will give me."

My arms wrap around his neck, and I run my nose along his. "Maybe we should practice, to be sure we've got it down when we're ready to start trying."

"Fuck me," he hisses under his breath.

"Yes, please."

Joseph

The sun reaches through my sleepy haze. It's early, too early. The warmth cuddled against me urges me to wake up and seize the day—or at least her ass—as I burrow my way deep inside her sweet pussy. My hand roams over her body as I stretch and blink against the morning light, fully opening my eyes for the first time.

She stretches and moans, pushing her ass into my awaiting erection—morning wood—gotta love it, especially when you have someone to share it with. And lucky for me, I have someone for the rest of my life.

"Good morning, Sweetness." I kiss along her neck.

"Morning, Caveman." She turns in my arms, her plump breasts nestled against my chest, her eyes locked on mine as her face tips upward.

"Do you know I could spend the rest of my life like this, with you in my arms?" I cup a breast and bend to lick and suck her nipple, relishing her gasp and thrust of her hips toward my cock. "Except I'd be cock deep inside you at all times."

"Hmm." She moans as I slip down to take care of her other breast. "It might be hard to walk like that."

"Who needs to walk? We'll have people bring us what we need. We can take bathroom breaks, but other than that, I don't see why it's not possible."

"I don't know that I can find any fault in that plan." She rolls to her back on a stretch.

I settle between her thighs, continuing to dine on her breasts. Her hands knead and pull at me as her legs run up and down mine. It's a slow and gentle build. A lazy morning of gasps and sighs, caresses and exploration, moans and beckoning. As my mouth moves to claim hers, my cock slides inside, nestling in its rightful place, what it was made to do—who it was made for.

"Joseph," she moans, wrapping her legs round me.

"My beautiful girl." My tongue delves deeper as my cock rocks home over and over again.

When she chants my name mixed with "oh god," I know she's close. My balls tingle in anticipation, holding out for that final signal that presents itself when she squeezes my cock as she comes undone and milks me, taking my seed, leaving me in a state of bliss.

On a groan, I roll to my back, pulling her close. From our bed, we can see the aqua blue of the ocean with sailboats floating across the horizon. It's heaven here. I can't believe I bought this island—a fucking island—for a steal. It was pure luck—preparation meets opportunity.

My Sweets slips out of bed and into the bathroom. I wander out on the deck and pee out over the side, watering the green bushes.

"You're such a boy." My girl giggles from behind me.

"You'd do it if you could."

She laughs again. "Yeah, I probably would."

I go inside to wash up and brush my teeth. I join her at the railing—where we've found ourselves every morning of our two weeks' stay—kiss her shoulder and nuzzle up to her naked backside. "What do you want to do on our last day?"

"I think I'd like more of what we just did." She looks over her shoulder and kisses my cheek. "If it's all the same to you."

My hands travel around her front, finding a nipple and slipping into her wet heat. "Sweets, didn't I make it clear I could spend a lifetime inside you and it wouldn't be near enough?"

She arches into my hands, her ass pushing back on my balls, my cock hard against her back.

"Spread your legs for me," I whisper in her ear.

She widens her stance and sighs when I run my fingers through her wet pussy, spreading her juices to her ass.

"Oh, god," she moans.

I nibble on her ear, lick the shell, and suck on her lobe. All while my thumb rubs her rosebud. "I want in here today, Sweets."

"Joseph."

"Shh, only my finger, baby." We've never gone further than that. Eventually, I'd like to claim her ass, but for now, I'll take this. I kiss her cheek. "I'll be right back."

When I pull away, she slumps against the railing, her body already revved up, ready to take me, ready to go off.

Returning, I trail kisses along her back, working my way down to her ass and then to her pussy. Nudging her legs apart, I lick her until her legs are shaking and she's begging me to fuck her. I love my girl and how hot she gets.

Standing, I lube up my finger and her ass. My other hand plays with her clit, slowly, enough to keep her on edge but not enough to send her over. Taking her ass gets easier each time, soon she's pushing back, ready for me, begging for me to fill her up. My cock bobs, doing its own begging. "That's it, Sweets. Push again and let me in."

"Oh, fuck!" she screams as my fingers breeches her ass and slip inside her pussy.

"Your ass is so hot and tight, baby. And your pussy is so wet and succulent, clenching my fingers with need." Fuck. I'm so turned on.

"Caveman, I want you inside me."

I alternate my fingers, in her ass, out her pussy. "I am inside you."

Squeezing the railing, she thrusts her pelvis like she's aching for more. "I want your cock."

She whimpers when I suck on her neck. "You'll have my cock soon enough, but I want you to come like this first."

I pick up the tempo, massaging her clit with my palm.

"Oh, god." Her head falls back, resting on my chest.

"I'm desperate for you, Samantha. Come for me, so I can sink inside my heaven."

"Joseph." Her hips gyrate, grinding against my palm.

"Fuck, yes. Just like that. Come all over my hand, baby." I increase the pace, suck and bite on her neck, shoulder, ear—anywhere I can reach.

Her whole body is trembling, and I worry her legs will give out, but before they do, she takes flight. "Oh, my god."

I hold onto her, slip my finger out of her ass, continue finger-fucking her pussy until her contractions subside. I kiss and nuzzle her neck, telling her how amazing she is and how fucking sexy she is.

Cradling her in my arms, I take her back to bed, lay her down, then wash my hands and grab a warm washcloth to take care of her.

I'd planned to have her ride my cock on a balcony chair. But truly, I want her in bed, underneath me, face to face, so I can see her, kiss her, and make love to her in my favorite way—with her arms and legs wrapped around me, holding me like she can't get me close enough.

I'm horny as hell and could pound away at her, but I don't. I kiss her tenderly, pulling her back from her orgasm-fog. I want her with me. Always with me. Always beside me. Never behind me. Not in front of me, but beside me—*with me*.

Partners.

Soul mates.

Husband and wife.

The yin to my yang.

My *Sweetness* to her *Caveman*.

I sink in slowly, she arches to meet me—pulling me in—welcoming me home.

My girl.

My love.

My *Sweetness*

My *Sweets*.
My *baby*.
My wife.
Forever.
Always.
I do.

The End

Bonus Scene

9 MONTHS AFTER WEDDING

HE TAKES MY BREATH AWAY. STILL. THE CUT OF HIS jaw. His dark hair that's grown to be a little unruly—just like him. His perfect mouth, not just its shape, but the words that come out of it, the things he *does* with it. The dimples that reach inside me and squeeze when they're aimed at me. The command in his voice, in every step he takes as he rounds his desk, his eyes, on his phone. He exudes confidence. Pure, unadulterated confidence of a man who knows where he belongs, does what he loves, and has the world at his fingertips.

This is the man I fell for, married nine months ago, and get to work and live with every single day. I'm one lucky girl. I bite the tip of my pen, my eyes, trained on him as he moves with the grace of an athlete, every step bringing him closer...

"Sweetness?" The husk in his voice does dirty things to my girly parts.

I flash to his emerald eyes that see me in a way I never will. "Yeah?" I pluck the pen from my mouth, realizing I was sucking on it.

He stops before me, his crotch at eye level as I sit on the couch in his office—our office. He insisted I have a desk in here even though I have an office down the hall and my own assistant. He prefers me close. The impressive bulge in his pants, not really the reason, but not to be negated either.

Tipping my chin with a finger, he leans down till we're face to face.

211

His crook of a smile with a barely-there dimple, alludes to his amusement and a knowing that my mind has drifted into a personal arena that has nothing to do with the new tech we were discussion moments ago as he read the latest update from one of our industry scouts. "Did you hear any of the recommendations?"

Hear? *Yes.*

Remember? *No.*

"How can I concentrate when you look like that?" I motion to his suit he wears like a second skin, a body armor decked out to slay the day, take no prisoners, securing the future of MCI and its employees. He's dedicated, but does he have to be so damn hot while he's doing it?

He drops his phone on the couch beside me and sits on the edge of the coffee table, sequestering my knees between his long, powerful legs. He grips my thighs as he leans in. "Did you notice the bulge in my pants, Sweets?"

I nod, swallowing the saliva that's pooled in my mouth.

"Then you know it's no walk in the park for me. You in heels, a pencil skirt, and blouse…" He motions to my head. "Your hair up, looking like the hottest fucking librarian I've ever only seen in my fantasies." He easer closer, his hands slowly sliding my skirt up as he goes.

Newsflash. "You fantasize about librarians?"

His chuckle does nothing to quell the need building in me. "I fantasize about *you* as a librarian. A teacher. A secretary. A flight attendant. Any stereotypical female role that makes me an asshole to think it, much less say it, has you in the starring role with my dick, my mouth, and my fingers."

I shake my head. "Not *my* mouth?" I'm poking the bear, knowing he's as turned on as I am. And that knowledge only makes me hotter.

His growl is immediate. His lips nearly to mine.

Put me out of my misery, Caveman. Kiss me. Then fuck me.

But he doesn't. He licks his lips and whispers his thumb across my mouth, barely a touch. "Always about your beautiful lips on me in any way you damn well please."

My heart hammering against my chest and erratic breaths seems so loud, I'm sure Teddy will hear from his desk on the other side of the door. "I want that."

"I know. So do I." He sits back, pulls my skirt down to a respectable position. "But we can't." He captures my hands. "We've managed to avoid office sex for four whole months since you started working here full-time."

I arch a brow.

His jaw ticks before he breaks into a full-fledged smile. "Okay." He stands, adjusting himself. "We've managed to avoid office sex during *business* hours."

"I should just work from my office. Why are we putting ourselves through this day in and day out?" I stand to collect my laptop, but he stops me.

"I need you here." Leaning on the edge of my desk, he pulls me between his legs. "I *want* you here." A punch of air cascades down my blouse as he leans his head against mine. "This beautiful brain of yours works in a way mine doesn't. We complement each other. If you weren't here, I'd be walking down to your office continually or booking you for hours upon hours of meetings. It would be no different. We've got this." He kisses me softly. Passion simmers, but this is a kiss of love and a promise: I'm his wife, and I'm also as his partner at MCI. He's not my boss. I'm an equal. At home *and* work.

"We got this," I affirm his conviction.

"Yeah, we do." He kisses up my jaw to my ear where his breath sends chills down my spine. "But I'm going to fuck you senseless when the clock strikes five."

I wouldn't want it any other way. Joseph and I have a connection that goes beyond our love for each other and flows into our love of MCI and all things techy.

He steps back, collecting his phone, and walks back to his desk. "Now try to pay attention when I read the update this time." He winks before his gaze lowers to his phone and he starts to read. His voice pulls me to him like a siren song, but this time, I am listening.

When I sit on his lap, he wraps an arm around my waist, and I cuddle close. We may not have a typical working relationship. But what we do works for us, works for MCI.

I get to see him day in and day out at home and in the office. For some that might be too much. For us, it's just right.

He's always been the yin to my yang.

My husband.

My Caveman.

And now, my co-worker.

Life is good, especially when I get to work from his lap.

1 WEEK LATER

She's crying. My wife, my everything, is crying, and it guts me. She left work early. Meeting Margot for some girl-time.

I'm going to rip someone's head off if they hurt my girl.

"Baby." My anguish is clear, but it's my presence that has her head popping up, her eyes wide. She didn't hear me come in because she was *crying*. Sobbing. "Sweetness, what's wrong?" I charge across our apartment, scoop her onto my lap before she can even hide the evidence of her tears or reply to my question.

Her curling into me gives me a peace I don't deserve, given she's so broken up over something I'm oblivious of.

"I thought I was ready. I thought I was over it. Over her—" her last word comes out on a sob.

I rack my brain, trying to figure out who *her* is. "Ready for what? Over what? Who's *her?*"

Samantha sniffs and takes stuttered breaths as she tried to calm down. I hand her a tissue from the end table and wait. She needs a second. I've promised her forever. I've got time.

Composed, she adjusts in my arms to meet my eyes. Her blues, so full of love with an undercurrent of hurt. She palms my cheek, like I'm the one upset. I guess I am. Her pain is mine. I wipe at her tears, unconvinced that's the last of them. My girl feels things deeply. Happy or sad, her tears are never far away. She was made to believe it made her weak. But it's her strength, her courage that allows her to be vulnerable enough to shed the emotions bubbling inside her. Not everyone gets that. I do, and I love that about her.

On a productive breath she licks her lips and begins. "I thought I was over my mom. I was fine without her at our wedding. I'm fine without her in our lives. I'm over it. I've accepted it. But…" Her chin trembles.

"But?"

"I didn't think I'd feel this way. I should be happy, but instead, here I am crying over *her*. Still." She hops off my lap, grabbing a few more tissues, and blows her nose with one hand and pats her face dry with the other. She begins to pace. "And I'm angry that after all this time, she's still hurting me." She stops at the window. "She's tainting my good news."

I stand and meet her reflection in the floor to ceiling window, wrapping my arms around hers crossed over her chest. "What news?"

Her chin starts to tremble again, and I swear I'm about to join her. "Baby. Fuck. You've got to tell me. Please, you're killing me." I can't help if I don't know what I'm dealing with.

"*Good* news, Caveman. Calm down." She turns in my hold, her hands landing on my chest, searing me through my dress shirt. "I'm pregnant."

I nearly buckle.

I smack a palm against the glass behind her, leaning in, my head next to hers. "Say that again."

I suck in air.

In.

Out.

In.

Out.

"I'm pregnant." She cradles my head on her shoulder.

Her touch is everything. Wrapping her in my arms, I take us to the floor before I fall.

We've been trying for six months, and once a month for every six months my girl cries when she finds out she's not pregnant by either starting her period or by a negative pregnancy test. It's three weeks of bliss as we fuck like rabbits, and a week of sorrow when her period comes… All tinged with sadness that it hadn't happening *yet*.

For six fucking months.

We said we were going to wait a few years, but once we got married and her graduation date neared, all bets were off.

"Are you sure? Were you late? Are you feeling okay?" Did I miss the signs like a selfish asshole?

She cups my face, her calmer state helping me find my center. "I'm good." My pleading stare gives her pause. "Really, Joseph. I'm good. I've felt a little off in the mornings. The smell of coffee makes my stomach churn. That, and the fact that I'm late, prompted me to take a test today when I got home."

I move us back to the couch, positioning us with my girl's legs across my lap and her back to the armrest. "And your mom?"

Twisting her lips, she shrugs a shoulder. "Yeah, my mom."

I bring our joined hands to my mouth and kiss her fingers, the back, the palm, her wrist, imbuing my love into every touch. "It's her loss. But I know it hurts to know she won't be here for you. If it helps, my mom will be excited enough for two moms."

My girl smiles, her eyes filling with tears. "She will. She'll be a wonderful grandmother. Your dad is going to have to love enough for two granddads too." A tear slips free and then another, and another.

This isn't just about our kids missing out on her parents. I know she loves me and my family as if we were her blood. But it's moments like this that are another level of disappointment. Another life event she has to face without her birth family by her side—the absence that much keener. The pain that much deeper. I'm thankful Jace has come around and their relationship is that much stronger for all the hardship they faced.

I pull her to me, hugging her as close as I can and not choke her out. "With Jace, Fin, Matt, Michael, Victor, and Sebastian, our kids are going to have lots of men who will love them like their own. Margot and whoever the guys end up with will love our kids too. They won't even realize they're missing a set of grandparents. I promise, Sweetness."

She nods. She knows. The hurt is still real, though. "Our family is big and will only grow bigger with each wedding, each baby born. I just need a minute to come to terms with my parents not being here. It's a reality check that sideswiped me. That's all."

"Take all the time you need. I'm not going anywhere." I kiss her forehead and sigh over the top of her head. She settles in close, and I relish every second of it.

She's pregnant. The thought fills me with a peacefulness I never thought was possible. "Thank you," I murmur against her brow.

"For what?" Her glistening eyes meet mine.

"For being mine. For marrying me. For loving me. For making me a daddy."

"You're making me a mommy." Her smile is the sweetest fucking thing ever.

I return it. "I am, aren't I." Pride wells as if I got her pregnant just by being in the same room with her.

She laughs and my heart soars. "You're such a caveman, Caveman."

"I am, but only for you, Sweets." I kiss her softly. "Only ever for you."

7 MONTHS LATER

Her pregnancy body is going to kill me. Downright give me a heart attack. I can't get enough of her new curves. I can't get my fill. I can't get deep enough. And when our son moves and stretches in her tummy like a scene from Alien, I get rock hard.

My Brady is a big baby. They think our son is ten pounds. The doctor is going to induce Samantha in two days if she doesn't go in to labor before then. Yeah, I'm a sick motherfucker to find pride in my woman carrying around a baby big enough to rip her to shreds on his way out.

I pray, *pray*, my girl will be alright. She has to be.

I'll remind Brady every damn day how much his mother sacrificed to bring him into the world—when he finally fucking comes.

"Here." My Sweets waddles toward me where I'm sitting on the edge of our bed. She holds out a tub of lotion she wants me to rub on her belly to save her from scarring stretch marks. And she's naked—completely—and ready to *pop*, as she likes to say.

"You want to lie down?" She won't, but I ask anyway. The sight of her makes me hard and so damn guilty for doing this to her. Every step hurts, she can't get comfortable, false labor is kicking her ass, she's barely eaten today, and she pees more than she drinks, if that's even possible.

She rubs her ginormous belly in circles and moans, "No," just as Brady's foot pushes in the spot she's rubbing.

Dipping my fingers into the tub, I come out with a heaping handful, rub my hands together and start massaging it into her taut skin. Brady moves from side to side like he's trying to mirror my movements from the inside. This kid, if he doesn't kill his mommy, is going to be my pride and joy. I can't wait to see the beast of a man he'll be one day. But for the moment, he's the source of my woman's discomfort.

I move lower, my eyes locked on her *Caveman's* tattoo below her bikini line. It's vibrant and shines from the liberal application of lotion, the top a bit distorted from stretching to accommodate Brady.

"What if they have to cut me there?" My Sweets worries her bottom lip as she holds my shoulders for support.

"They won't." I'm certain.

"But what if they do?" I catch the fear in her voice and it has nothing to do with her tattoo.

I continue to caress her silky skin as my eyes catch on her abundant breasts before locking on her troubled, blue eyes. "If they do, then our son will have a round head instead of a cone, and my girl will have a scar to brag about." I cup her breasts and squeeze, teasing the stiff peaks that are sensitive enough to make her come if given enough attention.

She gasps, her fingers digging into my shoulders.

"Whatever happens, Samantha, we've got this. I can't do this for you—and even if I could, I'm not sure I would. You're amazing. You're tough. You take everything in stride and giving birth will be no different. I'll be there the entire time, before, during, and after. I've got you. I promise."

A deep breath and a slight smile are all I get.

"And I will love your body in every stage of our lives. Scars and stretchmarks are nothing compared to the miracle you're giving us." I don't put lotion on her stretchmarks because I care about her having them. I put it on her because she asks, and any chance to get my hands on my girl is reason enough.

"Joseph," the wisp of her reply tugs at my heart.

I capture her cheek, keeping her eyes on me. "Don't you know by now, baby? I want you pregnant, not pregnant, scars, no scars, young, old. You get my cock hard, my heart racing, and my blood pumping. I'm the man I am because of you. The way you love me. The heat in your eyes and the swoon in your step when you catch me looking. Fuck, Sweets it's only you. Always has been. Always will be."

She leans in for a kiss, maneuvering around her tummy that hits me way before her mouth does. "The things you say," she whispers across my lips before she presses her mouth to mine.

I hold her close, supporting her pregnancy weight with my body, and suck her bottom lip, tugging lightly. Her moan has my cock dancing in my boxer briefs, and my hand sliding between her legs. I growl with satisfaction. "You're so fucking wet, Sweets."

"Your mouth—"

"Do you want my mouth on you, or—" I slip a finger inside her and then rub her clit. "Do you think you can stand while I make you come?"

I flick her nipple and fill her with another finger as I suck on her plump peak. She clenches around my finger, her moans ratcheting up as if she's ready to come. She probably is. My girl is hot when she's not pregnant but amp her up with hormones and she's purring and ready 24/7.

"Joseph," she warns.

"Can you stay on your feet, baby?"

"Yes. Just—"

"I know. I got you." Her head falls back as I suck and bite her nipples, her hands holding on like we're on turbulent seas.

Her trembling starts with gasps and sucked in breaths, her hips moving, her pussy gripping my fingers in an effort to keep them in as I pull out. "God, Sweets. You're so fucking sexy." I tug on her nipple, releasing it with a pop.

She cries out, begging me for more.

"You gonna come for me?"

"Yes."

"I need to bury my cock balls deep in you."

She shutters. My cock fights to rid itself of its clothed cage.

"But not before you come on my fingers." I suck on a nipple, tweak the other with my fingers, strum her insides, and press on her clit until she's shaking so hard, I'm sure she'll collapse.

"I'm..." she cries out. Moisture pools a second before she comes.

"Jesus, yes. Just like that, Sweetness."

Tremors rack her body. I wrap an arm around her back, suck a nipple till I'm sure I'll draw milk that's meant for my son. I hold my girl as she falls apart for me, one clench, one scream, one erotic shudder at a time.

Before she can come down, I've got her lying on her side with me kneeling over her, straddling her bottom leg and holding her open. Her other leg is cradled against my abdomen as I sink my aching cock in her an inch at a time. Taking it slow. I may have finger fucked her hard, but this close to giving birth, she's tender inside and my cock is bigger than my fingers.

I delve in, swivel my hips. Pull out and do it again, and again. She gasps and moans, clutching the covers and my thigh, moving her hips into me. Her belly moves, her tits bounce, and her eyes stare straight into my soul.

"Joseph?"

A shiver runs up my spine. "Yeah, Sweets?"

"I'm gonna come again." She arches. "I need to come again."

"Fuck." I'm not ready to blow. Not yet. But her body is talking to mine in a way that's too familiar and hard to resist.

I wrap my arm over her top thigh, holding her flush to me and rub her clit and use my other hand to tease her breasts in just the way she likes it—the way she needs it.

As she gets closer, I switch it up, giving up on her breasts and tease her ass, squeezing and kneading, my thumb rubbing over her tight ring that's so wet from her juices.

I thrust a little harder when a soft, "More," seeps out between her moans. My thumb slips through her rosebud, my balls tighten, and my girl asks for more.

"You want my cock here don't you, Sweets?" The idea has me gritting my teeth. I don't even need her answer, her body tells me all I need to know. I push a little farther, moving my finger in and out of her ass as my cock fills her pussy. So tight. Fucking heaven. I lean over her, careful not to squish her belly. I don't need it, but I definitely want to hear her say it. "Tell me."

She captures the back of my neck and pulls till we're nose to nose. "Yes." She licks across my lips.

"My dirty girl." I kiss her hard, possessively, as I rub her clit, surging inside her. "Soon, Sweets."

"Yes," she chants as I sit back, my abs clenching as I thrust, holding off what I can't wait to give her—my cock in her ass, my fingers in her pussy, riding her hard as she screams my name and begs for more. Everything.

On a moan that starts with the pointing of her toes and the shaking of her legs and works up her body, my beautiful, pregnant wife comes so hard, she rips my orgasm from me, pulling it right along with her own release. My groan is deep and savage and so fucking full of love and awe for the woman I've been blessed with.

I fall over, kissing her thoroughly as I pull her close and hold her as we catch our breath.

Life is never boring with my Sweetness.

The sex is off the charts.

She challenges me. She fulfills me. She's my partner in life—in good times and bad.

And our life is about to get even fuller with the birth of our son.

She snuggles in as close as her belly allows, throwing her leg over me, her wet heat tempting my cock. Her hips flex and that's all it takes to convince me we're not quite done. I push inside her with languid strokes, growing harder as she clenches around me. I lean over her and suck in a nipple and find her clit.

Stroking and sucking until she comes, and comes again.

Stroking and sucking until I come.

Stroking until she comes again and falls asleep in my arms.

My cock still inside her.

My son inside her.

My world is complete.

Author's Note

Do you want to see the birth of Joseph and Samantha's son?

Sign up for my Newsletter and receive a free Bonus Scene!

Free BONUS SCENE: dl.bookfunnel.com/khtau191ty

Continue reading with Fin and Margot's story in *Until You Believe*.

dmckdavis.com/all-books/series/until-you/uybelieve

Did You Enjoy This Novel?

This is a dream for me to be able to share my love of writing with you. If you liked my novel, please consider leaving a review on the retailer's site where you purchased this book (and/or on Goodreads).

Personal recommendations to your friends and loved ones are a great compliment too. Please share, follow, join my newsletter (dmckdavis.com/subscribe), and help spread the word—let everyone know how much you loved Joseph and Samantha's story.

Acknowledgements

Thank you to my husband, my children, my mom, my sister, and the rest of my family for their unwavering support. I do this for you because you believe I can.

To my follow writerly peeps: thank you to the MP group for your support and early critiques of *Until You Say I Do*. Thank you to Teddy—I could not do this without you by my side. You're my cheerleader, my confidant, my sister from another mister.

To my bulldog editor, Tamara, for putting up with my emotional, grammatically-challenged self. I wouldn't want to do this without you.

And lastly, to the readers—thank you for your kind words and support. It means so much to hear how much you love Joseph and Samantha. I hope their book three will fill all those gooey romantic parts of you with their love. It is a rather epic love story. One I have loved writing. I will miss them so much. But don't fear, Joseph and Samantha will continue to be integral players in the *Until You* series which continues with Fin and Margot's story in *Until You Believe*.

Until next time, I will continue to write...

"What only the heart hears..."

About the Author

D.M. Davis is a Contemporary and New Adult Romance Author.

She is a Texas native, wife, and mother. Her background is Project Management, technical writing, and application development. D.M. has been a lifelong reader and wrote poetry in her early life, but has found her true passion in writing about love and the intricate relationships between men and women.

She writes of broken hearts and second chances, of dreamers looking for more than they have and daring to reach for it.

D.M. believes it is never too late to make a change in your own life, to become the person you always wanted to be, but were afraid you were not worth the effort.

You are worth it. Take a chance on you. You never know what's possible if you don't try. Believe in yourself as you believe in others, and see what life has to offer.

Please visit her website, dmckdavis.com, for more details, and keep in touch by signing up for her newsletter, and joining her on Facebook, Twitter, and Instagram.

Additional Books by
D.M. DAVIS

Until You Series

Book 1—Until You Set Me Free

Book 2—Until You Are Mine

Book 3—Until You Say I Do

Book 4—Until You Believe

Finding Grace Series

Book 1—The Road to Redemption

Book 2—The Price of Atonement

Black Ops MMA Series

Book 1—No Mercy

Book 2—Rowdy

Book 3—Captain

Standalones

Warm Me Softly

Join My Reader Group

Stalk Me

Visit www.dmckdavis.com for more details about my books.

Keep in touch by signing up for my Newsletter.

Connect on social media:
Facebook: www.facebook.com/dmdavisauthor
Instagram: www.instagram.com/dmdavisauthor
Twitter: twitter.com/dmdavisauthor
Reader's Group: www.facebook.com/groups/dmdavisreadergroup

Follow me:
BookBub: www.bookbub.com/authors/d-m-davis
Goodreads: www.goodreads.com/dmckdavis

d.m. davis
SEXY WITH HEART
CONTEMPORARY & NEW ADULT ROMANCE AUTHOR

Made in the USA
Las Vegas, NV
20 April 2021